I Am a Cat
(III)

SŌSEKI NATSUME

I Am a Cat

(III)

translated by
Aiko Itō and Graeme Wilson

Published by Charles E. Tuttle Company, Inc.
of Rutland, Vermont & Tokyo, Japan
with editorial offices at
Suido 1-chome, 2-6, Bunkyo-ku, Tokyo

© 1986 by Aiko Itō and Graeme Wilson
All rights reserved

Library of Congress Catalog Card No. 85-051917
International Standard Book No. 0-8048-1503-1

First printing, 1986
Third printing, 1990

CHARLES E. TUTTLE CO.
Rutland/Vermont : Tokyo/Japan

Published by the Charles E. Tuttle Company, Inc.
of Rutland, Vermont & Tokyo, Japan
with editorial offices at
Suido 1-chome, 2-6, Bunkyo-ku, Tokyo

Library of Congress Catalog Card No. 85-051782
International Standard Book No. 0-8048-1860-6

First printing, 1986
Third printing, 1992

Printed in Japan

Introduction

THESE COMMENTS will be brief, primarily because we have nothing substantial to add to the observation on Sōseki's work in general and on *I Am a Cat* in particular which we have already offered in the Introductions to our three earlier translations of his prose: *I Am a Cat (I)* (Tuttle, 1972), *Ten Nights of Dream* (Tuttle, 1974) and *I Am a Cat (II)* (Tuttle, 1979).

Natsume Kin'nosuke (1867–1916) was the youngest and late-born son of a family of minor town-gentry whose hereditary occupation as ward-chiefs in Tokyo under the Tokugawa shogunate disappeared at the Imperial Restoration of 1868. Extensively educated in both the Chinese and the Japanese literary traditions, Sōseki early recognized the importance of English to any senior career under the westernizing influence of the restored regime and, specifically, to the entry requirements of Tokyo Imperial University. Hoping to become an architect, he entered that university's Department of Engineering in 1881 but soon transferred to the Department of Literature and, in September 1890, joined the Department of English Literature as a loan-scholarship student of the Ministry of Education. He graduated three years later and proceeded to try his luck, with little real success, first in journalism and then as a teacher. In 1896 he married Nakane Kyōko, the eldest daughter of the chief secretary of the House of Peers and, in 1900, reluctantly acceded to the ministry's proposal to send him (on a relatively niggardly scholarship of 1800 yen a year) to study in England, where, for two unhappy years in London, he devoted himself to intensive reading of books in English on almost every conceivable subject and at the same time made himself an authority on eighteenth-century literature. He arrived back in Japan in January 1903 and shortly thereafter, in fulfillment of the terms of his scholarship, entered upon a four-year stint of lecturing at Tokyo Imperial University. He disliked the work, but from those teaching years he later compiled two still-impressive volumes of academic studies: *Bungaku-ron (Comments on Literature)* of 1907 and *Bungaku Hyōron (Literary Criticism)* of 1909. In 1907 he resigned from the university and became the literary editor of the *Asahi Shimbun,* a daily newspaper in whose pages he thereafter serialized, until his death in 1916, some dozen major psychological novels on which his lasting reputation is securely founded.

I Am a Cat began as a single short story (now the first chapter of a very long comic novel) published in January 1905 by the literary magazine *Hototogisu (Cuckoo)*. The immediate public demand for further installments of the story led to an additional ten chapters in which the initial comic idea of a cat's-eye view of the lower reaches of the new Meiji middle class developed and widened into a satirical picture of mankind. In the final chapter Sōseki even ventured upon the tricky task, one no less tricky than satirizing satire, of a satire upon Zen. It was, of course, a field in which he had personal experience deriving from his ten-day sojourn beginning on December 27, 1894, at the Engaku-ji in Kamakura; but it is perhaps worth noting both that his Zen studies proved abortive (though he paid a further brief visit to the temple in 1898) and that he described himself in the temple register for Zen trainees as *Hokkaidō heimin* when, so far as we have been able to ascertain, he had never set foot, let alone held permanent residence, in that northern island.

Successively published as a three-decker novel in 1905, 1906 and 1907, *I Am a Cat* first appeared in a single-volume edition in 1911. It has remained popular in Japan to this day: and it is surely significant of the

8

Introduction

ever-increasing esteem which Sōseki commands in Japan that, in November 1984,
his portrait replaced that of the statesman
Itō Hirobumi on the 1000-yen banknote.
We will not here add any specific comments on the technique of translation
which we have adopted, if only because
the three earlier Introductions already
mentioned do include an account of our
approach; and that approach is maintained in this the concluding volume of
I Am a Cat. We will only say that we regard Sōseki as the greatest novelist ever
to have been born in Japan, the land where
the world's first novel was written, and that
we have consequently striven to ensure that
our versions of his writing keep true faith
with the Master.

—THE TRANSLATORS

Note: Japanese names throughout this book, except
on the cover and title page, are given in Japanese
order, that is, surname followed by given name.

WHEN I WAS describing my fence-
trotting exercises, I must have mentioned that bamboo fence which
encloses my master's garden. Beyond that
fence to the south of us there is another
dwelling, but it would be an error to assume
that our neighbors are just anybody. Admittedly, it is a low-rent area; but Mr. Sneaze is
a person of some standing, and certainly not
the sort of man to establish chatty relationships across a backyard fence with any old
Tom, Dick or Harry. On the other side of
our particular fence there is an open space
about thirty feet deep at the far end of which
stands a dark green row of five or six heavily
foliaged cypresses. If one looks at this scene
from our veranda, the impression it creates
is of a deep and thickly wooded forest, and
one feels that here is a lonely house in a glade
where some learned sage, indifferent to fame
and wealth, leads out his solitary life with
only a nameless cat for his companion. However, the cypresses do not, in fact, grow
quite as thickly as I'd like to make out, for
through their greenery one can with hurtful
clarity descry the undistinguished roof of a

cheap boarding-house of which the only redeeming feature is its soul-astounding name:
Crane Flock Manor. You will appreciate that
it consequently takes a real effort of the im-
agination to fit my master as I've hitherto
described him into such a high-falutin' background. Yet, if that crumby boarding-house
can bear so grand a name, then surely my
master's home deserves at least to be known
as the Cave of the Sleeping Dragon. Since
there's no tax on house-names, one might as
well select a name which sounds impressive.
Anyway, this open space to the south of us,
of a north-south depth of some thirty feet,
extends on an east-west axis for about sixty
feet along our bamboo fence and then turns
right-angularly northward to run along the
eastern side of the Cave of the Sleeping
Dragon. Now it is in this northern area that
trouble has arisen.

One might dare boast that this open space,
stretching as it does around two whole sides
of our dwelling, is big enough to please anyone; but in point of fact not only the master
of the house but even I, the dragon's resident
sacred cat, are often at our wits' end to know
what to do with so much emptiness. Just as
the cypress trees lord it to the south, so to
the north the scene is dominated by some
seven or eight paulownias standing in a row.
Since those trees have each now grown to be
a good twelve inches round, one could make
a pretty packet by selling their highly fancied
wood to the first clog-maker whom one cared

to call in. Unfortunately, even if my unworldly dragon could rise to such an idea,
being no more than a tenant of his cavern, he
couldn't put it into practice. My heart bleeds
for my half-wit master. Especially so when I
recall that only the other day some lowly
drudge of a porter at his school came round
and calmly cut a large branch from one tree.
On his next visit he was sporting an exceed-
ingly fancy pair of paulownia-wood clogs and
was boasting to everyone within earshot that
his clogs were made from the branch he'd
stolen. Such cunning villains flourish; but for
me and for the rest of my master's household, though those valuable paulownias are
within our daily grasp, they profit us nothing. There's an old adage that to hold a gem
invites misfortune, which is generally inter-
preted to mean that it is opportunity which
creates a thief. But in our sad case the plain
fact is that growing paulownias earn no
money. There they are, as pointlessly valuable as gold left in the ground; but the numbskull in this matter is neither myself nor my
master. It's the landlord, Dembei, a man so
dense, so deaf, that even when his trees are
positively shouting for a clog-maker, begging
aloud to be cut, he takes not the slightest
notice, but just comes and collects his rent.
However, since I bear no grudge against our
landlord, I'll say no more about his crazy
conduct and revert to my main theme, that
is to say, to the odd series of events whereby
that open space came to be the cause of so

much strife and tribulation. But if I tell you the inwardness of it all, you mustn't, ever, let on to my master. These words of mine, remember, are between you and me and the gate-post.

The immediately obvious snag about that open space is that it is indeed entirely open: unenclosed, no kind of fence around it. It is a breezy, easy, go-as-you-pleasy sort of right-of-way: it is, in short, a good, honest open space. I must, however, confess that my use of the present tense is misleading, for, more precisely, I should have said that it *was* a good honest open space. As always, one cannot understand the present situation without tracing its development back to causes rooted in the ancient past. Since even doctors cannot prescribe cures unless they first have diagnosed the causes of disorder, I will take my time and, beginning my story from its true beginning, go back to those days when my master first moved into his present home.

It's always pleasant in the humid days of summer to have plenty of airy space around one's house. Of course such open sites offer to burglars the advantage of easy access, but there's little risk of burglary where there's nothing worth the thieving. Hence my master's house has never stood in need of any kind of outer wall, thorn-hedge, stockade or even the flimsiest fence. However, it seems to me that the need for such defensive structures is really determined by the nature of whatever creatures, human or animal, which happen to live on the other side of any such open space. From which it follows that I must clarify the nature of the gentlemen dwelling to the north of us. It may seem rather rash to call them gentlemen before I have clearly established whether those beings are human or animal, but it's usually safer to start by assuming that everyone's a gentleman. After all, we have the authority of the Chinese classics for calling a sneak-thief hiding in the rafters a "gentleman on the beam." However, the gentlemen in our particular case are not, at least individually, criminal characters such as trouble the police. Instead, the criminality of these neighbors seems to be a function of their enormous number. For there are swarms of them. Swarms and swarms of pupils at a private Middle School which, rejoicing in the name of the Hall of the Descending Cloud, collects two yen a month from each of eight hundred young gentlemen in return for training them to become even yet more gentlemanly. But you'd be making a serious mistake if you deduced from the elegant name of their school that all its students were gentlemen of elegance and taste. Just as no crane ever flocks to the seedy roosts in Crane Flock Manor, just as the Cave of the Sleeping Dragon in fact contains a cat, so the tasteful name of our neighboring school is an unreliable indicator of the true degree of its occupants' refinement. Since you have already learnt that a madman like my master can be held to be included within the ranks of university men,

even of lecturers, you should have no difficulty in grasping what louts may well be
numbered among the inferentially polished
gentlemen in the Hall of the Descending
Cloud. If my point is still not clear, a three-
day visit to my master's house will certainly
drive it home.

As I've already mentioned, when my master
first moved into his house there was no fence
around the empty space; and consequently
the gentlemen of the Hall, just like Rickshaw
Blacky, used to saunter about among the
paulownias, chatting, eating from their lunch-
boxes, lying down on the clumps of bamboo-
grass, doing, in fact, whatever they fancied.
After a while they began using the paulownia
grove for dumping their discardable rubbish
—first the corpses of their lunch-boxes (that
is to say, the bamboo wrapping-sheaths and
odd sheets of old newspaper)—but soon they
took to dumping worn-out sandals, broken
clogs, anything in fact that needed pitching
out. My master, typically indifferent, showed
no concern about these developments and
did not even bother to lodge a protest. I don't
know whether he failed to notice what was
going on or whether, noticing, he decided not
to make a fuss. At all events, those gentlemen
from the Hall seem to have grown ever more
like gentlemen as they advanced in their education, for they gradually extended their disgusting activities on the northern side of the
open space to encroach upon its southern
area. If you object that a word like "en-

croach" should not be used in reference to
gentlemen, I am willing to abandon it; but
there is in truth no other word to describe
the process whereby these gentlemen, like so
many desert nomads, emerged from their
paulownia wastes to advance upon the cypresses. Inasmuch as the cypress trees stand
right in front of our living-room, it was at
first only the most daring of these elegant
young men who dared to venture so far, but,
within a matter of days, such daring had
grown general, and the more sturdy of the
venturers had moved on to greater things.
There is nothing quite so terrifying as the
results of education.

Having thus successfully advanced to the
actual side of the house, these educated
youths then launched upon us an assault of
song. I have forgotten the name of their song
but it was certainly not a classical composi-
tion, being distinctly lively in the catchy style
of certain popular ditties. My master was not
the only person who was surprised, for I, too,
was so much impressed by the range of talents displayed by these young gentlemen that
I found myself, in spite of myself, listening
to their singing. However, as my readers may
already know, it is perfectly possible to be
both impressed and seriously disturbed by
the same occurrences. Indeed, upon reflection, it strikes me as regrettable that, as in
the present case, the two reactions should so
often be simultaneously evoked; and I have
no doubt that my master shared my sense of

regret. Nevertheless he had no real choice but, on two or three occsions, to come rushing out of his study and drive them off his property with such stern rebukes as "This is not the place for you " and "I'd be obliged if you'd go."

Of course, since the offenders are educated gentlemen, they show no disposition meekly to obey my master's exhortations, so no sooner have they been turned out but back they come again. And once they're back they start again on their less than seemly singing interspersed with loud-voiced chat and banter. What's more, and of course because they're gentlemen, their language differs from that in common use. They use such words as "youse" and "dunno." Such words, I understand, were, until the Restoration, part of the professional vocabulary of footmen, palanquin-carriers and bathhouse attendants; but, in the present century, have become the only style of language deserving study by an educated gentleman. I've heard it said that a similar social climb can be observed in the matter of taking physical exercise, for physical jerks, once generally scorned as an activity proper only to the lower classes, are now most warmly smiled upon at the highest levels of society. However, on the occasion when one of my master's frantic sallies from his study actually resulted in the capture of a student skilled in this new language of the gentry, the prisoner, no doubt frightened into forgetting the subtleties of modern educated speech, offered an explanation for his intrusion in such extremely vulgar terms as "Please accept my most sincere apologies, but I had, Sir, the mistaken impression that this area was the school's botanical garden."

Having subjected his victim to a cautionary lecture, my master turned him loose. Which is a silly sounding form of words, more suited to the liberation of newly hatched baby turtles, but nevertheless appropriate in that my master kept a firm grip on his prisoner's sleeve throughout the process of his reprehension. Naturally enough, my master confidently expected that the force of his wingèd words would be sufficient to halt the nomadic inroads, but, as has been well known since the earliest days of recorded Chinese history, there is a vast difference between expectation and reality. At all events, my master's expectations were quickly proved misplaced. The young gentlemen now began to enter the open space from their northern side, walk boldly straight across it, then across our garden and complete their short cut into the road beyond by use of our front-gate. The sound of its opening naturally led us to expect the pleasure of visitors, so it was all the more infuriating in fact to receive nothing more than the noise of vulgar laughter from the direction of the paulownias. Things were clearly going from bad to worse. The effects of education grew daily more apparent until, recognizing that the situation had gone beyond his own powers of control, my master shut himself up in his study and there composed a politely worded letter to the headmaster of the Hall asking that a little closer control be exercised over the high spirits of his students. The headmaster, in similarly courteous terms, replied with an expression of regret for past intrusions and a plea for a little more patience pending the construction, for which he had already arranged, of a fence between the two properties. Shortly thereafter a few workmen turned up and, in a scant half day, set up along the borderline a so-called four-eye fence of open-work bamboo approximately three feet high. My master, poor old duffer, was delighted. Daft as ever, he glowed in the false conviction that the nomadic raids had now been walled away, but what man in his right mind could possibly believe that a real change in the behavior of gentlemen can be wrought by the flimsy magic of a dwarfish bamboo fence?

One must, of course, recognize that there is a vast fund of pleasure to be drawn from the provocation of human beings. Even a cat like myself sometimes derives amusement from teasing my master's otherwise uninteresting daughters. So it is entirely understandable that the bright young gentlemen at the Hall should have found it rewarding to tease such a dimwit as my master. The only person who objects to teasing is, of course, the person teased. Analysis of the psychology of teasing reveals two major aspects of its successful pursuit. First, the person or persons teased must never be allowed to remain calm. Secondly, the person or persons teasing must be stronger than the teasee(s) both in sheer power and in mere number. Only the other day my master, who had gone off to gawp in some zoo, came home to recount an incident there which had particularly impressed him. He had, apparently, taken time to watch some idiotic rumpus between a small dog and a camel. The small dog, barking like mad, had scampered like a whirlwind round and round the camel, while the camel, paying no whit of attention, had simply stood there, stolidly patient under the burden of its hump. Unable to provoke the slightest stir of interest from the camel, the little dog had eventually barked itself into a disgusted silence. My master, too dull to see the relevance of that experience to his own circumstances, had seen the camel's dull insensitivity as nothing more than comic; and he laughed a lot as he told his tale. However, that incident does clearly illustrate one major facet of the business of teasing. No matter how skilled the teaser, his efforts will be wasted if the teasee happens to be as dull (or as intelligent) as a camel. Of course, should the victim happen to be as inordinately strong as a lion or a tiger, the teaser will quickly find himself involved in the yet more total disappointment of being ripped to shreds. But when the teaser has accurately determined that his victim, however deeply

angered, still can do nothing in effective re-
taliation, then indeed the joys of provocation
can be drawn from a bottomless well.

Why, one may ask, does teasing offer such
endless pleasure? There are several reasons.
First and foremost, it is the most marvelous
way for killing time, better for the bored than
counting one's whiskers. Of all the tribula-
tions in this world, boredom is the one most
hard to bear. I've even heard that, long ago,
there was a prisoner so crazed by solitary
confinement that he passed his days in draw-
ing triangles, one upon another, all over the
walls of his cell. For unless one does something, indeed anything, to incite a sense of
purpose in one's life, one cannot go on living.
Thus, the amusement in teasing derives in no
small part from the stir, the stimulus, which
it gives to the teaser; but it is of course obvious that it's worthless as a stimulant unless it
successfully provokes in others a sufficient
degree of that irritation, anger, even distress,
which makes the teaser's life worth living.

Study of the annals of history discloses that
there are two main types of person disposed
to indulge in teasing: those of an utterly bored
or witless mind and those who need to prove
to themselves their superiority to others. The
first group includes such creatures as those
bored feudal lords who neither understood
nor cared about the feelings of other people,
a group which is nowadays best represented
by boys so infantile, so mentally stunted,
that, while having no time to think of any-

thing but their own fool pleasures, they have
insufficient intelligence to see how, even in
that sub-puerile pursuit, best to employ their
vitality. The second main group of teasers
realizes that one can demonstrate superiority
by killing, hurting or imprisoning other people but that such a proof only occurs as a
sort of by-product from situations where the
real objective is to hurt, kill or jail. Consequently, should one wish to demonstrate
superiority without going to the lengths (or
running the risks) of inflicting major damage,
the ideal method is by teasing. In practice it
is impossible to prove one's superiority without inflicting some degree of injury, and the
proof has to be practical because no one
derives adequate or pleasurable confidence
in his prowess from mere conviction thereof
within the privacy of his own mind. It is of
course true that the human creature characteristically prides itself on its self-reliance.
However, it would be more exact to say that
the creature, knowing it can't rely upon itself,
would very much like to believe that it could
and is consequently never at ease with itself
until it can give a practical demonstration to
some other such creature of how much it can
rely upon itself. What's more, those endowed
with the least intelligence and those least sure
of themselves are precisely those who seize
upon the slightest opportunity to demonstrate their entitlement to some sort of cer-
tificate of prowess. One can observe the same
phenomenon in the world of judo, whose

devotees, every so often, feel the need to heave someone or other over their buttocks and smack them down on the ground. The least proficient of these dedicated cross-buttockers wander about their neighborhoods looking for someone, even for someone not of their quaint fraternity, upon whose weaker person they can demonstrate their superiority in using their bottoms to sling the upright flat on their backs.

There are many other considerations which make teasing a popular and admirable activity, but, since it would take a long time to set them all down here, I will say no more upon the topic. However, anyone interested in deepening his understanding of this fascinating subject is always welcome to call upon me, bearing a proper fee in dried bonito, for further instruction.

Perhaps I might usefully offer the following succinct conclusion based upon my foregoing remarks, namely, that in my opinion the ideal subjects for teasing are zoo monkeys and school teachers. It would be disrespectful to compare a school teacher with a monkey in the Asakusa Zoo, disrespectful, that is, not to monkeys but to teachers. But truths will always out, and no one can deny how close is the resemblance. As you know, the Asakusa monkeys are restricted by link-chain leashes so that, though they may snarl and screech to their hearts' content, they cannot scratch a soul. Now, though teachers are not actually kept on chains, they are very effectively shackled by their salaries. They can be teased in perfect safety. They won't resign or use their teeth on their pupils. Had they sufficient spunk to resign, they would not originally have allowed themselves to sink into the slavery of teaching. My master is a teacher. Though he does not teach at the Hall, still he is a teacher and just the man for the job: inoffensive, salary-shackled, a man designed by nature for schoolboys to torment in total safety. The pupils at the Hall are gentlemanly youths who not only consider it proper to practice teasing as a part of their rite of passage into the superiority of manhood, but who also believe that they are of right entitled to be tormentors as a due fruit of their education. Moreover, a sizable proportion of these lively lads would not know how to occupy their limbs and brains through the long ten minutes of the morning break if a kindly nature failed to provide them with a target for persecution. In such circumstances it is as inevitable that my wretched master should be teased as that the yobbos from the Hall should do the teasing. Given that inevitability, it seems to me quite ludicrous, a new high point in his long ascent to the thin-aired peaks of pure fatuity, that my master should have allowed himself to be provoked into so much pointless anger. Nonetheless, I shall now recount in detail how those pupils teased him and with what boorish folly he responded.

I assume my readers need no description of

a four-eye fence. I, for instance, can move back and forth through its lattices with such complete freedom that it might as well not be there. However, the headmaster of the Hall did not have cats in mind when he arranged for the fence to be erected. His only concern was to provide a fence through which the young gentlemen of his school could not pass; and I must confess that, freely as the winds may move between its bamboo laths, I see no way in which a man or boy could do the same. Even for such an accomplished contortionist as Chang Shih-tsun, that Chinese magician who flourished in the days of the Ch'ing, it would be hard to weasel a way through a wall of apertures each no more than a tight four inches square. Being thus impenetrable by human beings, it is understandable that the fence when first erected left my master happy with the thought that he was safe at last. However there's a hole in the logic of my master's thinking, a hole far bigger than the squares in the four-eye fence. Indeed, the hole's so vast that it could easily let through even that monster fish which, in Chinese legend, once swallowed a whole ship. The point is this. My master assumes that a fence is something not to be crossed, from which follows his second assumption that no schoolboy worthy of that name would force his way past any fence which, however humble, can be recognized as indeed a fence and, as such, a clear identifier of a boundary-line. Even if my master were able temporarily

to set aside those two assumptions, he would
nevertheless still calculate that the smallness
of the open-work squares provided genuine
protection even against any such improbable
youth as might dare to contemplate forcing
his way through them. He all too hastily concluded he was safe simply because it was
obvious that not even the smallest and most
determined boy, unless he happened to be a
cat, could possibly squeeze through the fence.
But the massive flaw in his analysis lay in the
fact that nothing is more easy than to climb
or jump a fence but three feet high. Which,
quite apart from the fun of it, also offers excellent physical exercise.

From the day following the erection of the
fence the young gentlemen from the Hall
began jumping into the northern portion of
the open space with the same regularity as
they had previously just walked across. But
they no longer advance to their earlier forward positions right in front of our living-
room because, if they are now chased, it will
take them a little longer to reach the safety
of school-land by reason of the new need to
get back over the four-eye fence. So they loaf
about in the middle distance where they run
no risk whatever of being caught. From his
detached room on the east side of our house
my master cannot see what the boys are doing. For that purpose one must either go out
to the garden-gate and there look at a right
angle into the open space or else one must
go to the inside lavatory and peer out through

its little window. From that latter position my master can very clearly see what is going on, but, however many the intruders upon his property, nothing can be done to catch them. All he can do is to shout unheeded scoldings through the window-grille. If he tries a sally through the garden-gate into enemy-occupied territory, the sound of his approaching footsteps gives them ample time to scoot away, nimbly clear the fence and continue their hooting from the safety of school-land. My master's tactics of creep-and-rush are much like those adopted by sea-poachers trying to surprise seals as they bask in the sun. Naturally, my master cannot spend his whole life either peering from the loo or dashing out through the garden-gate in response to every stimulus of sound from the open space. He would have to give up teaching and concentrate on full-time self-employment as a yobbo-hunter. The weakness of his position is that from his study he can hear but not see his enemies, while from the lavatory he has them in plain view but can do nothing more effective than yell his silly head off. His enemies, full aware of his dilemma, have shaped their strategy to exploit his difficulties.

When the young gentlemen are sure that my master is in his study, they set up a racket of talk so deliberately loud that my master cannot avoid hearing the cracks they make about him. To salt his mortification, they vary the volume of their comments so that he can

never be certain whether their babble origi-
nates from his or their side of the four-eye
fence. When my master makes one of his
forays, they either scuttle off or, if they happen already to be in their own territory, they
stare at him with insolent indifference. When
my master is lurking in his lavatory—I regret,
indeed I would normally disparage, this constant use of that somewhat indelicate word,
but in battle reports one is duty-bound to
be topographically accurate—his tormentors
loaf about under the paulownias and take
pains to draw his attention to their unwel-
come presence. Then, as soon as he starts
raving at them through the window-grille,
they, cool as little cucumbers, let the roar of
his abuse flow over their heads to disturb the
whole neighborhood with its ugly echos while,
utterly unconcerned, they drift away into the
home ground of their Hall. These tactics are
reducing my master to a gibbering idiot.
Sometimes, sure that the little louts are on
his property, he dashes out with his walking-
stick at the ready, only to find the open space
deserted. At other times, confident of their
absence, he nevertheless takes a quick peep
from his lavatory window, and there they are,
a loathly gaggle of them, loitering on his
land. So he nips round to his garden-gate
and he squinnies from the john. He squinnies
from the john and he nips round to his garden-gate. Over and over and over again. If
you find my account repetitive, the simple
reason is that I am committed to recounting

·
吾輩は猫である

endless repetitions of the same inane and equally pointless alternative behaviors. My master, worn to a frazzle, is clearly approaching the point of nervous breakdown. He has become so frenziedly obsessed with his problem that one hardly knows whether he is still a professional teacher or now regards this crazy oscillation between peep and sally as his sole true calling. And then, as the tides of his frenzy rose ever closer to the neap of madness, the following incident occurred.

Some kind of incident almost always does occur when frenzy, brainstorm, wrong-way-upness, a rush of blood to the head—call the condition what you will—impairs the human power to reason clearly. All the authorities, Galen, Paracelsus, even such ancient Chinese quacks as Pien Ch'üeh, are at one in this prognosis. There does, of course, remain some scope for debate as to where the "inverse up-rush" actually starts and as to what it is that rushes. The long-outmoded lore of European medicine-men held that there are four different liquids, or humors, washing around in the human body. The first such liquid was that of choler which, when it rose inversely, produced fury. The second liquid, that of dullness, if inversely risen, brought on lethargy. The third, the fluid of melancholy, produced, as one might have expected, melancholia. While the fourth, blood, was responsible for the activity of arms and legs. The progress of civilization appears, for no discernible reason, to have drained away the

fluids of choler, dullness and melancholia, so
that, as I understand it, nothing now remains
to circulate in our bodies but residual blood.
Consequently, if any inverse rising does indeed take place, it must be a wrong-way-upness of the blood. There is, of course, a limit
to the amount of blood containable in the
human body and the precise volume varies
slightly as between individual specimens, but,
on average, every human being contains some
9.9 liters of the stuff. Now when that liter-
age rises inversely, the head, beyond which it
cannot rise, becomes heated and inordinately
active whilst the rest of the body, drained of
blood, numbs with cold. One may reasonably
compare this process to the happenings in
September 1905 when the populace of Tokyo,
dissatisfied with the terms of the Treaty of
Portsmouth, took to burning police-boxes.
On that occasion all the police conglomerated
at headquarters, leaving no single officer out
on the streets or even to defend their various
police-boxes. That rush to headquarters could
well, medically, be diagnosed as a rush of
blood to the head; and in both cases the
proper cure is to re-establish the normal
balanced distribution of blood (or of bloody
cops) throughout the body (or body politic).
To achieve that balance the blood, inversely
risen, must be drawn back down from the head,
and there are various treatments available.

For instance, I understand that my master's
deceased father was in the habit of wrapping
a cold wet towel round his head and then

toasting his feet on a charcoal foot-warmer, practices whose efficacy would seem to be well warranted by those passages in that Chinese medical classic, *Some Thoughts on Typhoid Fever,* which state that keeping the head cold and the feet warm ensures good health and guarantees longevity. A towel a day keeps the doctor away. Another much-favored method of treatment is that in common use among the priesthood. Indeed, it appears that, when on pilgrimage, wandering Zen priests would invariably pick out a place to rest or sleep where there was "a tree above and a stone beneath." That slogan refers neither to any aesthetic ideal nor to the self-mortifications of penitents but to a particular technique for reversing rushes of blood to the head which was first worked out, no doubt in his early days as a rice-pounding kitchen scullion, by the Sixth Patriarch of the Zen sect, His Ineffable Holiness Hui Neng. Test the method for yourself. Sit on a stone and, in the nature of things, your bottom will grow cold. As the buttocks chill, any heady sensations associated with risen blood will sink away to nothing. That too, beyond all shadow of doubt, is also in the nature of things. One marvels, does one not, at the percipience of the Sixth Patriarch.

Thus, while a number of methods have been devised for cooling down rushes of blood to the head, I regret to report that, as of the present time, no satisfactory way to incite them has yet been invented. It is per-

haps natural that people should generally assume that there's nothing to be gained from
rushes of blood to the head, but there's at
least one context where any such sweeping
judgement is like to prove unduly hasty. Indeed, many of those engaged in the activity
I have in mind would swear blind that without such rushes they could not even begin to
pursue their profession. I am speaking of
poets. Just as coal is indispensable to a
steamship, so to poets are rushes of blood to
the head. Bereft of that energy-source for so
little as one day, poets would deflate into
mediocrities capable of nothing but eating
and drinking in a lifelong haze of idleness. In
sober truth, a rush of blood to the head is
simply an attack of lunacy, but since no professional would care to admit that he cannot
pursue his profession except when in a state
of mental derangement, poets, even amongst
themselves, do not call their madness madness. By an arrangement privately arrived at,
a sort of literary conspiracy, they all seek to
dazzle the foolish public by describing their
derangement as inspiration. The fact remains
that we are speaking of madness. Nevertheless,
poets do have Plato on their side, for he called
their ailment a sacred madness, a divine
afflatus. Even so, and no matter what degree
of divinity may really be involved, people
would refuse to regard poetry with any
measure of respect if it were openly identified
with lunacy, and I therefore conclude that
poets are wise to cling to their inspiration

because, though "inspiration" sounds to me like the name of some newly invented patent medicine, it remains an impressive word, one behind which the pottiness of poets can most splendidly be sheltered. When exotic-sounding delicacies in fact consist of nothing more unusual than yams, when images of the Goddess of Mercy consist of nothing more than two brief inches of rotten wood, when game-soup specialities are cooked from common crow, when the best stewed beef in boarding-houses is horse flesh in hot water, why should one question the reality of inspiration? If its reality is, as it must be, madness, at least it quickly spends itself—lunacy by fits (especially fits) and starts. Indeed it is only because their manic possession is so signally short lived that poets are not all shut away in the loony-bin at Colney Hatch.

I think it fair to add that these short-term maniacs, these inspired idiots, appear to be extraordinarily difficult to produce. It is painfully easy to manufacture lifelong loonies, but even the most artful God seems to have trouble fashioning beings whose manic spells are limited to those periods during which the lunatic is holding a means to write and is confronted with blank paper. At all events, God seldom creates such specimens. Consequently, they have to be manufactured without divine assistance and, all down the ages, scholars have been obliged to devote quite as much time and effort to finding the best way to generate the flow of inspiration as they have to the problems of preventing rushes of blood to the head. One seeker after inspiration, convinced that the secret of its attainment lay in constipation, assiduously strove for that prior condition by eating a dozen unripe persimmons every day for fruitless years on end. Another aspirant to inspiration believed he could achieve his objective by literal hotheadedness and accordingly spent his days in an iron bathtub, heated from below, consuming enormous quantities of hot *saké*. Failing to achieve immediate success, he concluded that the flaw in his scheme must lie with the bath-water, but unfortunately, he died before he could gather sufficient money to afford the expense of bathing in boiling port. Yet another would-be poet placed his hopes for an inspiring rush of blood to the head in the long-received concept of acquisition through imitation. It is an ancient idea that imitation of the conduct of some acknowledged master will produce in the ape the same mental state as graced the model. According to this theory a man who behaves like a drunkard will eventually feel what a drunkard feels, while a man who squats sufficiently long in the attitudes of a Zen master, enduring the agony while a joss-stick burns itself to nothing, will, somehow or other, experience the master's experience of enlightenment. The adoption of that theory of imitation to the search for inspiration led to the conclusion that, if one imitated the conduct of some literary giant, one would experience the same rushes of blood to the head as had inspired his literary achievements. I am reliably advised that Victor Hugo used to think up his finest prose effects while lying on his back in a sailing-boat, from which it would follow that if one can board a yacht, lie on one's back and stare at the blue of sky, one may confidently expect an upflow of stupendous prose. Since Robert Louis Stevenson is said to have written his novels while lying flat on his belly, it should be possible by worming around on the floor to have one's brush construct whole archipelagoes of treasured islands.

You can deduce, even from the modest number of examples which I've cited, that many persons have devised methods for generating inspiration; but none has so far proved successful, and current opinion holds that its artificial generation is impossible. Which is, of course, sad, but nothing can be done about it. However, I am quite certain that, sooner or later, someone will find a way to produce the divine afflatus on demand and, for the sake of dull humanity, I sincerely hope that that desirable discovery is not too long delayed.

I feel that I have spoken at more than sufficient length about rushes of blood to the head, and I will therefore now revert to my account of the crisis mounting within my master. I must, however, first observe that any major event is invariably preceded by a series of minor happenings, tremors and smoke-puffs clearly indicative of the coming explosion, and that throughout the ages, the admirable efforts of a long succession of historians have all been flawed by their concentration upon major events to the near total disregard of the minor forewarnings in any developing situation. Thus in my master's case the vehemence of the rush of blood to his head increased with every minor brush with his tormentors, and that steady rise in pressure made the eventual eruption entirely predictable. If I am properly to convey the real extent of my wretched master's sufferings, if I am to avoid the possibility that my readers should look down upon his rushes of blood to the head as trifling bubbles popping in his veins, if the world at large is not to sneer at his conduct as an exaggerated re-action to petty pin-pricks, surely I must not scamp the ordered details of the development of his frenzy. Indeed, when one considers what agony is involved in the generation of the most modest inspiration, it would be a discouragement to many a budding talent if any manifestation of wrong-way-upness should be disparaged. However, I must confess that the chain of incidents, minor and major, which I am about to relate reflects no honor upon Mr. Sneaze. Nonetheless, though the incidents themselves are, by and large, disgraceful, I must make it clear that the frenzy is no whit less genuine, less pure, than the flow of inspiration in the very greatest of the madmen of the arts. Since my own old master has nothing else remarkable about him, were I not to laud his frenzy, I, his life's recorder, would have nothing much to record.

Our enemies who swarm all over the Hall of the Descending Cloud have recently invented a new sort of dumdum bullet which they mercilessly fire into the northern part of the open space not only during their ten-minute breaks between classes but also after their school hours end. This new dumdum is apparently called a ball and it is discharged at the foe by being struck with an object resembling a bloated pestle or rolling-pin. However, powerful as that weapon may be, the range from its point of discharge in the Hall's playground to the study where my master is normally entrenched is too far for him to be in any personal danger. Our enemies are, of course, fully aware of the range-problem and have accordingly developed a tactic which exploits the limitations of their weapon. I understand that the Japanese triumph at the battle of Port Arthur was due in no small part to the indirect gunfire of our Navy. Correspondingly, even a dumdum struck no further than into the open space must surely contribute something to the discomforture of my master; especially when, presumably as an expression of the solidarity of the swarm, every missile is accompanied by a loud and menacing cry of "Wow" uttered in unison from every hostile throat. You can imagine with what terror my master is overwhelmed, how pitifully contracted are the blood-con-

duits to his arms and legs, and how inevita-
ably, under the pressures of agony, all the
blood at large within him begins to flow in
the wrong direction upwards to his head.
One must concede the artful ingenuity of
those young schemers in the Hall.

Long ago in Greece there lived a writer
named Aeschylus whose head was of the kind
common to all scholars and writers—that is
to say, it was bald. If you should wonder why
such persons should all lack head-hair, the
reason is that scholars and writers are usually poor (and therefore ill nourished) and
that their work is all in the head (so that what
little nourishment reaches their heads is all
so rapidly there consumed that only a very
small proportion of it survives to nourish the
hair-roots in their scalps). Writers and scholars are all characteristically both undernour-
ished and bald. It follows that Aeschylus,
being a writer, had no hair on his head. Indeed, he was renowned for his magnificently
smooth pate, hairless as a kumquat. One day,
with his usual head (I do not mean to imply
that one can change heads as one changes
hats, wearing at will a party head or an everyday head or a Sunday-go-to-meeting head,
but simply that on this occasion the head of
Aeschylus was as bald as ever), this famous
writer went out walking in the streets, where
he allowed the brilliant Grecian sunshine to
be reflected from his scalp. Which was a very
bad mistake. Bright light reflected from a
smooth bald head can be seen from an enor-

mous distance. It is the top of the tallest tree which takes the wind's worst force, so the top of earth's most shining man may well expect attentions no less fierce. At all events, it then so happened that an eagle with a captured tortoise clutched in its talons came cruising through the skies directly above the scintillating Aeschylus. Tortoises and turtles make delicious eating, but even in the days of the early Greeks they had already so far evolved as to be very hard-shelled creatures; and shells so hard, however delicious the meat within, make it equally hard for meals to be made of tortoises or turtles. It is perfectly true that lobsters grilled in the shell are a popular dish today, but no one's ever heard of tortoise stewed in the carapace, and I doubt if they ever will. Certainly no such item appeared on the menus of ancient Greece, and that cruising eagle was beginning somewhat embarrassedly to wonder what on earth he should do with his pendant tortoise when his eye was caught by a brilliant glittering from the distant earth below him. "I've got it," thought the eagle. "If I drop this tortoise on that shiny thing, its shell must surely break, and, once the shell is broken, I can plummet down and gorge to my heart's content on the so-unshielded meat. Nothing more simple. Here we go!" And, aiming skillfully for the effulgent center of the Aeschylean skull, he straightway dropped the tortoise. Unfortunately, both for Aeschylus and for the disappointed eagle, the skulls of writers are softer than the carapace of a tortoise; and so it was that, with his bright head smashed in smithereens, that luminary of literature came to his pitiful death.

My readers may be wondering how this long digression into death from the sky relates to my master's troubles; but, all in good time, I have reasonable hope that the connections will declare themselves. First, however, I feel bound to comment that I find it hard to determine the true intent of that eagle. Did he drop the tortoise in full awareness that the shiny object was the head of a writer, or did he genuinely believe his target was bare rock? Depending on the way in which one interprets the bird's intention, one either can or cannot draw a useful parallel between the eagle and those boy-faced harpies from the Hall. Moreover, any attempt fully to understand the problem must take due account of a variety of conflicting factors. For instance, it is a matter of fact that my master is not bald, and consequently, his head, unlike those of Aeschylus and other distinguished writers and scholars, emits no brilliant light. However, he does possess (though it is a pitiably small example) that *sine qua non* of any writer or scholar, a study. In addition, though he is normally to be found asleep in front of it, he does actually spend much of his time with some difficult book propped up before his nose. One must accordingly regard him as a person of at least the scholarly type. The fact that his head is not of a scholarly baldness does not necessarily mean that he is unqualified for such nudity: it could simply be that he is not yet fully unfledged. However, at his present rate of losing his wig, he can confidently expect soon to be as bald as any coot of a professor. If his depilation is the battle-objective of those hooligans at the Hall, one must acknowledge that they would be acting shrewdly if they concentrated their dumdum-fire on my master's head. Two weeks of such bombardment would so terrify the man that his contracted veins would cease to nourish him properly and his head would quickly come to resemble a kumquat or a kettle or a bright round copper pot. Two further weeks of bombardment and the kumquat would be squashed, the kettle spring a leak and the copper pot crack open. Faced with such a battle-plan, the only person who could fail to predict its inevitable success, the only fathead who would soldier on regardless, would be, of course, my madman of a master.

There came an afternoon when, taking my usual snooze on the veranda, I dreamt I was a tiger. "Bring me," I growl at my master, "buckets brimming with chicken-meat," which he, crawling toward me in a pleasing tremble of terror, immediately supplied. Waverhouse then appeared and I promptly snarl, "Get yourself down to the Wild Goose Restaurant, for I want, and you shall fetch, goose-flesh of the best."

"Pickled turnip and rice-crackers," comes the expectable blather of Waverhouse response, "have a savor strikingly similar to that of the wild goose."

Not deigning even to comment on his presumptuous prevarication, I simply open wide my cavern of a mouth and shake him silly with a single shattering roar.

Waverhouse turns pale and placatingly continues, "The Wild Goose Restaurant on Yamashita Street has, I much regret to report, just gone out of business. What other fare, most honored Sir, would you allow me to procure for you?"

"Shut, is it? Well, in that case I'll let you off with beef. Don't just stand there. Be off to Westbrooks and hurry back here with a pound of the finest roasting-beef. Hurry," I said, "or I'll gulp you where you stand." Waverhouse shoots out of the house at the double, the back of his gown tucked up into his girdle to free his legs for a truly astonishing turn of speed. My enormous body sprawled at ease along the veranda, I am lying there waiting for the return of Waverhouse when, all of a sudden, a hideous shouting fills the house and, without so much as a nibble of beef, I was jerked awake from my flesh-delicious dream. For my master, who only a moment back had been prostrating himself before me in a cringe of juddering terror, came rocketing out of the lavatory, kicked me aside with a savage toe in the ribs and, before I even recovered from that shock, had slipped on his outdoor clogs, whizzed out through the garden-gate and was off at his ungainliest gallop toward the Hall of the Descending Cloud. It is distinctly disconcerting to find oneself so quickly shrunken from a tiger to a cat, but I confess I was also somewhat tickled by this latest weird development. Indeed, the combination of the sight of my master's ferocious countenance with the pain of his vicious kick soon wiped from my mind all memory of tiger-time. My lightheartedness derives from the likelihood that, if my master is at last really going into action, there'll be some fun when the sparks start flying. So disregarding my aching ribs, I limp along in his wake and, as I come to the backyard gate, I hear him barking, "Thief!"

Up ahead, just scrambling over the four-eye fence with his Hall school-cap still stuck on his head, there's a sturdy lad aged about eighteen or nineteen. As the intruder drops into safety and scampers off to his base-camp in the playground, I sigh that he's got away, but my master, encouraged by the success of his shout of "Thief," shouts it once again and thunders on in hot pursuit. Which brings him to the fence. If he keeps on going, he too will trespass into thievery and, in his present transport of frenzy, it looks as though the passion of the chase and his own Dutch courage may actually carry him up and over the barricades. Certainly he shows no sign of wavering as his spindly legs bring him to the point where the bamboo stakes stand planted on the border. One more climbing step and my normally craven master will have gradu-

ated into villainy. At that moment one of the
enemy generals, some scurvy usher with a
droopy thin moustache, moved up to the
frontier, where he and my master, each on
his own side of the fence, engaged in the
following utterly fatuous parlay.

"Yes, he is a student of the Hall."

"Then, like all good students, he should
conduct himself correctly. How does he come
to be trespassing on someone else's prem-
ises?"

"He was collecting a ball that had rolled
onto your land."

"Why, then, did he not simply come and
ask my permission to retrieve it?"

"I will ensure that the boy is reproved."

"Well, in that case, all right."

The negotiations which I had happily an-
ticipated developing into outright battle thus
quickly petered out in a dull exchange of the
prosiest kind of chicken-chat. My master's
fire-breathing threats are mere bravado. When
it comes to action, nothing ever happens. It's
not unlike my own reversion from a dream-
tiger to an actual cat. At all events, the foregoing happenings constitute that "minor
incident" of which I wished to tell you, and
I will now proceed to the tale of the major
incident which followed.

My master is lying flat on his belly in the
living-room with the sliding-door left open.
He is deep in thought, probably devising
ways to defend himself against those hooligans at the Hall where, it would seem, classes

must be in progress because no noise whatever is coming from the playground. Instead, through the unwonted quiet comes a voice, which by its resonance I immediately recognize as the voice of the enemy general at yesterday's conference, delivering a clear and closely reasoned lecture upon ethics.

"Thus, public morality is so important that you will find it practiced everywhere: in Europe, in France, in Germany, in England, everywhere. Furthermore, everyone in Europe, even the most humble persons, pays deep respect to this public morality. It is all the more regrettable that we, in Japan, are still unable to match the civilizations of foreign countries in this matter. Some of you may perhaps think that public morality is an unimportant concept newly imported from abroad; but if you do so think, you are mistaken. Our own forebears were proud to be guided by the teachings of Confucius, which in every context emphasize the importance not only of faithfulness but of true understanding of the needs of other beings; and it is upon precisely such an understanding that public morality is founded. Since I am human, there are times when I feel like singing in a loud voice. But if I were studying and someone in the next room started singing loudly, I'd find it impossible to concentrate on my reading. Therefore, even though I would like to refresh my mind by quoting aloud from some anthology of classical Chinese poetry, I restrain myself from doing so because I know how infuriating I would find such a disturbance of my own studies. In brief, your own national tradition of public morality must always be observed and you should never do things which might be a nuisance to others. . . ."

At that point my master, who had been listening carefully to the lecture, broke into so broad a grin that I feel I must explain the inwardness of his reaction. A cynical reader might well suspect some element of sarcasm in my master's grinning, but the reality is that his nature is too simple, even too sweet, to accommodate the sour subtleties of doubt. He simply does not have the brainpower to be bad. He grinned for no more complicated reason than that he was pleased by what he'd heard; and, in his pitiful simplicity, he genuinely believed that since the ethics teacher had given such a poignant exhortation to the students, the hail of dumdums would now cease and he could snooze along forever in the recovered safety of his study. He need not yet, he reasoned, lose his hair. His frenzies may not instantly be cured, but, with the passing of the days, their violence will abate. He can dispense with wet towels round his brows and a charcoal-burner for his feet. And he need not sleep with a tree for his only shelter and a stone beneath his bum. Cozy in such delusions, of course the fathead grinned. It is in the not unworthy nature of the man that my master should have taken that lecture seriously. Indeed, though he lives in the

twentieth century, he still quite honestly be-
lieves even that debts should be repaid.

In due time the school's class-hours must
have ended, for the lecture on ethics came to
a sudden stop. I assume all the other classes
finished at the same time, for, quite suddenly,
with hideous whoops and shouts some eight
hundred young gentlemen came tumbling out
of the building. Buzzing and whirring like a
swarm of bees whose hive has been knocked
over, they poured from the windows, door-
ways and indeed from every least gap in the
fabric of the school. And it was with that
eruption that the major incident began.

Let me begin with an account of the battle-
formation of these human bees; and, should
you think it overblown to use specialized
military terms to describe such a piffling
business as my master's scufflings with mere
schoolboys, well, you'd be quite wrong. When
ordinary people think of warfare, their idea
of battle is of such bitter encounters as those
which took place during our recent war with
Russia at Shaka, Mukden and Port Arthur.
Less ordinary persons, notably those barbari-
ans who have some feel for poetry, associate
warfare with particular colorful incidents or
feats of derring-do: with Achilles in his char-
iot dragging the corpse of Hector round the
walls of Troy, or with Chang Fei of Yen
standing alone with his four-yard, snake-
shaped halberd on the Ch'ang-pan Bridge
and glaring down the milling hordes of Ts'ao
Ts'ao's army. However, though every man is

perfectly entitled to fashion his individual
notion of the nature of warfare, it would be
outrageous to lay down that the only real
wars are those of the kinds to which I've just
referred. One would like to think that totally
foolish wars only took place in antiquity and
that today, in the capital city of Imperial
Japan and during a period of peace, such
barbaric behavior were inconceivable. Even
though riots do occasionally occur, there's no
real danger of the disorder going beyond the
burning of a few police-boxes. Against that
background there can be no doubt that the
battle between Mr. Sneaze, Captain-General
of the Cave of the Sleeping Dragon, and the
eight hundred stalwart youths from the Hall
of the Descending Cloud must be recognized
as one of the most important conflicts fought
out in Tokyo since the foundation of that
city.

Tso Shih's account of the battle of Yen
Ling opens with a description of the enemy's
forces and their disposition; and, since all
subsequent historians of any repute have followed his example, I see no reason not to
begin with a description of the battle-forma-
tion of the Bees. In the van, disposed in line
close against their own side of the four-eye
fence, there is an advance-guard of students
whose probable function is to lure my master
forward into artillery-range. "D'you think
the old nut knows when he's beaten?" "Too
much of a fool." "Hasn't the guts to come
against us." "Where's he skulking now?"

"You'd think he had enough of his stinking loo." "Not him." "Maybe he's stuck there." "Silly old twerp." "Let's try barking." "Bow-wow-wow." "Yap-yap-yap." "Bow-wow-wow." These educated observations culminated in a long yowling war-cry of derision from the whole detachment. Stationed slightly apart to the right and rear of the advance unit in the general direction of the playground, a battery of artillery has taken up a commanding position on a bump of higher ground. The chief gunner, armed with an enormous rolling-pin, stands facing toward the Dragon's den; a second officer, with his back to the den, faces his colleague at a distance at some forty feet; and directly behind the bludgeon-bearer, similarly facing toward both the den and the second officer, a third artilleryman crouches like a frog. I have been told that persons so aligned are not necessarily preparing for battle and are probably practicing a game newly imported from America which is called baseball. Being myself an ignorant creature, I know nothing whatever about that game, but it is said to have become the most popular of all sporting activities in the middle schools, high schools and universities of modern Japan. America has a peculiar bent for the invention of fantastic things and I suppose it was only in kindness of heart that she taught Japan a game which can so easily be mistaken for gunnery and which causes so much annoyance in an otherwise peaceful neighborhood.

I imagine the Americans honestly think their game is no more than that; but even the most gamesome game, if it is able to disrupt an entire neighborhood, can hardly avoid being regarded as bombardment. In my view the lads at the Hall schemed for the results of bombardment under the guise of good clean fun. The truth is that by the infinite flexibility of interpretation one can get away with anything. Some people perpetrate fraud in the name of charity, others justify their obvious lunacy by calling it inspiration. Could it not be that others practice warfare in the guise of baseball? Baseball as I've hitherto described it is the normal form of the game, but the variety which I'll now describe is nothing less than the gunnery aspects of siege-warfare. I shall commence with an account of the gunnery-drill for firing dumdums. The second officer in the three-man crew which I've already described takes a dumdum in his right hand and slings it straight at the bludgeoneer. None but the initiated know the precise contents of the dumdum, so, as a non-professional, I can only say that the missile is round and hard like a stony dumpling and that its contents are extremely carefully sewn tight within a leather casing. As I was saying, this dumdum comes whistling through the wind toward the bludgeoneer who, brandishing his rolling-pin, slams the missile back. Every so often there is a misfire when bludgeon and dumdum fail to connect and the frog-like figure is then supposed to stop the ball and toss it back for the first officer again to start the firing-procedure. However, in most cases the connection is achieved and, with a savage cracking sound, the dumdum is discharged. The force thus generated is truly enormous and the kinetic energy stored in the missile could easily smash the thin skull of a neurotic dyspetic like my master. The main three-man gun-crew is all that is fundamentally necessary for the weapon to go into action, but the master-gunners are supported by droves of reinforcements who stand around the gun-site and, whenever the crack of pestle on sturdy dumpling reports a successful firing, burst into a chorus of raucous shouts and a rapid fire of hand-claps.

"Strike," they bellow.

"A real home-slam."

"Had enough yet?"

"We've got you licked."

"Go, go, go!"

"Get on back, you fool!"

Such a tempest of insults to my master would be bad enough, but injury is added to that offensiveness by the fact that, out of every three struck dumdums, at least one rolls onto the dragon's land. And that penetration is not accidental. On the contrary, it is the entire reason for the use of the baseball weapon. The weapon's bullets are nowadays manufactured all over the world, but they still remain extremely expensive, so that even in times of war, their supply is limited. Normally each artillery unit is provisioned with no more than one or two dumdums, and they cannot afford to lose their precious missile every time it's fired. These units consequently always include a platoon of ball-pickers, whose sole duty is to retrieve fallen balls. That duty is relatively easy when the dumdums happen to fall in plain view on accessible ground, but when they land in long grass or on hostile territory, the platoon has an unenviable task demanding speed, ingenuity and often a willingness to face real danger. It is thus the gunners' normal tactic to aim the weapon in such a way that its projectile can be readily recovered but, in the present context, their usual practice is deliberately reversed. They are no longer playing a game: they are engaged in warfare. They aim to fire their dumdum into my master's property so as to provide an excuse, the need to retrieve it, for crossing the four-eye fence. The constant irritation of dumdums landing in his property immediately to be followed by hordes of howling schoolboys leaves my master with a hideous choice between unventable anger and that resignation to fate which is surrender. Under such strain his baldness, surely, can only be a matter of time.

Then it was that a particularly well-struck dumdum came whistling over the four-eye fence, slashed off a few leaves from the lower branches of a paulownia and, with tremendous noise, landed full-toss against our inner castle-wall; that is to say, against that bamboo fence around our garden which I use for my exercises. We know from Newton's First Law of Motion that a body remains in its state of rest or of uniform motion unless acted upon by some external force. If the movement of matter were governed only by that Law, my master's skull would at this very moment be sharing the fate of Aeschylus, so he was fortunate that Newton was kind enough to save him from such a shattering experience by the establishment of a Second Law to the effect that change in motion is proportional to, and in the same direction as, the applied force. This, I'm afraid, is all a bit too difficult to follow, but the fact that the dumdum failed to pierce our garden-fence, failed to rip on through our paper-window and failed to smash my master's skull must, with our deepest gratitude, be attributed to Newton. In next to no time, as was only to be expected, the intrepid ball-pickers were in action on our property. One could hear them thrashing about with sticks in the clumps of bamboo-grass to the accompaniment of such screeched comment as "It landed about here" and "Rather more to the left." All enemy penetrations of the frontier in hot pursuit of their dumdums are conducted with maximum noise, since to sneak in for a secret retrieval would be to fail in their real mission. It is, of course, important to recover a costly missile, but it is even more important to tease my master into frenzy. Thus, on this particular occasion the ball-pickers knew perfectly well where to look for their ball. They'd seen its original line of flight, they'd heard it smack against our garden-fence and, therefore knowing the point of impact, they also knew precisely where it must have dropped to the ground; so it need have been no trouble at all to pick it up quietly and to depart in peace. We are indebted to Leibniz for the observation that any form of coexistence depends upon the maintenance of formal order. Thus, the letters of the alphabet, like the symbols of a syllabary, must always, in accordance with his Law of Systematic Order, occur in the same sequential relationship. Similarly, the relationships established by convention, proverb and received wisdom should not be disturbed: good luck demands that under a willow tree there should always be a loach, while a bat and the evening moon are necessarily linked. There is no such obvious connection between a ball and a fence, but persons who have accustomed themselves by daily baseball-practice to regular inroads into our property do acquire a sense of order in such a relationship, from which it follows that they always know exactly where to spot their fallen dumdums. It further follows that, since Leibniz has told them where to look, their unwillingness to do so clearly shows that the fuss they make is directed not toward finding their ball but to provoking my master into warfare.

Things have now gone so far that even a

man as mild and as naturally sluggish as my master cannot fail to respond to the challenge. Can it only have been yesterday that this suddenly berserk man of action was grinning so amiably to himself as he eavesdropped upon ethics? Swept to his feet by pure rage, he ran out roaring from the house; and so savagely sudden was his counter-attack that he actually took a prisoner. One cannot deny the brilliance, for my master, of this feat, but a beardless little lad of fourteen, maybe fifteen, summers makes a captive unbecoming to a fully whiskered man. Unbecoming or not, it was good enough for my master as, despite its pitiful pleas for mercy and forgiveness, he dragged the wretched child into his very den and onto the veranda.

At this point I should perhaps offer some further clarification of the enemy's tactics. They had in fact deduced from my master's ferocious behavior on the previous day that he was now close to the breaking-point and that it was a near certainty that today he could easily be needled into another lunatic charge. If such a sally led to the capture of some laggard senior boy, there would obviously be trouble; but they calculated that the risk of trouble would be minimized to virtually nothing if they used as ball-pickers only the smallest of their first- and second-year juniors. If my master succeeded in catching such a minnow and then kicked up a whale of a fuss, he would merely succeed in disgracing himself for childish behavior, and no

reflection whatever would be cast upon the
honor of the Hall. Such were the calculations of the enemy and such would be the
calculations of any normal person; but their
planning failed to take account of the fact
that they were not dealing with an ordinary
human being, and they should have realized
from his extraordinary performance yesterday that my master lacks the common sense
to see anything ludicrous in a full-grown
man pitting himself against some squitty
little schoolboy. A rush of blood to the head
will lift a normal person into flights of ab-
normality and transmute level-headed creatures into raving loonies; but so long as a
victim of frenzy remains capable of distin-
guishing between women, children, pack-
horse-drivers and rickshawmen, his frenzy
remains a paltry possession. True frenzy, the
divine afflatus, demands that its possessed
possessor should, like my frenzied master, be
capable of capturing alive some snotty little
schoolchild and of keeping him close as a
prisoner of real war. The capture has been
made. The trembling captive had been ordered forth to pick up balls like a common
soldier ordered into battle by his senior officers, only to be cornered by the inspired
battlecraft of a mad opposing general. Cut
off from escape home across the frontier, he
is caught and held in durance vile on the garden veranda of his captor. In such circumstances, my master's enemies cannot just sit
back and watch their friend's disgrace. One

after another, they come storming back over the four-eye fence and through the garden-gate until some dozen doughties are lined up in front of my master. Most of them are wearing neither jacket nor vest. One, standing with his white shirt-sleeves rolled up above his elbows, folds defiant arms. Another carries a worn-out cotton-flannel shirt slung across one shoulder. In striking contrast, yet another, a right young dandy, wears a spotless shirt of whitest linen hem-piped in black with its owner's initials in tasteful matching black embroidered as large capital letters above his heaving chest. Every member of the detachment holds himself like a soldier, and, from the tanned darkness of their sturdy bulge of muscle, one might guess them to have arrived no later than last night from the rough warrior-breeding uplands of the Sasa-yama mountains. It seems a shame to waste such splendid material on a middle school education. What an asset to the nation they could be as fisherfolk or boatmen. They were all bare-footed with their trouser-ends tucked high, as though interrupted on their way to fight some fire in the neighborhood. Lined up in front of my master, they glared at him in silence; and he, equally silent, glared belligerently back. Through what seemed hours of steadily increasing tension their eyes remained locked and the atmosphere built up toward a pressure only to be relieved by the letting of blood.

"Are you," suddenly snarled my master

with truly draconian violence, "also thieves?" His fury, like a blast of flame, vented itself from nostrils flared back from the sear of passion. The nose of the lion-mask used in lion-dances must have been modeled from an angered human face, for I can think of nowhere else where one could find so vicious an image of the mindless savagery of anger.

"No, we are not thieves. We are students of the Hall of the Descending Cloud."

"Not just thieves but liars too! How could students of that school you mention break into someone else's garden without permission?"

"But you can see the school-badge on the caps we're wearing."

"Those could be stolen too. If you are what you claim to be, explain how pupils at such a respectable school could be such thieves, such liars, such disgusting trespassers?"

"We only came to get our ball."

"Why did you allow the ball to come upon my property?"

"It just did."

"What a disgraceful lot you are."

"We shall be more careful in future. Please forgive us this time."

"Why on earth should I forgive a gang of young hooligans, all complete strangers, who come rampaging over fences to muck about on my property?"

"But we really are students of the Hall."

"If you are indeed students, in what grade are you?"

"The third year."

"Are you certain of that?"

"Yes."

My master turned his head toward the house and shouted for the maid, and almost immediately, with a questioning "Yes?" that idiot O-san stuck her head out of the door.

"Go over to the Hall of the Descending Cloud and fetch someone."

"Whom shall I fetch?"

"Anyone, but get him here."

Though O-san acknowledged these instructions, the scene in the garden was so odd, the meaning of my master's orders so insufficiently clear and the general conduct of the matter so inherently silly that, instead of setting off for the school, she simply stood there with a half-baked grin on her face.

We must remember, however, that my master thinks he is directing a major war-operation in which his inspired genius is in fullest flower. He naturally expects that his own staff should be flat out in his support and is far from pleased when some menial orderly not only seems blissfully unaware of the seriousness of warfare but, infinitely worse, reacts to action orders with a vacuous grin. Inevitably his frenzy mounts.

"I'm telling you to fetch someone from the Hall, anyone, no matter who. Can't you understand? One of the teachers, the school secretary, the headmaster, anybody."

"You mean the schoolmaster?" In respect of school matters that oaf O-san knows nothing of heirarchy and no school-title save schoolmaster.

"Yes, any of the schoolmasters, or the secretary or the head. Can't you hear what I'm saying?"

"If none of those are there, how about the porter?"

"Don't be such a fool. How could a porter cope with serious matters?"

At this point, O-san, probably thinking there was nothing more she could usefully do on the veranda, just said, "Right," and withdrew. Quite plainly she hadn't the foggiest idea of the purpose of her mission, and, while I was pondering the likelihood of her returning with the porter, I was surprised to see the lecturer on ethics come marching in by the front-gate. As soon as the new arrival had composedly seated himself, my master launched out upon his pettifogging impeachment.

"The clepsydera has barely dripped two shining drops since these brute fellows here broke in upon my land. . . ." My master opened his indictment in such archaic phraseology as one hears at kabuki plays about the forty-seven masterless *samurai* who attracted so much attention by their carryings-on in the early days of the eighteenth century, and wound his wailings up with a modest touch of sarcasm: ". . . as if indeed such persons could possibly be students of your school."

The ethics instructor evinced no obvious

signs of surprise. He glanced over his shoulder at the bravos in the garden and then, returning his eyes to focus on my master, indifferently answered, "Yes, they are all students from the Hall. We have repeatedly instructed them not to behave in the manner of which you complain. I deeply regret this occurrence. . . . Now, boys, for what conceivable reason do you even want to go beyond the school-fence?"

Well, students are students, everywhere the same. Confronted with their lecturer on ethics, they seem to have nothing to say. Silent and huddled together in a corner of the garden, they stand as though frozen, like a flock of sheep trapped by snowfall.

Self-defeatingly, my master proved unable to hold his tongue. "Since this house stands next to the school, I realize it's inevitable that balls from the playground will sometimes roll in here. But, the boys are really too rowdy. If they must come over the fence, if they only collected their balls in decent silence and left without disturbing us, then I might be content not to pursue the matter, but . . ."

"Quite so. I will most certainly caution them yet again. But you'll appreciate there are so many of them sculling about all over the place that it's difficult for us teachers to. . . . Listen, you lot: you must take far more care to behave properly. If a ball flies into this property, you must go right round to the front door and seek the master's permission to retrieve it. Understand?" He turned again to my master. "It is, good sir, a big school and our numbers give us endless, endless trouble. Since physical exercise is now an integral part of the educational system, we can hardly forbid them playing baseball even though we realize that the particular game can so easily prove a nuisance to your good self. We can thus only entreat you to overlook their intrusions in a benign awareness that high spirits do sometimes overflow into misconduct. For our part, we will ensure that they always present themselves at your front-entrance and request your generous permission to enter upon your land and retrieve their balls."

"That will be perfectly satisfactory. They may throw in as many balls as they wish. If in future the boys will present themselves properly at the front-door and properly ask permission, everything will be fine. Perhaps I may now hand these particular miscreants back into your charge for supervised conduct back to school. I am only sorry that it has proved necessary to put you personally to the inconvenience of coming over here to cope with this business." As always, my master, though he went up with the flash and sizzle of a rocket, came down like a dull old stick. The teacher of ethics led off his mountain-troopers through the front-gate; and so this major incident drooped to its tame conclusion.

If you laugh at me for calling it a major

event, well, you are free to laugh. Should it, for you, seem trivial, then so indeed it is; but I have been describing what seemed to my master, not perhaps to anyone else, events of enormous magnitude. Anyone who sneers at him as, at best, an arrow shot from a possibly once-strong bow but now so far gone as to be spent and feeble, should be reminded that such spent-arrowness is the essence of the man, and, moreover, that his peculiar character has made him the star-figure in a popular comic novel. Those who call him a fool for wasting his days in crazy quarrels with the younger kinds of teenage schoolboys command my immediate assent, for he is undoubtedly a fool. Which, of course, is why certain critics have said that my master has not yet grown out of his babyhood.

Having now described the minor and major events in my master's war with the Hall, I shall close that history with an account of their aftermath. Some of my readers may choose to believe that I'm having them on with a history of pure balderdash but, I do assure you, no cat, and least of all myself, would be so irresponsible. Every single letter, every single word which I set down implies and reflects a cosmic philosophy and, as these letters and words cohere into sentences and paragraphs, they become a co-ordinated whole, clear and consistent, with beginnings and ends skillfully designed to correspond and, by that correspondence, to provide an over-all world view of the condition of all creation. Thus, these close-written pages, which the more superficial minds amongst you have seen as nothing better than a tiresome spate of trivial chit-chat, shall suddenly reveal themselves as containing weighty wisdom, edifying homilies, guidance for you all. I would therefore be obliged if you would have the courtesy to sit up straight, stop lolling about like so many sloppy sacks and, instead of skimming through my text, study it with close attention. May I remind you that Liu Tsung-yüan thought it proper actually to lave his hands with rose-water before touching the paper lucky enough to carry the prose of his fellow-poet and fellow-scholar, Han T'ui-chih. The prose which I have written deserves a treatment no less punctiliously respectful. You should not disgrace yourselves by reading it in some old dog-eared copy of a magazine filched or borrowed from a friend. Have at least the grace to buy a copy of the magazine with your own money. As I indicated at the beginning of this well-constructed paragraph, I am about to describe an aftermath. If you think an aftermath could not possibly be interesting and consequently propose to skip reading it, you will most bitterly regret your decision. You simply must read on to the end.

On the day following the major showdown I took myself off for a walk. I had barely set out when, on the corner across from my master's house where a side-street joins the road, whom should I see but Goldfield and his toady Suzuki engaged in earnest conversation. Lickspittle Suzuki had in fact just left the Goldfield mansion after some obsequious visit there, when its flat-faced owner, homebound in his rickshaw, stopped to speak with him. Though I have lately come to find old Goldfield's household something of a bore and have therefore discontinued calling there, the sight of the old rogue himself stirred in my heart an odd warmth toward him. I even feel sufficient interest in Suzuki, whom I haven't seen for several weeks, to sidle across for a closer look; and it was thus natural that, as I drifted toward them, their conversation should fall upon my ears. It's not my fault, but theirs, if in a public place I happen to hear their talk. Goldfield, a man whose broad concept of decency permits him to hire narks to spy upon my master, would, I feel quite sure, extend his sympathetic understanding to any chance coincidence of presence which narrower minds might consider common eaves-dropping. I'd be disappointed if he displayed such lack of balance as to cut up rough. At all events, I heard their conversation—not, I repeat, of my own will or by my own scheming, simply because their talking was rammed into my ears.

"I've just been to your house. How fortunate to have met you here." Suzuki performs his usual series of overhumble bows.

"Fortunate indeed. As a matter of fact I've been wanting to see you."

"Have you, Sir? How lucky then. Is there anything I can do for you?"

"Well, nothing serious. Quite unimportant really. But it's something only you could do."

"You may be assured that anything I can do, most happily I will. What have you in mind?"

"Well now . . . ," grunted Goldfield as he searched for the right words.

"If you prefer, I could come back any time which happens to suit you. Would you care to suggest a time?"

"No, no; it's not all that important. Indeed, I might as well tell you now."

"Please don't hesitate."

"That crazy fellow, that friend of yours . . . what's his name now . . . Sneaze I think it was . . ."

"Oh, him. What's Sneaze been up to now?"

"Nothing really, but I've not entirely got over that last annoying business. It's left a nasty taste in my mouth."

"I quite understand. Vainglory such as his is positively sickening. He should see himself and his social status realistically; but no, stupid and stuck-up, he carries on like the lord of all creation."

"That's just it. His insolent disparagement of the business community gets my goat. All that rant about never bowing to the might of money. So I thought I'd let him see what a businessman can do. For quite some time now I've been putting spokes in his wagon, modest irritations involving no more than modest expenditure, but the man's incredibly stubborn and I find myself stumped by his sheer block-headedness. He can't, apparently, grasp that he's being got at."

"The trouble is that he has no real understanding of profit and loss. He is incapable of appreciating, let alone weighing, the balance of his own advantage and disadvantage. So he goes his own mad road, feeble but persistent in resisting redirection, totally oblivious to his own best interest. He's always been like that. A hopeless case."

Goldfield burst into genuine laughter at the portrait drawn by Suzuki of a character so ludicrous to them both that cachinnation was their only possible reaction. "You've hit the nail on the head. I've tried all sorts of tricks to shake him up. Knowing the level of his intelligence, I've even hired schoolkids to play him up with pranks."

"That was a bright idea! Did it work?"

"I think it's working. Certainly it's put him under strain, and I fancy it's now only a matter of time before he cracks under the pressure."

"Under sheer weight of numbers! How clever you are."

"Yes, I think that he's beginning to feel the effects of his singularity. Anyway, he's pretty weakened and I want you to go along and see how he is."

"Gladly. I'll call on him right away and

let you have a report on my way back. This should be interesting. It must be quite a sight to see that bull-headed fellow down in the dumps."

"Very well, then. See you later. I'll be expecting you."

"All right, Sir."

Well, well! So here we are again with another pretty plot. The power of a businessman is indeed formidable. By its frightening force my clinker of a master has been set afire with frenzy; his thatch of hair is well on its agonized way to becoming a skating rink for flies; and his skull can soon expect an Aeschylean bashing. Considering how much has been achieved by the power of a single businessman, I am obliged to conclude that, though I'll never know why the earth spins round on its axis, it's certainly cash that motivates this world. None know better than businessmen what power money buys. It is by their nod that the sun comes up in the east and, by their decision, goes down in the west. I have been very slow to learn the divine right of businessmen, and I attribute my backwardness to the atmosphere, the cultural effluvia from a poor pig-headed schoolie, in which I have been reared. The time has clearly come when my dimwitted bigot of a master simply must wake up to the realities of this world. To persevere in his present attitudes could well prove dangerous; dangerous, even, to that dreary, dull, dyspeptic life which he so desperately treasures. How, I wonder, will

my master cope with the coming visitation
of Suzuki? Believing that the style in which
that visitor is received will be an accurate
indicator of the degree to which my master
has learnt to recognize and accept the power
of businessmen, I know I must not loiter.
Though merely a cat, I accept the impera-
tives of loyalty and am worried for my master's safety. I slink around the nauseating
Suzuki and, at a scamper, got back home
before him.

Suzuki proves as smooth and slippery as
ever. No mention of the Goldfields soils his
subtle lips, but he chats away, amused and
even amusing, on matters of no importance.

"You don't look too well. Is anything
wrong?"

"No, I'm quite well."

"But you're pale. Must take care of yourself. The weather's not been good. Are you
sleeping all right?"

"Yes."

"Perhaps you have some worry. If there's
anything I can do, just tell me."

"Worry? What worry?"

"Oh, if you're so lucky as to be quite
worry-free, that's fine. I only spoke of worry
in the hope that I might help. Worry, you
know, is the worst of poisons. It's much more
profitable to live one's life with gaiety and
laughter. You seem to me a bit depressed,
gloomy even."

"Laughter's no joke; sometimes positively

harmful. Men have died from too much laughter."

"Nonsense. Remember the saying that luck arrives through a merry gate."

"It sounds to me as though you've never heard of Chrysippus. Have you? An ancient Greek philosopher?"

"Never heard of him. What did he do?"

"He died of laughter."

"Really? How extraordinary! But that was long ago."

"What difference does that make? Chrysippus saw a donkey eating figs from a silver bowl and thought the sight so funny he laughed and laughed and couldn't stop laughing. Eventually he laughed himself to death."

"Well, that's certainly a very funny story, but I'm not suggesting you should laugh your life away. But laugh a little, moderately, a little more than you do, and you'll find you feel wonderful."

Suzuki was watching my master through intently narrowed eyes, but his concentration was broken by the noise of the front-gate opening. I thought, with pleased relief, that one of my master's friends had chosen this happy moment to drop in. But I was wrong.

"Our ball's come in. May I go and get it?"

O-san answered from the kitchen, "Yes, you may"; and the schoolboy pads around to the back-garden.

Suzuki distinctly puzzled, asks, "What was all that about?"

"The boys from the school next door have batted one of their balls into my garden."

"Schoolboys next door? Do you have schoolboys for neighbors?"

"There's a school out back, the Hall of the Descending Cloud."

"Oh, I see. A school. It must be very noisy."

"You've no idea how noisy it is. I can't even study. If I were the Minister of Education, I'd order it closed forthwith."

Suzuki permitted himself a burst of laughter sufficiently long to increase my master's irritation. "My goodness," he observed when his cackling ceased, "you really are worked up. Do the schoolboys bother you all that much?"

"Bother me! They certainly do! They bother me from morning till night."

"If you find it all so irritating, why don't you move away?"

"You dare suggest that I should move away! What impertinence!"

"Steady on, now. There's no point in getting angry with me. Anyway, they're only little boys. If I were you, I'd simply disregard them."

"Yes, I expect you would; but I wouldn't. Only yesterday I summoned one of the teachers here and lodged a formal complaint."

"What a lark! He must have been ashamed."

"He was."

Just then, we heard again a voice and the

sound of the front-door opening. "Our ball's rolled in. May I please go and fetch it."

"Golly," said Suzuki, "not another with another lost ball."

"Yes, I've agreed that they should come by the front-gate."

"I see, I see. They do keep coming, don't they? One after the other! I've got it. Yes, I see."

"What is it that you see?"

"Oh, I meant I see the reason for this stream of schoolboys coming to collect lost balls."

"That's the sixteenth time today."

"Don't you find it a nuisance? Why don't you keep them out?"

"Keep them out? How can I keep them out when their ball keeps flying in? They'd come in anyway."

"Well, if you say you can't help it, I suppose you can't. But why get so tense and stiff-necked about it? A man with jagged edges is permanently handicapped: he can never roll smoothly along in this rough world. Anything rounded and easy-going can easily go anywhere, but angular things not only find it hard to roll but, when they do roll, get their corners snagged and chipped and blunted. Which hurts. You see, old chap, the world's not made simply and solely for you. You can't always have things your way. In a nutshell, it doesn't pay to defy the wealthy. All you'll achieve are strained nerves, damaged health and an ill name from everyone. Whatever you do and however much you suffer, those with money won't care a damn. All they have to do is to sit back and hire others to work for them, including whatever dirty work they happen to want done. It's obvious that you can't stand up to people like that. Dogged adherence to high moral principle is all very well in its way; but it seems to me that the price you might have to pay, indeed the price you are apparently paying, is a total disruption of both your private studies and your daily employment. You'll finish up completely worn out for no gain whatever."

"Excuse me, but another ball's come in. May I go round to the back and get it?"

"Look," said Suzuki with a knowing laugh, "here they are again."

"The impudent brats," my master shouted from a face stung red with rage.

The purpose of his mission now achieved, Suzuki made polite excuses and, as he left the house, invited my master to call upon him sometime.

No sooner had Suzuki gone but we had another visitor, the family physician, Dr. Amaki. The record of history since the most ancient times shows very few persons describing themselves as frenzied; and it's obvious that when they can recognize themselves as a bit odd, they've passed the peak of their derangement. My master reached and passed that peak during yesterday's major incident, and, though he started off all flame and fury only to settle down in dust and ashes, the

fact remains that he did achieve a settlement.
Yesterday evening, as he ruminated over the
business of that busy day, he recognized there
had been something odd about it. Whether
the oddness lay with himself or with the in-
mates of the Hall—that, naturally, remained
in doubt; but there was no least doubt at all
that something very odd was going on. In
the course of his ruminations, he even realized that, despite the constant provocation
which having a middle school for a neighbor
must inevitably generate, it was nevertheless
a bit peculiar to have lost his temper, to have
been dispossessed of his self-possession, day
in day out, for weeks on end. If the oddity
lay in himself, something must be done about
it. But what, he wondered, what? In the end
he concluded he had no choice but to seek
some drug or medicine which would suppress
or tranquilize his irritation at its internal
source. Having reasoned thus far, my master
decided that he'd call in Dr. Amaki and ask
for a physical checkup. We need not concern
ourselves with the wisdom or folly of that
decision, but my master's determination to
cope with his frenzy once he'd noticed it commands, unquestionably, respect and praise.

Dr. Amaki is his usual smiling self as he
serenely asks, "And how are we today?" Most
physicians ask that curious question in the
plural, and I wouldn't trust a doctor who
didn't.

"Doctor, I'm sure my end is near."

"What? Nonsense. That's impossible."

"Tell me frankly, do doctors' medicines ever do one good?"

Dr. Amaki was naturally taken aback by the form of that question but, being a man of courteous disposition, he answered gently without showing any annoyance: "Medicines usually do some good."

"Take my stomach trouble for instance. No amount of medicine produces the least improvement."

"That's not quite true."

"No? Do you think my medicine is making me feel better?" He's off again about his blessed stomach, inviting external opinions on an internal condition about which his nervous system sends him regular on-site reports.

"Well," says the doctor, "no cure comes in the twinkling of an eye. These things take time. But you're already better now than you used to be."

"Really? Do you think so?"

"Are you still easily irritated?"

"Of course I am. I fly off the handle even in my dreams."

"Perhaps you'd better take more exercise."

"If I do that, I'll lose my temper yet more quickly."

Dr. Amaki must have felt exasperated, for he said, "Let's take a look at you," and began examining my master. As soon as the examination was over, my master suddenly asked in a very loud voice, "Doctor, the other

day I was reading a book about hypnotism
which claimed that all sorts of ailments, including kleptomania and other strange disorders, respond well to hypnotic treatment.
Do you think it's true?"

"Yes, that treatment has been known to
effect cures."

"Is it still practiced today?"

"Yes."

"Is it difficult to hypnotize a person?"

"No, quite easy. I often do it."

"What? You do it?"

"Yes, shall I try it on you? Anyone can be
hypnotized, at least in theory. Would you
like me to try?"

"Very interesting! Yes, please do try. I've
always wanted to be hypnotized, but I
wouldn't care to remain in a permanent
trance, never to wake up."

"You needn't worry about that. Right
then, shall we start?"

Knowing my master, I was surprised at
the speed with which he had agreed to this
somewhat unusual form of treatment. I've
never seen a hypnotist in action, so, thrilled
by this exciting chance to witness a wonder
for myself, I settled to watch from a corner
of the room. Dr. Amaki began by stroking
my master's upper eyelids in a downward
direction. Though my master kept his eyes
shut tight, the doctor continued his downward stroking as though endeavoring to close
the lids. After a while, the doctor asks, "As

I stroke your eyelids down, like this, you feel the eyes are getting heavy, don't you?"

"True, they are becoming heavy," answers my master.

The doctor continues stroking and stroking, and eventually says, "Heavier and heavier, your eyes feel heavier and heavier, you feel that heaviness, don't you?"

My master, no doubt feeling just as the doctor suggests, is silent. The stroking continues for a further three or four minutes, and then the doctor murmurs, "Now you can't open your eyes."

My wretched master! Blinded by his own physician!

"You mean my eyes won't open."

"That's right. You can't open them."

My master, his eyes closed, makes no reply. And I watch this fearful scene in the compassionate conviction that he has now become blind. After a while the doctor says, "Just try to open them—I bet you can't."

"No," replies my master. No sooner had he spoken than both his eyes pop open; and, with a happy smirk, he comments, "You didn't do me, did you?"

"No," says Dr. Amaki, laughing in reply, "it seems I couldn't." So the experiment with hypnotic healing proved a flop, and Dr. Amaki left on some other mission of medical mercy.

Soon another visitor arrived. Since my master has very few friends, it's almost unbelievable that so many of those he has should choose to call today: indeed, I've

never known such numbers visit in the space
of a single day. Still, there it is. The visitors
did come, and this particular visitor was a
very rare specimen. I hasten to clarify that I
shall be writing about him at some length
not because of his rarity but because he has
a significant part to play in that promised
aftermath which I am still in process of describing. I do not know the man's name, but
he looks about forty and sports a smart
goatee on his long face. Just as I think of
Waverhouse as an aesthete, I see this new arrival as a philosopher. It's not that he's laid
any kind of claim to philosophic status or
blown his own trumpet in the Waverhouse
style, but simply that, as he talks to my master, he looks to me as a philosopher should
look. I deduce that he must be another of my
master's school-mates, for they speak to each
other in the familiar manner of very close
old friends.

"You mentioned Waverhouse. Now there's
an extraordinary man, as light and flossy as
goldfish food floating around on a pond.
Don't you agree? Someone was telling me
that only the other day he went out walking
with a friend and, as they passed the gates of
some peer or other, no one of course whom
Waverhouse had ever met, he dragged his
companion right into the house on the
grounds that it would be pleasant to call on
the owner and take a dish of tea. He really
is the giddy limit!"

"And what happened?"

"I didn't bother to find out. Something eccentric, I've no doubt. The man was born that way, not a thought in his head; unadulterated goldfish-food. And Suzuki? You see him here? Well, well. That one's clever all right, but not a man of the mind, not the kind I'd have thought you'd care to have around. He's the type to whom money and a gold watch seem to gravitate. Worldly-wise but ultimately worthless. A shallow man, and restless. He's always talking about the importance of smoothness, of doing things smoothly, smoothing one's way through life. But he understands nothing. Nothing at all. Not even the meaning of smoothness. If Waverhouse is goldfish food, Suzuki's common jelly-paste: a thing unpleasantly smooth which shakes and trembles, a thing fit only to be stringed on straw, available for sale to any passer-by."

My master seems to be much impressed by this flow of denigrating simile for, which he rarely does, he broke into hearty laughter and enquires, "That's Waverhouse and Suzuki. Now what about you?"

"Me? Well, maybe I'm a yam—long in shape and buried in mud."

"At least you seem carefree, always so self-controlled and self-composed. How I envy you."

"But I'm much the same as anyone else. There's nothing about me particularly to be envied. Still, I have the luck not to envy anyone. Which is just about the only good thing about me."

"Financially, are you now well off?"

"No, the same as ever. Little enough, but just sufficient to eat, so there's nothing to worry about."

"Myself, I feel so deeply discontented that I'm always losing my temper. I grouse and grumble and hardly anything else."

"There's nothing wrong with grumbling. When you feel like grumbling, grumble away. At least it brings one interim relief. You see, everyone is different. You can't re-fashion others to be like you. Consider chopsticks and bread: you've got to hold chopsticks as everyone does or you'll find it hard to eat rice; but bread can be cut, and is best cut, in accordance with your own particular liking. A suit made by a good tailor fits like a glove from the moment you put it on, but something run up by a shoddy craftsman takes years of tiresome wearing before it adjusts itself to your own particular bone-structure. If competent parents produced children all neatly shaped to fit the ways of our present world, all would be happily well. But if you have the misfortune to be born bungled, your only choice is either to suffer as a misfit or to hang on grimly until the world so changes its shape as to suit yours."

"I see no prospect that I shall ever fit in. It's a depressing prospect."

"If one forces one's way into a suit too

small for one's body, of course one tears the stitchings, by which I mean that persons violently ill suited to the world they seek to inhabit are those who pick quarrels, commit suicide, even incite real riots. But you, to be frank, are merely discontented. You're not going to do yourself in and you're not a natural brawler. You could be a lot worse off than you are."

"On the contrary, I find I'm picking quarrels morning, noon and night. When I lack a subject on whom to vent my spleen, I live in a constant fume of anger. Even such undirected ire amounts to brawling, doesn't it?"

"I see; you brawl with yourself. Interesting. But what's wrong with that? Brawl away to your heart's content."

"But I've grown bored with brawling."

"Then just stop it."

"I understand what you're driving at; but whatever you may say, one cannot do what one likes with one's own mind."

"My point is that one can. But leaving that aside, what do you think is the root-cause of your self-wounding discontent?"

In response to that sympathetic invitation, my master poured out before his friend the long sad catalogue of his woes and grievances. Beginning with an account of his war with the schoolboys, he proceeded to list, in manic detail and a neatly ordered reverse chronology, every single fretfulness, right back to the days of the terracotta badger, Savage Tea and his petty provocations by

conniving colleagues on the staff of his own
school.

The visiting philosopher listened in complete silence, but, allowing a long pause after Mr. Sneaze had finished his jeremiad to add its weight to his response, offered the following sagacities. "You should pay no regard whatever to the things said by your staff colleagues, which were anyway all complete rubbish. The schoolkids from the Hall are not to be taken seriously, grubby little vermin, existences not worthy even to be noticed by a man at your level of intellectual attainment. What? You insist that they disturb you? Tell me then, have your demeaning counter-activities, even your formal complaint, even that so-called settlement of the matter led to any lessening of disturbance? In all such matters I believe that the ways of our ancestors are wiser and much more effective than the ways of Europe, that so-called positivism which has lately attracted so much faddish attention. The main snag with positivism is that it acknowledges no limits. However long you may persist in positive action, the craving for ultimate satisfaction remains unsatisfied, the quest for the ideal eternally unrealized. You see those cypresses over there? Let us suppose you decide that they obstruct your view and you clear them away. Then you'll find the boarding-house behind them has become a new interruption of your view. When you've eliminated the boarding-house, the building next beyond begins to niggle you. There's no end to your search for a perfect view, and your ultimate dissatisfaction is the fate implicit in the European hankering for incessant progress toward an imagined ideal. Nobody at all, not even Alexander the Great or Napoleon, has ever felt satisfied with his conquests. Take a more homespun case. You meet a man, you take a scunner to him, you get into a quarrel, you fail to squash him, you take him to court, you win your case: but if you imagine that that's an end to the matter, you're most lamentably mistaken. For the real issue, the problem in your mind, remains unsettled, however hard you wrestle it around, until your dying day. The same truth applies in every context you may care to posit. You happen perhaps to live under an oligarchic government which you dislike so much that you replace it with a parliamentary democracy, but, finding you've only hopped out of a frying-pan into a fire, you run the risks of civil commotion merely to find another no less searing form of government. Or you find a river troublesome, so you bridge it; you are blocked by a mountain, so you tunnel through; it's a bore to walk or ride, so you build a railway. On and on it goes, with no solution solving the real problem of a positivist's dissatisfaction. Surely it's obvious that no human individual can ever have the whole of his heart's desire. The progressive positivism of Western civilization has certainly produced some notable results, but, in the end, it is no more than a civilization of the inherently dissatisfied, a culture for unhappy peoples. The traditional civilization of Japan does not look for satisfaction by some change in the condition of others but in that of the self. The main difference between the West and Japan is that the latter civilization has developed on the basic assumption that one's external environment cannot be significantly changed. If father and son cannot get along together, Westerners seek to establish domestic peace and quiet by changing the parent-child relationship, whereas we in Japan accept that relationship as immutable and strive, within that fixed relationship, to find a workable pattern for the restoration of domestic harmony. We take the same attitude toward any difficulties that may arise in such other fixed relationships as those between husband and wife, between master and servant, between the merchant and the warrior classes. We hold our attitude to be consonant with, indeed a reflection of, Nature itself. If some mountain-range blocks our free passage to a neighboring country, we do not seek to flatten the mountain, to re-structure the natural order. Instead we work out some arrangement under which the need to visit that neighboring country no longer arises.

"This method of fostering happiness, whereunder a man becomes perfectly content not to cross mountains, is perhaps best understood by Confucianists and Buddhists of the Zen sects. Nobody, however mighty, can do as he likes with the world. None can stop the sun from setting, none reverse the flow of rivers. But any man is able to do as he likes with his own mind. Thus, if you are prepared to undergo the disciplines that lead to control of the mind, indeed to its ultimate liberation, you would never even hear the racket kicked up by those graceless imps at the Hall; you would care no whit to be called a terracotta badger; and, knowing your fellow-teachers for mere fools, you would smile your disconcern upon their pitiful pavinities. As an example of the efficacy of the course of conduct I suggest, may I remind you of the story of the Zen priest Sogan who, in the turbulent times of thirteenth-century China, was threatened with decapitation by some berserk Mongol swordsman. Sitting unmoved in the posture of meditation, Sogan spoke, extempore, this verse which, in my opinion, can never be too often quoted.

Though, like a lightning-flash, some
    sword
May lop my head, it were as though
Spring winds were slashed. One is
    not awed
By threats of such a blowless blow.

As you will recall, the Mongol swordsman was so discountenanced by that calm asserva-tion of the power of Mind, of the life no kill-ing sword can kill, that he simply ran away. Perhaps, after years of the hardest training of

the mind, we too might reach that ultimate
passivity where, with the same empowered
disconcern so spiritedly shown by Sogan, we
too might understand how, like a flash of
lightning, the sword cuts through the breeze
of spring. I do not pretend yet to understand
anything so difficult, but of this I'm certain:
that it is dangerously mistaken to place your
entire trust in Western positivism. Your own
case proves my point. However positively
you struggle, you can't stop the schoolboys
teasing you. Of course, if you had the power
to close the school or could prove such serious wrong-doing as would merit police attention, things might be different. But things are
not that different and, as things actually are,
you have no chance, however positivist your
actions, of coming out on top. Any positivist
approach to your problem involves the question, and the power, of money; and it also
involves the fact that you are in a minority
of one against heavy odds. In brief, if you
continue to behave as a Westerner would,
you'll be forced to knuckle under to the rich
man and, by sheer weight of their numbers,
to be humiliated by the little boys. The basic
reason for your baleful discontent lies in the
fact that you are a man of no wealth seeking,
all on your own, to pursue a quarrel on positivist lines. There," he concluded his lengthy
dissertation, "you have it in a nutshell. Do
you understand what I've been saying?"

My master, who had listened in attentive
silence, said neither that he understood nor

that he didn't; but after this extraordinary
visitor had taken his leave, my master retired
to sit in his study where, without even opening a book, he seemed to be lost in thought.
Suzuki had preached that the wise man goes
with the tide and always truckles to the
wealthy. Dr. Amaki had given his professional opinion that jangled nerves may be
steadied by hypnotism. And our last visitor
had made it very clear that in his remarkable
view a man can only attain to peace of mind
by training himself to be passive. It remains
for my master to decide which course of action or inaction he wishes to follow. But one
thing's certain: he cannot go on as he is, and
something must be done.

MY MASTER is pockmarked. Though I hear that pockmarked faces were well regarded in the days before the restoration of the Emperor, in these enlightened times of the Anglo-Japanese Alliance, such cratered features look distinctly out of date. The decline of the pockmark began precisely when the birth-rate started to climb, so one may confidently expect that it will soon become extinct. This conclusion is an inescapable deduction from medical statistics; and these, being thus scientifically established, even a cat, a creature as penetrating critical as myself, would not dare cast doubt upon it. I cannot, offhand, quote statistics of the current incidence of pockmarks among the population of the world, but in my own district and among my many associates, no single cat and only one human being is so grievously afflicted. That human oddity is, I am deeply sorry to say, my poor old pitted master.

Every time I catch sight of it, I am moved by that pot-holed visage to reflect upon the dire ill luck which brought my master to live and breathe the air of this twentieth century through a face so anachronistic. Once upon a long time back he might have made a brave showing of his disastrous dimples; but in these present times when, by virtue of the vaccination laws of 1870, all pockmarks have been ordered into reservations on the upper arms, the determined squatting of such sunkennesses on the wan wastes of his cheeks and on the very tip of his nose, while perhaps admirable for their resistance to the drifts of change, is in fact a slur upon the honor of all pockmarks. I think it would be best if my master just got rid of them. And as quickly as he can. It seems to me that those pockmarks must feel lonely. Or could it be that they crowd together in a clutter on his face as for some final gathering of doomed clans still driven by a mad ambition to restore their fallen fortunes to a former state of glory? If that should be the case, one should not slight these pockmarks. There they are, a rallying of eternal dents, last-ditch indentations entrenched to block the march of time and rapid change. Such deep redoubts deserve our deep respect. The only snag is that they are also so deeply dirty.

Now there flourished in the days of my master's childhood a certain noted physician of Chinese medicine, Asada Sōhaku, who lived in Ushigome. When that old man went out upon his rounds, he invariably traveled, very very slowly, in a palanquin. As soon as he was dead and his adopted son had taken over the practice, the palanquin was put

away in favor of a rickshaw. No doubt in
time's due course the adopted son's adopted
son will put away the invariable herb-tea of
his predecessors and start prescribing aspirin;
but even in the first Sōhaku's heyday, it was
regarded as shabbily old-fashioned to be trun-
dled through the streets of Tokyo in a palanquin. Only long-established ghosts, dead pigs
on their way to freight-yards and, of course,
Sōhaku's doddering self saw nothing unpre-
sentable about it. I tell you this because my
master's pockmarks are as datedly unseemly
as Sōhaku's palanquin. Persons who clap eyes
upon my blighted patron naturally feel a little
sorry for him; but every day my master, no
less obstinate and insensitive than that trun-
dled quack of a herbalist, serenely saunters
off to school, his lone and helpless pockmarks
bared to a dumb-struck world, there to in-
struct his dullard students in the mysteries of
the English Reader. And precisely because he
is their teacher, the lessons to be learnt from
a now-departed era, deeply graven on his
hapless face, are, in addition to his intended
instruction, usefully imparted to his pupils.
Again and again, reading from his treasured
texts, his mouth transmits the precious truth
that "monkeys have hands," but all the time
his silent skin gives out its clear and frightening answer to unasked questions about the
effect of smallpox on the face. Were men as
warningly disfigured as my master to abandon the teaching profession, students concerned with the smallpox problem would be

obliged to hie themselves off to libraries and museums there to expend as much mental energy on visualizing pockmarks as we are forced to expend in our attempts to visualize the men of ancient Egypt by staring at their mummies. Considered from this angle, my master's blemishes, albeit unintentionally, are virtuous in performance.

However, it was not as an act of virtuous performance that my master plowed his face and scattered thereupon the tiny seeds of smallpox. It's barely credible, but the fact is that my master was actually once vaccinated. Unfortunately, the vaccine planted in his arm contrived, I know not how, to evade the intended localization and, instead, burst forth in ugly flower all over his face. Since this apparently happened when, being a child, he had neither the least romantic inclination nor any consciousness of our present high evaluation of a clear complexion, he consequently scratched away at his face wherever it felt itchy. Like volcanoes his many boils erupted and, as their yellow lava trickled down all over his face, the original appearance given him by his parents was irremediably wrecked. Every now and again my master still assures his wife that, before that business of the smallpox, he was a striking boy. At times he even boasts that he was indeed so remarkably beautiful that Europeans were wont to turn round in the street simply to take a second look at him. It is, of course, quite possible. But, sad to say, there's no one who can vouch for it.

Nevertheless, no matter how virtuous or how pregnant with admonitory truths a thing may be, if it is a dirty thing it still remains disgusting. Consequently, from as far back as his memory can reach, my master has been niggled by his pockmarks and has examined every conceivable method by which his tangerine appearance might be chamfered down to a texture less offensive. However, his pockmarks cannot just be garaged out of sight like Sōhaku's palanquin. They manifest themselves, and their blatant self-exposure so weighs upon his mind that, every time he walks along a street, he carefully counts the number of pockmarked persons he may be so lucky as to see. His diary logs the details. How many pockmarked persons, male or female, met that day, the place of the encounter, perhaps the general store at Ogawa-machi, perhaps in Ueno Park. Sometimes he cheats with a specific count of pockmarks, but usually contents himself with a slight exaggeration of the general intensity of the pocking. Where pockmarks are concerned, he reckons himself an authority second to none. The subject so obsesses him that the other day, when one of his friends just back from foreign travels called round to see him, he opened their conversation with the question "Are there pockmarks to be seen in Europe?"

His friend first answered, "Well," and then, tilting his head, gave himself up to long consideration before replying, "They are very seldom seen."

"Very seldom," repeated my master in despondent tones, "but," and a note of hope strengthened his voicing of the question, "there are, aren't there, just a few?"

"If there are, their owners will be either beggars or tramps. I doubt whether any pockmarks can be found on members of the educated classes," came the indifferent reply.

"Really?" said my master. "Then it must be very different from how things are in Japan."

Accepting the philosopher's advice, my master has given up quarreling with those little louts from Cloud Descending Hall and, since that act of abrogation, has secluded himself in his study to brood about something else. He may indeed be following the philosopher's recommendation that he should sit in silence and by negative activity advance the mental training of his soul; but whatever he's up to, I'm sure no good can come of encouraging a cabbage, that creature born to craven passiveness, to indulge himself in loafing gloomy idleness. I have come to the conclusion that he'd be far better off if he pawned his English books and took up with some geisha who might at least teach him how far it is to Tipperary. But bigots such as he would never listen to a cat's advice; so I decided to let him stew in his own dull juice and have accordingly not been near the man for the last six days.

Today's the seventh day since I left him stewing. Since Zen practice includes the discipline of sitting in cross-legged meditation for a week-long stretch, a discipline designed to bring divine enlightenment by sheer determination, I thought it possible that, by now, my master, dead or alive, might have meditated to some real effect. Accordingly, I slouched my way from the veranda and, peering in through the entrance to his study, looked for any sign of movement in the room. The study, a modest area of some hundred square feet, faces south with a big desk planted in its sunniest spot. "Big" is an understatement, for the desk is truly vast. Six feet long and nearly four feet wide, it stands proportionately high. Naturally, this mammoth object was not ready-made but, the bespoke handiwork of a neighboring cabinet-maker, it was most curiously required to serve both as a desk and as a bed. Never having discussed the matter with my master, I cannot possibly tell you how he came to order such an acreage of wood or why he ever contemplated sleeping on it. It may have been some passing whim which led to this enormity, the product of that process whereby certain types of lunatic associate two unassociable ideas. Certainly the association of the concept of a desk with the concept of a bed is genuinely remarkable. The trouble is that, for all its striking remarkability, the thing is virtually useless. Some time ago I happened to be watching while my master lay at snooze upon this ludicrous contraption. As I watched, he turned in his sleep, tumbled off and rolled out onto the veranda. Since that day he seems only to have used it as a desk.

In front of the desk lies a skimpy cushion whose cover of pure-wool muslin is decorated with three or four small holes, all in one area, burnt there by his cigarettes. The cotton stuffing leaking through these holes looks distinctly grimed. The man so ceremoniously sitting on this cushion, with his back and foot-soles turned toward us, is, of course, my master. His sash is knotted just above his bottom, and the two sash-ends of some grubby gray material dangle down limply against his staring soles. Only the other day he gave me a savage smack just because I tried to play with those dangling ends. Those ends are ends strictly not to be touched.

He seemed still to be lost in meditation, and, as I moved to look beyond his shoulder, I recalled the saying that pointless pondering is a waste of time. I was accordingly surprised to see something gleaming strangely on his desk. In spite of myself I blinked and blinked again. Very strange it was, indeed a thing to blink at. Withstanding the glare as best I could, I studied this glittering object and suddenly realized that I was being dazzled by his manipulation of a mirror on his desk. What on earth, I naturally wondered, is my master doing with a mirror in the study? Mirrors

belong in the bathroom. Indeed, it was only
this morning that, visiting the bathroom, I
saw this mirror there. My powers of recognition are, of course, remarkable; but I hardly
needed to exercise them, for the bathroom
mirror is the only one in the house. My
master uses it every morning when, having
washed his face, he proceeds to comb a parting into his hair. My readers may well wonder
that a man of my master's character should
bother to part his hair but, though he is indeed bone-idle about all other aspects of
personal grooming, he really does take trouble with his hair. Never since I joined this
household, not even in the broiling heat of
summer, have I seen my master's hair
cropped close against his skull. Invariably,
his hair is long, three inches long, carefully
parted on the left with an inappropriately
cocky quiff turned up in a ducktail on the
right side of his scalp. This hair-style may,
of course, be nothing more than another
symptom of mental disease. However, though
this flash coiffure hardly accords with the
antique dignity of his desk, it harms nobody
and no one ever carps about it. Leaving aside
all further discussion of the weird modernity
of his parting, one may more usefully turn to
consider the reason for his bizarre behavior.
The fact is that his pockmarks do not merely
pit his open face but, ever since early childhood, have extended their erosions right up
over his scalp. Consequently, if he cut his
hair like a normal man to a mere half inch

or less, dozens and dozens of pockmarks would then be visible among the roots of his crop. No matter how hard he brushed or smoothed a close-cut head of hair, the spotty dots of his pockmarks would still shine whitely through. The effect could well be quite poetic, like a swarm of glow-worms in a stubble field, but certainly his wife would not appreciate the spectacle. With his hair long, his scalp could be inalveolate. Why then should he go out of his way to expose his pitiable deformity? Indeed, he would, if he could, grow whiskers all over his face. Would it not then be crazy to spend good money on hair-cuts that can only expose his pitted pate to general derision, when hair that grows cost-free will hide what best were hid? That, then, is the reason why my master keeps his hair long. Because it's long, he needs must part it. Because he parts it, he needs must peer in a mirror and keep that mirror in the bathroom. Hence also why the bathroom mirror is the only pier-glass in the house. How then comes that sole existing mirror, that characteristically bathroom feature, to be glinting about in the study? Unless the glass has sickened into somnabulism, my master must have brought it there. And if so, why? Could it be that he needs a mirror as an adjunct to his spiritual training in negative activity? I am led to recall the ancient story of the scholar who visited a Buddhist priest far-famed for his great virtue and enlightenment, only to find him sweating away

at polishing a tile. "What are you doing?"
asked the scholar. "I'm doing my best to
make a mirror." In some surprise the scholar
pointed out that, though the priest was a
man of marvelous parts, no man in the world
could ever polish a tile to be a mirror. "In
that case," said the priest, "I'll stop the polishing. But," and he burst out laughing, "the
parallel would seem to be that no man learns
enlightenment by scholarly perusal of whole
libraries of books." It may be that my master has heard some version of this tale about
the uselessness of scholarship and, armed
with the bathroom mirror, now seeks trium-
phantly to demonstrate that nothingness is
all. I watch him cautiously, suddenly conscious that his mental instability may well be
taking a dangerous turn.

My master, oblivious of my presence and
my thinking, continues to stare, transfixedly
and with an air of wild enthusiasm, into our
one and only mirror. Actually, a mirror is a
sinister thing. I'm told it takes real courage,
alone at night, in a large room lit by a single
candle, to stare into a mirror. Indeed the
first time that my master's eldest daughter
shoved a mirror in front of my face, I was
so simultaneously startled and alarmed that
I ran around the house three times without
stopping. Even in broad daylight, anyone
who stares into a mirror with the fixed ab-
sorption now being displayed by my master
will end up terrified of his own reflected face;
and I am bound to observe that my master's

face, even at first glance, is not exactly lacking in immediate sinisterity. I sat and watched. After a while my master began talking to himself. "Yes," he said, "I can see that it's a dirty face." I must say his acknowledgement of his own repulsiveness merits praise. Judging by appearances, his behavior is that of a madman, but what he says rings true. It struck me that if he goes one step further down this thorny path, he will be horrified by his own ugliness. Unless in his heart of hearts a man knows himself for a black-guard, he will never be wise in the ways of this world; and a man who lacks that wisdom will never sufficiently rid himself of passion as to attain enlightenment. My master, having come thus far toward recognizing his intrinsic blackguardism, should now be shuddering back from the mirror with some cry from the heart such as "Ah, how terrifying." He has, as you know, said nothing of the sort. Instead, having got so far as to admit out loud the nastiness of his face, he does no more than to start puffing out his cheeks. I cannot tell why he so ballooned himself. Next, with the palms of both hands, two or three times, he slapped his bloated chops. Perhaps, I thought, some ritual act of sorcery; and at the moment of so thinking I had the feeling that, somewhere, somewhere, I had seen that pursy face before. From my ransacked memory the sudden truth emerged. His is the face of O-san.

It would, I think, be proper if I here devoted a few lines to describing the face of my master's female servant. It is a tumid face, a face like that bulbous lantern made from a dried and gutted blowfish which someone bought while visiting a fox-god's shrine and then, when visiting this house, unloaded on my master. Her face is so malignly puffy that both her eyes are sunken out of sight. Of course the puffiness of a blowfish is evenly distributed all over its globular body; but in the case of O-san's mug, the underlying bone-structure is angularly fashioned so that its overlying puffiness creates the effect of an hexagonal clock far gone in some dread dropsy. If O-san were to hear these comments, she'd be so actively angered that I deem it prudent to resume my interrupted account of my seemingly sorcerous master.

As I have already mentioned, first he blew his cheeks out, then he started slapping them. That done, he began once more to babble to himself. "When the skin is stretched," he said, "one hardly sees the pockmarks." Next, turning sideways to present his profile to the light, he pored upon his image in the glass. "This way, very bad. The side-light shows them up. It seems that, after all, they look least there when the light's from dead in front. But even then," and he spoke as if quite genuinely impressed, "they're still extremely nasty." He then stretched out his right hand holding the mirror as far as it would go. He scrutinized the glass. "At a distance, not so bad. As I thought, it's the close-up view that's awful. Still, that's true of most things. Not," his mumblings came out clearly as though he'd lighted upon some marvelous long-hid truth, "just of pock-marked faces." Next, he suddenly laid the mirror glass-upward flat on the desk and began contracting his facial muscles so that his brows, his eyebrows, even his very eyes, all seemed drawn in one wild whorl of wrinkles around the crease where his nose springs out from his skull. How hideous, I thought. My master, too, seemed shaken by the sight, for he muttered, "That won't do," and ceased his vile contractions. "I wonder," he went on, lifting the mirror up to a point but three short inches from his pot-holed skin, "why my face is so extraordinarily repulsive." He sounded as though honestly perplexed. With his right index-finger he begins to stroke the wings of his nose. Breaking off, he presses his fingertip hard down on his blotting-pad. The grease appeared as a round blob on the blotter. He has indeed some charming little ways. Next he raises his nose-greased fingertip and hauls down on his right lower eyelid daringly to produce a red-fleshed goblin look, an ugly trick which, very understandably, is commonly described as making a hare's face. It is not entirely clear whether he is studying his pockmarks or merely trying to stare his mirror down.

Let us, however, be generous. He is a quirky man, but at least it seems that in his case such staring at a bathroom mirror does induce original ideas, even original actions. Nor is that all. Such quaint behavior could be seen, by well-disposed and drolly natured persons, as the means by which my master moves, madly gesticulating and with a mirror for companion, toward a revelation of his inmost nature—toward, in Zen terms, his Original Face. All studies undertaken by human beings are always studies of themselves. The proper study of mankind is self. The heavens, earth, the mountains and the rivers, sun and moon and stars—they are all no more than other names for the self. There is nothing a man can study which is not, in the end, the study of the self. If a man could jump out of his self, that self would disappear at the moment of his jumping. Nor is that all. Only oneself can study one's self. It is totally impossible for anyone else to do it. Totally impossible, no matter how earnestly one may wish either to study another or to be studied by another. Which explains why all great men invariably achieve greatness solely by their own efforts. If it were true that you could learn to understand yourself by virtue of someone else's helping effort, then you could, for instance, declare whether some hunk of meat were tough or tender by getting someone else to eat it for you. But hearing truths preached in the morning, listening all evening to learned expositions of the Way, reading scholarly tomes the night long in your study—all these worthy activities are nothing but disciplines designed to facilitate your perception of your own true self. Yet that true self of yours cannot conceivably exist in the truth preached at you by some other person, or in the Way some other man expounds, or in ancient books however heaped upon you. If your own self exists, it is your personal phantom, a kind of doppelganger. Indeed, it's often the case that a phantom has more substance than a soulless person. For if you dog a shadow, one fine day you may well find its substance. Indeed, as a general rule, shadows adhere to their substances. If it is as a reflection of such concepts that my master's toying with the bathroom mirror should be seen, then he may be someone to be reckoned with. For surely those who seek the truth in themselves are wiser, better men than such fool scholars whose only claim to wisdom is that they have gulped down all that Epictetus scribbled on that subject.

A mirror is a vat for brewing self-conceit, yet, at the same time, a means to neutralize all vanity. Nothing shows up the absurd pretensions of a show-off more incitingly than a mirror. Since time began, the pretentious and the vainglorious have gone about the world inflicting damage both upon themselves and upon others, and the first cause of at least two-thirds of that injury undoubtedly lay in mirrors. Like that wretched Dr. Guillotin, who unintentionally caused himself, quite apart from many others, so much painful inconvenience during the French Revolution by inventing an improved method of decapitation, the man who invented the mirror must almost certainly have lived to regret it. On the other hand, for persons beginning to sicken into self-disgust and for persons already feeling spiritually shriveled, there's nothing quite so tonic as a good long look in a mirror. For any such observer cannot fail to realize as a staggering fact the effrontery of his having dared to go about for years with such an appalling face. The moment of that realization is the most precious moment in any man's life, and none looks more exaltedly transfigured than a fool grown self-enlightened to his own intrinsic folly. Before this self-enlightened fool all the world's vainglorious ninnies should, in the deepest awe, abase themselves. Such ninnies may indeed sneer in contempt at the enlightened one, but in reality their triumphing contempt is an expression, however unwitting, of an awed submission. I doubt whether my master has the depth to realize his foolishness by staring into a mirror, but he is at least capable of acknowledging the ugly truth pox-graven on his phiz. Recognition of the loathliness of one's face often proves a first step forward toward realizing the depravity of one's soul. My master shows promise. But this glint of wisdom may, of course, be nothing more than a fleeting consequence of his having been put down in his recent encounter with that Zen-bent chum of his.

Musing idly along these lines, I went on

watching my master. Unaware of my surveillance, he continued happily tugging at his eyelids to produce a series of increasingly horrible caricatures of his naturally nasty features. "They seem," he suddenly said, "distinctly bloodshot. Chronic conjunctivitis." He closed his eyes and thereupon began to frot their reddened lids with the flank of his index-finger. I imagine they must be itching, but eyes already so irksomely inflamed are hardly likely to be soothed by such vigorous abrasion. If he keeps it up, it won't be long before his eyes just decompose like those of a salted bream. After a bit he re-opened his lids and peered back into the mirror. Just as I'd feared, his eyes have all the glassy leadenness of the winter sky of some northern country. As a matter of fact, whatever the season, his eyes are never exactly bright or even clear. They are, to coin a term, nubeculoid: so muzzily inchoate that nothing differentiates their pupils and their whites. Just as his mind is dim and vaporous, so too his eyes, cloudily unfocused, drift pointlessly around. Some say this eye-defect was caused by infection contracted when still in the womb, others that it is an after-effect of his childhood smallpox. At all events he was thoroughly dosed as a tot with decoctions of red frogs and of those insects found on willow-trees. Perhaps because such cures are properly intended to eradicate peevishness in children, the doubtless loving care of his doubtless loving mother seems to have been wasted upon him, for, to this day, his eyes have remained as swimmingly vacuous as on the day he was born. My personal conviction is that neither antenatal poisoning nor infantile smallpox are in any way responsible for his inner blear of eye. That lamentable condition, the persistent drifting of his gaze, the dark turbidity of his eyeballs, are all no more than external signs of the darkly turbid content of his mind. Indeed, since he is responsible for the long gray drizzle of his own dismal thoughts, he should be chided for their outward manifestations which occasioned so much needless worry to his innocent mother. Where there's a drift of smoke, there you will find a fire. Where there are drifting eyes, there you will find a half-wit. Since his eyes reflect his mind, which is about as much use as a hole in the head, I can understand why his goggle eyes, the shape and size of those old-time coins with holes right through them, are as totally vacuous as they are unsuited to these times.

My master next began to twirl his moustache. It is, by nature, an unruly growth, each individual hair sticking out in whatever direction happens to take its surly fancy. Though individualism is currently very much the fashion, if every moustache-hair behaved thus egotistically, gentlemen so adorned would be sadly inconvenienced. Having given the matter considerable thought, my master has recently begun trying to train his various tufts into some sort of general order and, to be fair, he's had a modest measure of success, for his whiskers have of late shown signs of acquiring a certain sense of cooperative discipline. Originally, the growth was a mere haphazard extension of hair through the skin of his upper lip, but now it is possible for him to claim with pride that he keeps a moustache. All determination is strengthened by success. And my master, conscious that his moustache has a promising future, gives it every encouragement, not just in the mornings and at bedtime, but on every possible occasion. His dearest ambition is to sport twin upturned spikes like those on Kaiser Bill, so, disregarding the random inclinations of his pores, some pointed sideways, some straight down, he hauls his tuft-growths hideously heavenward. Which must be very painful for those wretched hairs. Indeed, it's clear that even my master sometimes finds it painful. But that, of course, is the essence of training. Willing or not, in pain or not, the tufts are being disciplined to stick straight up. To any objective observer this drill must seem a silly sort of occupation, but to my master it makes good sense; and one can hardly reproach him when the whole educational system of this country is similarly designed so that teachers may go about bragging that they can twist their student's real characters into upward aspirations as daft as a waxed moustache.

My master was thus brutally drilling his whiskers when the hexagonal O-san advanced from the kitchen and, sticking a raw red hand into the study with her customary lack of ceremony, abruptly stated, "The mail, master." My master, still holding his moustache uptwisted in his right hand and the mirror in his left, turned round toward the entrance. As soon as O-san, who knows that growth for the ragged flop it is, clapped eyes upon what looked like two fish snuggled under my master's nose with their tails frisked up on either side of it, she threw down some letters and scuttled off back to the kitchen where, her whole fat body bent across the lid of the rice-cooker, she lay convulsed with laughter. My master, nowise perturbed by her performance, put down the mirror with the utmost composure and gathered up the scattered post.

The first letter is a printed communication imposingly heavy with formal Chinese characters. It reads as follows:

Dear Sir,

May we offer you the compliments of the season. Please permit us to congratulate you upon your present prosperity, and long may it continue. As we are all aware, the Russo-Japanese War has ended in our complete and total victory, and peace has been restored. Most of our officers and men, loyal, brave and gallant, are singing victory-songs amidst that incessant cheering which signifies the heart-felt joy of all our people. At the call to arms, these officers and men, selflessly sacrificing themselves for the public good, went forth to endure the broiling heat and the piercing cold in foreign parts thousands of miles from home. There, unstintingly, they risked their lives, fighting on our behalf. Such faithful devotion to duty must never be forgotten. We should carry a living consciousness thereof, always, close to our hearts.

By the end of this month the last of our triumphant troops will have returned. Accordingly, our association, which represents this district, proposes to hold, on the 25th instant, a major victory-celebration honoring the thousand or so officers, non-commissioned officers, petty officers and private soldiers who hail from our district. We would also wish to welcome to this occasion all those bereaved families whose dear ones fell on the field of battle. We desire thus to express with human warmth our sympathy with them in their loss and our sincere gratitude to them for their menfolk's sacrifice and valor.

It would give our association the greatest pleasure, indeed it would do us credit, if we could carry out the proposed ceremony in the knowledge of your approval. We therefore sincerely hope you will signify your approval of our proposal by a generous subscription to this worthy cause.

The letter is signed by a peer. My master, having read it through in silence, replaces it in the envelope. He looks quite unconcerned and shows no sign whatever of any readiness to cough up cash. The other day he did actually contribute a few pence for the relief of those whom the poor crops in the north-east had exposed to famine. But ever since he made that gift he has bombarded everyone he meets with complaints that the subscription was a robbery. If he voluntarily subscribed, he can't possibly call it robbery. It is, indeed, most improper to use a word with such criminal implications. However, my master really does seem to think he really was robbed. I consequently think it most unlikely that he will part with his precious money in response to a mere printed letter, certainly not to a letter so civilly written and unperemptory, even though the cause is as noble as a victory-celebration and its canvasser as noble as a nobleman can be. As my master sees it, before honoring the army, he'd like to be honored himself. After he has been sufficiently honored, he well might honor almost anything; but so long as he continues having to scrape along in penny-pinched obscurity, he seems content to leave the honoring of armies to peers who can afford it.

"Oh dear," he said as he picked up the second envelope, "another printed letter." He then began, with steadily growing interest, to read what it said.

We offer our congratulations that you and your family should be enjoying good prosperity at this season of chilly autumn.

As you are aware, over the past three years the operation of our school has been greatly hindered by a few overacquisitive men. Indeed at one stage, things looked very serious. However, having realized that all those difficulties originated in certain of my own failings, I, your humble servant Shinsaku, communed and expostulated most deeply with myself in respect of those regrettable deficiencies and, having endured unspeakable self-criticism, hardships and privations, I have at long last found a way unaided to obtain sufficient funds to construct the new school-building in a style compatible with my own ideals. The fact is that I am about to publish a book entitled *The Essentials of the Secret Art of Sewing: A Separate Volume.* This book which I, your humble servant Shinsaku, have composed at immense trouble, is written in strict accordance with that theory and those principles of industrial art which, for many years, I have so painfully been studying. I hope that every household will buy a copy of this book, the price of which is no more than the actual cost of producing it with little or nothing added as profit. For I am convinced that this book will serve to advance the art of sewing. At the same time, the modest profits I anticipate from its sale should be sufficient to finance the needed extensions to the school-buildings.

Therefore I should be most grateful and

honored if you would, by way of making
a donation toward the construction ex-
penses of the school-house, be so kind as
to purchase a copy of the aforementioned
Essentials of the Secret Art, a book which
you could, for instance, advantageously
put in the hands of your maidservant. I do
most humbly and sincerely hope you will
grant me your support in this matter.

With the utmost respect and good will,
and with nine respectful bows,

Nuida Shinsaku
Principal
Great Japan Women's High
Graduate School of Sewing

My master indifferently crumpled this courteous letter into a ball and pitched it lightly
into the waste-paper basket. I am sorry to
say that Mr. Shinsaku's nine respectful bows
and his many unspeakable hardships all came
to nothing.

My master then took up his third letter.
This one gleams with quite extraordinary lus-
ter. Its envelope is brightly colored with red
and white stripes and looks as gay as a sign-
board advertising boiled sweets. Right in the
center of these dazzling slats there is written
in a thickly flowery calligraphic style, "O
Rare Dr. Sneaze! With Deep Respect."
Whatever this envelope may contain, its ex-
ternalities are extremely grand.

Sir,

If I am to dominate the universe, then I would, in one swift go, swallow up the whole world. But if the universe is to rule over me, then I would become no more than a mote of dust. Tell me, I entreat you, what is the correct relation between myself and the universe.

The person who first ate sea-slugs deserves respect for his daring. The man who first ate blowfish should be honored for his bravery. He who added sea-slugs to our diet performed a service for the nation comparable to Shinran's founding of the Pure Land sect, and the contributor of blowfish may fairly be compared with such a courageous religious innovator as the great Priest Nichiren. But you, dear Dr. Sneaze, your gastronomic genius stretches no further than to dried gourd-shavings dressed with vinegared bean-paste. I have yet to meet a man of parts whose prowess was advanced by eating dried gourd-shavings dressed with vinegared bean-paste.

Your closest friend might betray you. Your very parents might turn cold toward you. Even your own true love might cast you off. No man, naturally, can put his trust in wealth or worldly honors. Lands and peerages can vanish in the twinkling of an eye. Even a lifetime's scholarship treasured in one's head goes moldy in the end. On what, then, Dr. Sneaze, do you intend to rely? What is there in the whole wide

God is a mere clay figure fabricated in the depths of their despair by dreggy persons, by beings themselves so terrified as to be nothing more than stinking lumps of shit. Could it be that you claim nevertheless to find some ease of mind by putting your trust in objects that you know to be untrustworthy? Ah, what a depth of folly! A staggering drunkard, babbling senseless words, totters, however weavingly, straight toward his grave. The oil is all used up. As the wick gutters into darkness, so even one's passions die down and are gone. When your destined course is run, what flicker of your self will remain or be remembered? Respected sir, had you not better take a sip of tea?

If you disdain others, you have nothing to fear. Why is it, then, that you, who do disdain all others, are nonetheless enraged at the world which disdains you? High-ranking and distinguished persons seem to be puffed up by their disdain for people. However, as soon as they feel themselves disdained, they flare up in real anger. Let them flare up. They are all idiots!

When due regard is given to other people but those other people do not reciprocate, then, instead of just complaining, the discontented are liable, every now and again, to seek redress of their grievance by some positive action. Such spasmodic action is called revolution. Revolutions are not the work of mere grumblers, but are the happy handiwork of high-ranking and distinguished persons who enjoy promoting them.

Honored sir, there is a great deal of ginseng in Korea. Why, dear Dr. Sneaze, don't you give it a try?

*Written from Colney Hatch
and dispatched with two respectful bows
by* Providence Fair

The needle-plying Shinsaku had offered nine such bows, but Providence Fair produces only a measly brace, and, since his letter does not ask for money, he must, to the extent of seven respectful bobbings, be that much the more arrogant. Still, even though the letter does not scrounge for cash, its vile construction and indigestible contents make it equally painful to receive. Were it submitted to a magazine, even the scurviest, it would undoubtedly be rejected; and I felt consequently sure that my master, who never likes to put the least strain on his gray matter, would just tear it up. To my immense surprise he reads it over and over again. Perhaps he cannot credit that a posted letter might actually have no meaning and is determined to discover what this one seeks to convey. The world is crammed with conundrums, but none of them are totally meaningless. No matter how incomprehensible a phrase may be, a willing listener can always wring some kind of message out of it. You can say mankind is stupid or that mankind is astute: either way, the statement makes some sense. Indeed, one can go much further. It is not incomprehensible if one says that human beings are dogs or pigs. Nor would it occasion any surprise if one stated that a mountain was low; or that the universe is small. One could well get away with claiming that crows are white, that living dolls are dead ugly, even that my master is a man of worth. It follows that even a letter as weird as Mr. Fair's could, if one really bent one's mind to the effort, be twisted to make sense. And a man like my master, who has spent his whole life explaining the meanings of English words which he does not understand, naturally has small difficulty in wrenching meaning out of mumbo-jumbo totally uninterpretable by anyone else. He is, after all, the very fellow who, when one of his pupils asked why people still say "Good morning" when the weather happens to be bad, pondered that knotty problem for seven days at a stretch. I remember, too, that he once devoted three whole days and three long nights to an attempt at establishing the correct way for a Japanese to pronounce the name of Columbus. Such a man finds no trouble at all in making free interpretations of anything he comes across: he could, for instance, interpret a habit of eating dried gourd-shavings dressed with vinegared bean-paste as a sure indicator of inherent ability to achieve world fame, and with similar ease he could identify ginseng-eaters as the instigators of revolutions. At all events, it soon became clear that my master, demonstrating yet again that perspicacity and depth of mind which he once bought to bear on the knotty matter of saying "Good morning" at times of nasty weather, has penetrated to the inner meanings of the crazy letter sent him with two respectful bows. "This letter," he breathed in tones of the deepest admiration, "is fraught with profound significance. Whoever wrote these words is an adept of philosophies. The sweep, the range, the grasp of the mind behind this letter are truly stupendous." Which only goes to show how daft my master is. But, on second thought, perhaps he isn't quite so stupid at all. Habitually he values whatever he does not understand, but he is by no means alone in that behavior. Something unignorable lurks in whatever passes our understanding, and there is something inherently noble in that which we cannot measure. For which reason laymen are loud in their praises of matters they do not understand and scholars lecture unintelligibly on points as clear as day. This lesson is daily demonstrated in our universities, where incomprehensible lectures are both deeply respected and popular, while those whose words are easily understood are shunned as shallow thinkers. My master admired his third letter, not because its meaning was clear, but precisely because large tracts of it were utterly incomprehensible. He was touched, I would

say, by the total lack of reason for the letter's sudden irrelevant sallies into such matters as the first consumption of sea-slugs and
its description of theists as terror-frantic shit.
Thus, as Taoists are most deeply ravished by
the most gnomic sayings of Lao-tzu, as fol-
lowers of Confucius laud the *Book of Changes*
and as Zen priests dote on the *Collected
Thoughts* of Lin Chi, so my master admires
that letter because he hasn't the faintest idea
what it means. Of course, it wouldn't do not
to understand it at all; so, reading its nonsense
in accordance with his gift for free interpretation, he manages to convince himself that
he's grasped its real intent. Well, it's always
pleasant to admire something incomprehensible when you think you understand it. So
it was with understandable reverence that my
master refolded the florid calligraphy of that
precious letter and placed it gently down
upon the desk before him. He sits there, lost
in meditation, head bowed and his hands
sunk deep within his clothing.

Suddenly, there came a loud voice from the
entrance. "Hello there! Can I come in?" It
sounds like that of Waverhouse, but most
uncharacteristically, it keeps on asking for
admission. My master obviously hears the
constant calling, but, keeping his hands
buried in his clothes, makes no move whatever. Perhaps he holds it as a principle that
the master of a house should not answer a
caller, for in my experience he has never, at
least not from his study, ever cried, "Come

in." The maidservant has just gone out to buy some soap and Mrs. Sneaze is busy in the lavatory, so that leaves only me to answer the door. But, frankly, I do not care to. The matter was, however, settled when the visitor, grown impatient, stepped up onto the veranda by the door, walked in uninvited and left the door wide open. In the matter of civilities, my master and his visitor seem a perfect match. The visitor first went into the living-room but, having fruitlessly opened and shut various of its sliding-doors, then marched into the study.

"Well, really! What on earth are you doing? Don't you know you've got a visitor?"

"Ah, so it's you."

"Is that all you have to say? You should've answered if you were in. The house seemed positively deserted."

"Well, as it happens, I've got something on my mind."

"Even so, you could at least have said, 'Come in.' "

"I could have."

"The same old iron nerves."

"The fact is that lately I've been concentrating on training my mind."

"Fantastic! And what will become of your visitors if your trained mind makes you incapable of answering the door? I wish you wouldn't sit there looking so smugly cool. The point is that I'm not alone today. I've brought along someone very unusual. Won't you come out and meet him?"

"Whom have you brought?"

"Never mind that. Just come out and meet him. He's most anxious to meet you."

"Who is it?"

"Never mind who. Just get up. . . . There's a good fellow."

My master stood up without removing his hands from his clothing. "I'll bet you're pulling my leg again," he grumbled as, passing along the veranda, he walked into the drawing-room with the clear expectation of finding it empty. But there, politely facing the alcove in the wall, sat an old man whose stiffly upright posture expressed both a natural courtesy and a certain solemnity of mind. Involuntarily, my master first brought his hands into view and then immediately sat down with his bottom pushed hard up against the sliding-door. By this precipitate action my master finished up facing in the same westerly direction as the old man, so that it was now impossible for them to bow to each other in formal greeting. And the older generation remains extremely rigid in matters of etiquette.

"Please be seated there," said the old man urging my master to take his proper place with his back to the alcove.

Up till a few years ago, my master assumed that it did not matter where one sat in a room; but since the day when someone told him that an alcove is a modified form of that upper room where envoys of the Shogun were accustomed to seat themselves, he avoids that place like the plague. Consequently, and especially now that an unfamiliar elderly person is present, nothing will induce him to sit down in the place of honor. Indeed, he cannot even manage a proper greeting. He just bowed once and then exactly repeated the words used by his visitor. "Please be seated there."

"I beg of you. I am at a loss to greet you properly unless you sit over there."

"Oh no, I beg of you. Please, you sit over there." My master seems unable to do anything but parrot his guest.

"Sir, your modesty overwhelms me. I am unworthy. Please don't stand on ceremony. And please do sit there."

"Sir, your modesty . . . overwhelms you . . . please," came the jumbled answer from my scarlet-faced master. His mental training does not seem to have had much useful effect. Waverhouse, who has been delightedly watching this ridiculous performance from a position just outside the door, evidently thought it had gone on long enough.

"Move over. If you plant yourself so close to the door, I shan't be able to find a place to sit down. Get along with you, don't be shy." He prodded my master with his foot and then, bending down, unceremoniously shoved at my master's bottom from behind until he was able to force himself between the two seated figures facing the alcove. My master reluctantly slid forward.

"Sneaze, this is my uncle from Shizuoka of

whom you've often heard me speak. Uncle, this is Mr. Sneaze."

"How do you do? Waverhouse tells me that you have been very kind and that you let him come on frequent visits. I've been meaning myself to call on you for a long time and today, as I happened to be in the neigh-borhood, I decided to come and thank you. I beg to be favored with your acquaintance." The old man delivers his old-fashioned speech of greeting with great fluency.

Not only is my master taciturn by nature and possessed of few acquaintances, but he has rarely if ever met anyone of this anti-quated type. He was thus ill at ease from the start, and became increasingly scared as the old man's flood of language washed about his ears. All thoughts of Korean ginseng, of the shining stripes of that red and white en-velope or of other aids to mental discipline have slipped from his mind, and his inco-herent stutter of response betrays his desper-ation. "I, too . . . yes, I also . . . just meant to call on you . . . pleased . . . yes, indeed . . . most glad to make your acquaintance." This babble was delivered with his head bowed down to the floor. When he fell silent, he half-lifted his nut only to find the old man still bent politely flat. Jittering with embarrass-ment, he promptly lowered his head back onto the floor.

The old man, timing it beautifully, lifts his head. "In the old days," he remarked, "I too had a place up here in Tokyo and for many years used to live close to the Shogun's residence. However, when the shogunate collapsed, I left for the country and have, since then, only seldom visited the capital. Indeed, I find that things have changed so much that now I cannot even find my way around. If Waverhouse is not there to help, I'm as good as lost. Great, great changes." He shook his head and sighed. "The shogunate, you know, had been established in the castle here for over three hundred years . . . ."

Waverhouse seems to feel that the old man's observations are taking a tiresome turn, so he quickly interupts. "Uncle, though the shogunate was no doubt a very excellent institution, the present government is also to be praised. In the old days, for instance, there was no such thing as the Red Cross, was there?"

"No, there wasn't. Such things as the Red Cross didn't exist at all. There are other welcome innovations. Only in this present time has it become possible actually to lay one's eyes on members of the imperial family. I'm lucky to have lived so long and I'm especially fortunate to have attended today's general meeting of the Red Cross where, with my own two ears, I heard the voice of the Crown Prince. If I die tonight, I shall die a happy man."

"It's good that, once again, you can see the sights of Tokyo. D'you know, Sneaze, my uncle came up from Shizuoka specially for today's general meeting of the Red Cross in

Ueno, from which we are in fact now on the
way home. It's because of the meeting that
he's wearing that splendid frock-coat which
I recently ordered for him at Shirokiya's."

is wearing a frock-coat all right. Not
that it fits him anywhere. The sleeves are too
long, the lapels are strained back too far;
there's a dent in the back as big as a pond
and the armpits are too tight. If one tried
for a year to make an ill-cut coat, one could
not match the mis-shapen marvel on Waverhouse's uncle. I should add that the old man's
white wing-collar has come adrift from the
front stud in his spotless shirt so that, whenever he lifts his head, his Adam's apple
bobbles out between the shirt-top and the
levitating collar. At first I couldn't be sure
whether his black bow-tie was fastened
around his collar or his flesh. Moreover,
even if one somehow could contrive to overlook the enormities of his coat, his topknot
of white hair remains a spectacle of staggering singularity. I notice, too, that his famous
iron fan, more precisely his famous iron-
ribbed fan, is lying close beside him.

My master has now at last managed to
pull himself together and I observed that, as
he applied the results of his recent mental
training to his study of the old man's garb,
he looked distinctly shaken. He had naturally taken Waverhouse's stories with several
pinches of salt but now, with the old man
dumped down before his very eyes, he recognizes that the truth of the man is stronger

than any of Waverhouse's fictions. I could see my master's thoughts moving behind his cloudy eyes. If my wretched pockmarks, he was thinking, constitute valuable material for historical research, then this old man's get-up, his topknot and his iron fan, must be of yet more striking value. My master was obviously yearning to pose a thousand questions about the history of the iron fan, but equally obviously believed it would be rude to make a blunt enquiry. He also thought it would be impolite to say nothing, so he asked a question of the uttermost banality. "There must," he said, "have been a lot of people there?"

"Oh, an awful lot of people, and all of them just staring at me. It seems that men have grown too greatly and far too blatantly inquisitive. In the old days of the shogunate, things were very different."

"Quite so. In the old days things were not like that at all," says my master as if he too were venerable with years. To be fair, however, I must assert that, in speaking as he did, my master was not trying to show off. It's just that the words came out like that, random fume-drifts from the dingy cloud-wastes of his brain.

"What's more, you know, all those people kept gawping at this helmet-cracker."

"Your iron fan? It must be very heavy," says my master.

"Sneaze, you try it. It is indeed quite heavy. Uncle, do let him hold it."

Slowly the old man lifts it up and, with a
courteous "Please," hands it to my master.
He, like some worshiper at the Kurodani
Temple who has been allowed briefly to hold
the long sword treasured there, holds the
iron fan for several minutes and finally says,
"Indeed." Then, reverently, he passed the
ancient weapon back to its ancient owner.

"People call it an iron fan but actually it's
a helmet-cracker. A thing quite different from
an iron fan."

"Ah yes? And what was it used for?"

"For cracking helmets. And while your
enemy is still dazed, you just finish him off.
I believe this particular fan was in use as
long ago as the early fourteenth century,
possibly even by the great General Masashige
himself."

"Really, Uncle? Masashige's helmet-cracker?"

"It is not known for certain to whom this
beauty belonged. But it's certainly an old
one. Probably fangled in 1335."

"It may be quite as ancient as you say,
but it surely had that bright young Coldmoon worried. You know, Sneaze, since we
happened today to be passing through the
university grounds on our way back from
Ueno, I thought it would be pleasant and
convenient to drop in at the Science Department. We asked to be shown round the
physics laboratory and, because this helmet-
cracker happens to be made of iron, every
magnetic device in the place went completely

crazy. We caused a most almighty stir."

"It couldn't have been the fan. It's pure iron of the Kemmu period. Iron of superior quality. Absolutely safe."

"It's not a question of the quality of the iron. Any iron would have the same effect. Coldmoon told me so himself. So let's not quibble about that."

"Coldmoon? Is that the fellow we found polishing a glass bead? A sad case, that. For he is very young. Surely there must be something better he could do."

"Well," said Waverhouse, "I suppose it is pretty heart-rending; but that's his speciality and, once he's got his polishing right, he can look forward to a fine future as a scholar."

"How very extraordinary. If one can become a fine scholar by rubbing away at a glass bead, the road to intellectual eminence must be open to us all. Even to me. Indeed the owners of toy-shops that sell glass marbles to schoolboys would be particularly well advantaged in the quest for professorships. You know," he went on, turning to my master as if seeking the concurrence of that noted academic, "in old Cathay such polishers of stony baubles were known as lapidaries and, I fancy rightly, their standing in the social scale was really rather low."

My master lets his head droop slowly downward in a gesture of respectful assent. "Quite so," he said.

"Nowadays all learning seems to be concentrated on the physical sciences which, though there's superficially nothing wrong with them, are, when it comes to the crunch, totally useless. In the old days it was different. One trained for the profession of arms at literal risk of one's life, and one consequently disciplined one's mind to ensure that in moments of supreme effort or danger one did not lose one's head. I imagine you would agree that such a training was noticeably more rigorous than buffing up beads or winding wires round an armature."

"Quite so," my master once again observes with the same air of respect.

"Tell me, uncle, that discipline of the mind which you mentioned, wasn't it a matter, totally different of course from buffing up beads, of sitting around dead still with your hands tucked into your bosom?"

"There you go again! No, the disciplining of the mind was not just a simple matter of sitting still and saying nothing. More than two thousand years ago Mencius is said to have impressed upon his pupils that a freed mind must then be returned to examine its liberator's self. This wisdom was re-iterated, at least in part, by Shao K'ang-chieh, that eminent scholar of the Sung dynasty, who insisted that the highest achievement of human aspiration was the liberated mind. He, of course, was a Confucian; but even among the Chinese Buddhists you will find that such worthies as the Zen master Chung Feng have always taught that a steady and devoted mind was all important. Such teachings, as I'm sure you will agree, are by no means easy to understand."

"If you're asking me," said Waverhouse, "I'd say they were absolutely incomprehensible. What are the recipients of such teachings supposed to do with it?"

"Have you ever read Priest Takuan's discourses upon Zen doctrines?"

"No, I've never even heard of him, let alone his book."

"Takuan, who also wrote importantly upon the seasoning of turnips, was basically concerned with the focusing of mind. If, he says, one focuses one's mind upon the movements of an enemy, then the mind will be entrammeled by and subject to such movements. If upon a foeman's sword, then mind will be subjected to that sword. Correspondingly, if one's mind is concentrated upon the thought of wishing to kill an enemy, that thought will dominate all else. If concentrated upon one's own sword, then it will become effectively possessed by one's own sword. If one's mind centers upon the idea that one does not wish to be killed, then it becomes possessed by that idea. If one's mind is bent solely upon someone's posture, then one's mind will be absorbed to be that posture. In brief, there is nowhere that a mind can be directed without ceasing to be itself. Thus, wherever the mind is, it becomes, by definition, non-existent."

"Quite remarkable. Uncle, you must have astonishing powers of memory to be able to

quote such complicated stuff at such impressive length. Now, tell me, Sneaze, did you
follow the reasoning of that turnip-pickling
priest?"

"Quite so," replied my master, employing
his stock answer to good defensive effect.

"But don't you agree with its truth? Where
indeed should one place one's mind? If one
focuses one's mind upon the movements of
an enemy, then the mind will be entrammeled
by and subject to such movements. If upon
a foeman's sword . . ."

"Come now, uncle. Mr. Sneaze is already
deeply versed in such concepts. In fact, he's
only just emerged from his study where he
was busy training his mind. As you may yourself have noticed, he's getting so regularly to
abandon his mind that he wouldn't even answer the door to a visitor. So don't worry
about Sneaze. He's perfectly all right."

"I'm relieved to hear what you say. It's
highly commendable that he should so often
go out of his mind. You'd do well to do as he
does."

Waverhouse giggled, half in horror, half in
embarrassment; but then, as ever, rose to
the occasion. "Alas," he said, "I haven't got
the time. Just because you, uncle, live in a
leisurely style, you shouldn't assume that
others can afford to fritter their hours away."

"But are you not, in truth, idling your life
away?"

"On the contrary. I manage to cram busy
moments into my leisured life."

•
吾輩は猫である

"There you go again. You're a scallywag and a scatterbrain. That's why I keep telling you to discipline your mind. One often hears it said that someone manages to secure odd moments of leisure in a busy life, but I've never heard anyone brag of his ability to cram busy moments into his leisured life. Have you, Mr. Sneaze, ever heard such a thing before?"

"I don't believe I have."

Waverhouse laughed again, this time in genuine amusement. "I'd hoped that wouldn't happen, you two ganging up on me. By the way, uncle," he immediately continued, "how about having some Tokyo eels? It's a long time since you tried them. I'll stand you a meal at the Chikuyo. If we take the tram, we can be there in next to no time."

"Eels would be delightful, and that eel restaurant is undoubtedly the best. Unfortunately, however, I have an appointment with Suihara, and indeed I must be off immediately."

"So you're seeing Mr. Sugihara? Is that old fellow keeping well?"

"Not Sugihara—Suihara. Once again, I catch you in an error, and it's especially rude to make errors about a person's name. You should be more careful."

"But it's written Sugihara."

"It is indeed written Sugihara but it is pronounced Suihara."

"That's odd."

"Not odd at all. It's technically known as

a nominal reading. The common stonechat for instance, is called a wheatear, but its name has nothing to do with either wheat or ears. The bird is really a kind of sparrow with particularly pallid feathers on its rump. Its name, in fact, means white arse."

"How extraordinary!"

"Similarly, the magpie was originally a maggot-pie, not because it had anything to do with either maggots or meat-pies, but because this pied, this black-and-white crow, was still earlier named a Margaret-pie; just as the sparrow was dubbed Phillip, the redbreast Robin and some tits Tom. Margaret and its associated nicknames seem to have been particularly fruitful in this field of linguistics, for it was also from that name that the owl came to be called a madge. So to go around referring to Suihara as Sugihara marks you as a provincial, as much a laughable yokel as someone from the backwoods who still clumps round counting maggot-pies for luck."

"All right, all right. I defer to your superior knowledge of patavinities. But if you're going off to see your old friend, how shall we arrange things?"

"If you don't want to come, you needn't. I'll go by myself."

"Can you manage alone?"

"I doubt that I could walk so far. But if you would be so kind as to call a rickshaw, I'll go directly from here."

My master bowed respectfully and quickly

arranged for O-san to go and find a rickshaw. When it arrived, the old man delivered the expectedly long-winded speech of departure and, having settled his bowler hat comfortably over his top-knot, left. Waverhouse stayed behind.

"So that's your famous uncle."

"The very one."

"Quite so," said my master who, re-seating himself on a cushion, then sank back into thought with his hands tucked back in his bosom.

"Isn't he an astonishing old fellow? I'm lucky to have such an uncle. He carries on like that wherever he goes. You must have been a bit surprised, eh?" Waverhouse evidently likes the idea that my master should have been taken aback.

"No, not at all surprised."

"If that old uncle of mine didn't at least startle you, you must have got uncommonly steady nerves."

"It seems to me that there's something magnificent about your uncle. For instance, one could but admire, admire and deeply respect, his insistence on the necessity of training the mind."

"You think that admirable? Maybe when you're well into your sixties, like my uncle, you will be able to afford to be old-fashioned. But for the time being you'd do better to keep your wits about you. You'll do yourself no good if you get yourself known as devoted to old-fashioned notions."

"You worry too much about being con- 133
sidered old-fashioned. Sometimes, in particular cases, being old-fashioned is far more
admirable than being up-to-date. Modern
education, for instance, attempts too much,
and people, ever grasping for more and more,
never once question the wisdom of its limit-
less spread. By comparison, a traditional,
even an old-fashioned, Oriental education is
less aggressive and, by its very passivity,
produces a more discriminating taste. For the
traditional education trains the mind itself."
Glibly exact, my master trots out as his own
views the twaddle that he has only recently
picked up from his philosophizing friend.

"This," said Waverhouse in genuine concern, "is getting serious. You sound like
Singleman Kidd."

At mention of that name a look of real
shock came over my master's face. For the
sage philosopher who so recently visited the
Cave of the Sleeping Dragon and who, having there converted my master to new styles
of thinking, then serenely went upon his way,
bore that very name. And Waverhouse had
been dead right in his comparison, for my
master's words, solemnly spoken as his own
original conclusions, were in fact all straight
cribs from Kidd's unhinging homily. Since
my master had not realized that Waverhouse
knew Kidd, the speed with which Waverhouse
attributed such ideas to their true source reflected unflatteringly on the superficiality of
my master's grasp of them. Indeed, my mas-

ter actually seems bright enough to regard Waverhouse's comment as a slight upon himself. To establish how much Waverhouse really knew, my master point-blank asked him, "Have you ever heard him explaining his ideas?"

"Have I ever heard him! That man's ideas haven't changed one whit in the long ten years since first I heard them in our own undergraduate days."

"Since truth does not change, perhaps that very lack of variance at which you sneer is, in fact, a point in favor of his theories."

"Oh dear, oh dear. Look, it's because men like you lend a sympathetic ear to his ravings that he keeps on raving away. But just consider the man. His family name suggests that he's descended from goats, and that straggly beard, a billy's goatee even in college days, confirms his bloodstock. And his own name too, is singular beyond the point of simple idiosyncrasy. Now let me tell you a story. One day some years ago he came to visit me and, as usual, lectured me at length on the marvels of his mental training and his consequent passive discipline. He went on and on. All the same old tripe and he simply wouldn't stop talking. Eventually I suggested it was getting late, but he wouldn't take the hint. He said he didn't feel at all sleepy and, to my intense annoyance, rattled ever on about his cranky notions. He became so much of a nuisance that I finally told him that, however wakeful he might feel, I was dead tired. I begged and coaxed him to go to

bed, and at long last he went. So far, so good.
But in the middle of the night there was a
major disturbance. A rat, I'm almost sorry
to say, came and bit him on the nose. Now,
although he'd worn my ears off with his repetitive accounts of his spiritual enlightenment, of the way his training had lifted him
above all concern with merely mundane matters, as soon as the rat had nipped his nose
he displayed a tremendous interest in worldly
realities. He was even worried lest his life
should be in danger. What, he demanded, if
the rat's teeth were infected? The poison, he
whimpered, would be spreading through his
system while we wasted time in idle talk. Do
something, he pestered me, do something and
do it quickly. Well, I didn't know what to do.
But, after racking my brains, I staggered off
into the kitchen and pressed some grains of
boiled rice onto a piece of paper; and that
did the trick."

"How can boiled rice-grains cure a rat
bite?"

"I told him that the gooey mash was an
imported ointment recently invented by a
famous German doctor and that it had
proved an immediate and sovereign cure
when applied, in, I think, the State of Hy-
derabad, to persons fanged by venomous
serpents. Provided you clap this on, your life,
I told him from the bottom of my heart, will
be entirely safe."

"So even in those early days you had a
knack for bamboozlement."

"Well, it set Kidd's precious mind at rest.

The simpleton believed me and dropped off, smiling, into sleepybyland. When I woke next morning, I was particularly delighted to notice that a trickle from my ointment had dried into a thread and solidified among the darker threads of his daft goatee."

"I see your point. But he was younger then. It seems to me that he has matured into a man of serious worth."

"Have you seen him lately?"

"He was here about a week ago, and spoke for some long time."

"Ah, that explains why you've been so actively brandishing the childish negativities of the Kidd School."

"It so happens that I was much impressed by his ideas, and I am currently considering whether I myself should make the effort demanded by his mental discipline."

"Making an effort is always a good thing. But you'll only make a fool of yourself if you persist in swallowing every tinseled tale that's flashed in front of you. The trouble with you is that you believe anything and everything that anyone says. Though Kidd talks loftily about freeing himself from coarse realities by the disciplined power of his mind, the truth is that, in a real crisis, he'd be no different from the rest of us. You remember that big earthquake about nine years ago? The only person who jumped from an upstairs window and so broke his leg was your imperturbable Kidd."

"But, as I recall it, he has his own explanation of that incident."

"Of course he has. And a wonderful explanation naturally it is! Kidd's version of that scaredy-cat reality is that the working of the Zen-trained mind is so sharp that, when faced with an emergency, it reacts with the terrifying speed of a bullet fired from a rifle. While all the others, he says, were fleeing helter-skelter during the earthquake, he simply leapt down from an upstairs window. This pleased him very much, for it was a proof that his training had resulted in a truly fantastic immediacy of reaction. Kidd was thus pleased but limping. He refuses to admit defeat. As a matter of fact, you may have noticed that those who make the greatest fuss about the unworldliness bestowed upon them by Zen practices and even by ordinary Buddhism are always the least reliable of men."

"Do you really think so?" asks my master who is patently beginning to wobble.

"When Kidd was here the other day I'll bet he said all sorts of things which you'd only expect from a Zen priest babbling in his sleep. Well, didn't he?"

"In a way, yes. He emphasized the particular significance of a phrase which went something like, 'As a flash of lightning, the sword cuts through the spring wind.' "

"That same old flash of lightning. It's pitiful to think upon, but that's been his pet stock phrase throughout the last ten years. Not his own phrase, of course. He lifted it from the sayings of Wu Hsüeh, who thought it up in China more than a thousand years ago. We even nicknamed Kidd with an ap-

propriate pun on the sound in Japanese of
Wu Hsüeh's Chinese name; and I do assure
you that the Reverend No-perception left
scarcely one of his fellow-lodgers in our student boarding-house unstruck by his tedious
lightning. We used to tease him into a frenzy
because he then got his patter so properly
mixed up that he became quite funny. 'As a
flash of spring,' he would shout at us, 'the
sword cuts through the lightning.' Try it on
him the next time he calls round. When he
sits there calmly propounding nonsense, interrupt and contradict him. Keep it up till he
gets rattled and in no time at all he'll start
spouting the most amazing balderdash you've
ever heard."

"Nobody's safe with a tricky rascal like
you around."

"I wonder who, really, is the trickster. As
a rational man, I very much dislike Zen
priests and all that riff-raff with their pre-
posterous claims to intuitive enlightenment.
Living in a temple near my house there's an
old retired priest, maybe eighty years old. The
other day when we had a heavy shower, a
thunderbolt fell in the temple-yard, where it
splintered a pine-tree in the old man's garden.
People were at pains to tell me how calm,
how unperturbed throughout that frightful
happening the good old man had been, how
in his spiritual strength he had shown himself serenely indifferent to a terrifying act of
nature which had scared everyone else clean
out of their wits. But I found out later that

this spiritual colossus was in fact stone-deaf.
Naturally he wasn't shaken by the fall of a
thunderbolt of which he was totally unaware.
And all too often that's how it really is. I'd
have no quarrel with Kidd if he did no more
than derange himself in his efforts to find enlightenment, but the trouble is that he goes
around involving other people. I know of at
least two persons who, thanks to Kidd, are
now stark raving mad."

"Who, for instance?"

"Who? One was Rino Tōzen. Thanks to
Kidd, he became a fanatic Zen believer, and
went to the Zen center at Kamakura and
there became a lunatic. As you may know,
there's a railway crossing in Kamakura right
in front of the Engaku Temple. Well, one day
poor old Rino went and sat down there to do
his meditation. He made a thorough nuisance
of himself, telling everyone not to worry because, such were his spiritual powers, he could
bring to a halt any train that dared to approach him. In the event, since the train stopped of itself, his stupid life was spared; but
he then went around saying that he had a
holy body of immortal strength which could
neither be burnt with fire nor drowned in
water. He actually went so far as to submerge
himself in the temple's lotus-pond where he
bubbled about below the water for quite some
time."

"Did he drown?"

"Again he was lucky. He was hauled out by
a student priest who happened to be passing.

After that he returned to Tokyo and eventually died of peritonitis. It is true, as I've just said, that he died of peritonitis, but the cause of his sickness was that he ate nothing but boiled barley and pickles throughout his time at the temple. Thus, though at several removes, it was Kidd who killed him."

"Overenthusiasm is not, it seems, an unmixed blessing," said my master looking as if he suddenly felt a bit creepy.

"Yes, indeed. And there is yet another of my classmates whom Kidd's meddlesome ministrations brought to an unhappy end."

"How terrible! Who was that?"

"Poor old Pelham Flap. He, too, was egged on into intemperate enthusiasms by that cranky Kidd, and used to come out with pronouncements such as 'The eels are going up to Heaven'; and, in a sense, they eventually did."

"What d'you mean by that?"

"Well, he was obsessed by food, the most gluttonous man I've ever met. So when his gluttony became linked with the Zen perversities he learnt from Kidd, there wasn't much hope for him so far as this world is concerned. At first, we didn't notice anything, but, now that I come to think back upon it, he was, even from the beginning, given to saying the strangest things. For instance, on one occasion when he was visiting me at home, he warned me somewhat ponderously that beef cutlets might soon be coming to roost in my pine-trees. On another occasion

he mentioned that in the country district
where his people lived it was not uncommon
for boiled fish-paste to come floating down
the river on little wooden boards. It was still
all right when he contented himself with mere
bizarre remarks, but when one day he urged
me to join him in digging for sugared chest-
nuts and mashed potatoes in a ditch that ran
in front of the house, then I reckoned things
had gone too far. A few days later they carted
him off to the loony-bin at Colney Hatch
and he's been there ever since. To tell the
truth, an earth-bound greedy pig like Flap
wasn't entitled to rise so high in the spiritual
hierarchy as even to qualify to become a lunatic, so I suppose he ought to thank Kidd for
that ludicrous measure of advancement. Yes,
indeed, the influence of Singleman Kidd is
quite something."

"Well, well. So Flap is still confined in an
asylum?"

"Oh yes; he's very much at home in there.
He's now become a megalomaniac, and finds
full scope in that institution for the exercise
of his latest bent. He recently came to the
conclusion that Pelham Flap was an unim-
pressive name; so, in the conviction that he
is an incarnation of Divine Providence, he's
now decided to call himself Mr. Providence
Fair. He's really putting on a terrific performance. You ought to go and see him one of
these days."

"Did you say 'Providence Fair'?"

"Yes, that's his latest moniker. I must say

that, considering he's a certified lunatic, he's picked on a clever name. Anyway, his fancy is that we are all living in darkness, a condition from which he yearns to rescue us. Accordingly, he fires off enlightening letters to his friends or, in fact, to just anyone. I myself have several of his demented encyclicals. Some are extremely long, so long that I've even found myself obliged to pay postage due."

"Then the letter I've just received must have come from this unbalanced Flap!"

"Ah, so you've heard from him too. That's odd. I bet it came in a scarlet envelope."

"Red in the center and white on both sides, a rather unusual looking envelope."

"D'you know, I'm told he has them specially imported from China. The color-scheme is supposed to symbolize one of his pottier maxims: that Heaven's way is white, Earth's way is white and that the human way turns red between them."

"I see. Even the envelope is pregnant with transcendental meaning."

"Being that of a lunatic, his symbolism is incredibly elaborate. But the quaint thing is that, even though he's gone completely out of his mind, his stomach seems to have maintained its gluttonous appetites. All his letters somewhere mention food. Did he refer to food in his letter to you?"

"Well, yes; he did say something about sea-slugs."

"Quite. He was very partial to sea-slugs.

It's only natural he still should think about them. Anything else?"

"The letter did contain some passing references to blowfish and Korean ginseng."

"That combination is rather clever. Perhaps in his lunatic way he's trying to advise you to take infusions of ginseng when you poison yourself by eating blowfish."

"I don't think that was quite what he meant."

"Never mind if he didn't. He's a lunatic anyway. Nothing more?"

"One thing more. There was a bit toward the end of his letter where he advised me, most respectfully, to drink tea."

"That's amusing. Advising you to drink tea, eh? Pretty tough talk, that, at least when it comes from Flap. I imagine he sees himself as having snubbed you. Well done, Providence Fair!!" Goodness knows what Waverhouse finds so funny, but it certainly makes him laugh.

My master, having now realized that the writer of that letter which he had read and re-read with such immense respect is a notorious maniac feels distinctly annoyed with himself, not least because his recent enthusiasm and his spiritual endeavorings have all been a waste of time. He is also somewhat ashamed of himself for having, after assiduous study of the material, so strongly admired the scribblings of an insane person. And to top off his discomforture, he harbors a sneaking suspicion that anyone so impressed by a madman's

・吾輩は猫である

work is himself likely to be not altogether right in the head. He consequently sits there looking decidedly upset in a mixed condition of anger, humiliation and worry.

Just at that moment we heard a sound of the entrance-door being roughly opened and the sound of heavy boots crunching on the step-stone. Then a loud voice shouted, "Hallo! Excuse me. Is there anyone at home?"

Unlike my sluggish master, Waverhouse is a buoyant person. Without waiting for O-san to answer the caller, he calls out, "Who is it?" Up on his feet in a flash, he sweeps through the neighboring anteroom in a couple of strides and disappears into the entrance-hall. The way he comes barging right into someone else's house without being announced or invited is, of course, annoying; but, once inside, he generally makes himself useful by performing such houseboy functions as answering the door. Still, though Waverhouse does in truth make himself useful, the fact remains that in this house he's a guest; and it is not proper that, when a guest flits out to the entrance-hall, the master of the house should just stay sitting, disturbingly undisturbed, on the drawing-room floor. Any normal person would at least get up and follow a guest, any guest, out to the entrance-hall. But Mr. Sneaze is and always will be his own obdurate self. Seemingly totally unconcerned, he sits there with his bottom planted on a cushion; but though such steadiness of bottom might be thought to imply some steadiness of nerve, he was inside a simmer of emotions.

Waverhouse can be heard conducting an animated conversation at the entrance, but eventually he turns to shout back into the drawing-room. "Sneaze," he yells, "you're wanted. You'll have to come out here. Only you can cope with this."

My master sighs in resignation and, his hands still tucked inside his robe, slowly shuffles his way to the entrance. There he finds Waverhouse, holding the visitor's card in his hand, crouched down in the polite posture for receiving visitors. Seen from the back, however, that posture looks extremely undignified. The visiting card informs my master that his latest visitor is Police Detective Yoshida Torazō from the Metropolitan Police Office. Standing beside Torazō is a tall young man in his mid-twenties, smartly dressed in a kimono ensemble of fine striped cotton. Quaintly enough, this personable young fellow is like my master in that, similarly silent, he also stands with his hands kept tucked inside his robe. The face strikes me as vaguely familiar and, looking at him a little more closely, I suddenly realize why. Of course! It's the man who burgled us a short while back and made off with that box of yams. And here he is again, by broad daylight, standing there as calm as you please, this time, too, at the front entrance.

"Sneaze," says Waverhouse, "this person is a police detective. He has called specially to tell you that the man who burgled you the other night has now been caught. So he wants you to come to the police station."

My master seems at last to understand why he is being raided by the police, and accordingly, turning to face the burglar, bows politely. An understandable mistake, since the burglar looks decidedly more presentable than the detective. The burglar must have been very surprised but, since he can hardly be expected to identify himself as a burglar, he just stands there calmly. He still keeps his hands buried in the fold of his kimono but, being handcuffed, he cannot take his hands out even if he wants to. Any sensible person could correctly interpret the situation by the appearances of the individuals concerned but my master, out of touch with modern trends, still makes much too much of officials and the police. He thinks the power of the authorities is really terrifying. Though he is just capable of grasping that, in theory at least, policemen and other such creatures are no more than watchmen employed by us and paid by us, in actual practice he is ready to drop on his hands and knees at the first sight of a uniform. My master's father, the headman of a district on the outskirts of some minor town, quickly developed the ugly habit of creeping to his superiors. Perhaps as an act of divine justice, his son was born with that cringing streak which one can but notice in my master's character. I find this very pitiful.

The police-detective must have had a sense of humor, for he was grinning when he said, "Please be at the Nihon-zutsumi police sub-station tomorrow morning at nine o'clock. Would you also please tell me precisely what goods were stolen from you?"

"The stolen goods," my master promptly responded, "consisted of . . . ," but having forgotten most of them, his voice petered out. All he could remember was that ridiculous box of yams. He didn't really care about the yams, but he thought he would look silly and undignified if, having started to identify the property stolen, he suddenly had to stop dead. After all, it was he who had been burgled, and he was conscious of a certain responsibility deriving from his burgled status. If he could not give a precise answer to the policeman's question, he would feel himself to be somehow less than a man. Accordingly, with sturdy resolution, he completed his sentence. "The stolen goods," he said, "consisted of a box of yams."

The burglar seemed to think this answer was terribly funny, for he looked down and buried his chin in his kimono collar. Waverhouse was less restrained and burst into hoots of laughter. "I see," he squawked, "the yams were really precious, eh?"

Only the policeman looked at all serious. "I don't think you'll recover the yams," he said, "but most of the other things will be returned. Anyway, you can find out about all that at the station tomorrow. Of course, we shall need a receipt for everything you re-possess, so don't forget to bring your personal seal. You must arrive not later than nine in the morning at the aforementioned substation, which lies within the jurisdiction of the Asakusa Police Office. Well, goodbye." His mission completed, the policeman walked out of the front door. The burglar followed him. Since he couldn't take his hands out of his kimono, the burglar couldn't close the door behind him; so after he'd gone, it just stood open. Though my master had conducted himself throughout the incident with awe-filled diffidence towards the police, he seemed annoyed by that parting rudeness: for, looking unpleasantly sullen, he closed the door with a vicious sliding slam.

"Well, well," said Waverhouse, "you do seem awed by detectives. I only wish you'd always behave with such remarkable diffidence. You'd be a marvel of good manners. But the trouble with you is that you're civil only to coppers."

"But he'd come a long way out of his way to bring me that good news."

"It's his job to come and tell you. There was no need whatever to treat him as anyone special."

"But his is not just any ordinary job."

"Of course it's not an ordinary job. It's a disgusting job called 'being a detective.' An occupation lower and dirtier than any ordinary job."

"If you talk like that, you'll land yourself in trouble."

Waverhouse snorted disrespectfully. "Very well then," he grunted, "I'll lay off slandering detectives. But, you know, it's not really a matter of respecting or not respecting those insufferable sneakers. What really is shocking is this business of being respectful to burglars."

"Who showed respect to a burglar?"

"You did."

"How could I conceivably number a burglar among my friends? Quite impossible!"

"Impossible, is it? But you actually bowed to a burglar."

"When?"

"Just now; you bowed down like a hoop before him."

"Don't be silly. That was the detective."

"Detectives don't wear clothes like that."

"But can't you see, it's precisely because he is a detective that he disguises himself in clothes like that."

"You're being very pig-headed."

"It's you who's being very pig-headed."

"Now do just think. To start with, when a detective visits someone, do you honestly imagine he will just stand there with his hands in his robes?"

"Are you suggesting detectives are incapable of keeping their hands in their robes?"

"If you get so fierce, I'll simply have to break this conversation off. But think, man.

While you were bowing to him, didn't he just stand there?"

"Not surprising if he did. After all, he is a detective."

"What glorious self-assurance! You're totally deaf to reason, aren't you?"

"No, I'm not. You keep saying that fellow was a burglar, but you didn't actually see him committing burglary. You just imagine he did so, and you're being extraordinary obstinate about it."

It was at this point that Waverhouse abandoned hope and accepted my master as dim beyond redemption. He fell unwontedly silent. My master, interpreting that silence as an admission of defeat, looks uncommonly pleased with himself. But in proportion to my master's self-elation, Waverhouse's assessment of the wretched man has dropped. In Waverhouse's view my master's fatheaded obstinacy has considerably lowered his value as a man; but in my master's view his firmness of mind has, by a corresponding amount, lifted him above the level of such pifflers as poor Waverhouse. Such topsy-turveydoms are not unusual in this imperfect world. A man who sees himself as magnified by his display of determination is, in fact, diminished in the public estimation by that demonstration of his crass wilfulness. The strange thing is that, to his dying day, the mulish bigot regards his dull opiniatrety as somehow meritorious, a characteristic worthy to be honored. He never realizes that he has

made himself a despised laughing-stock, and
that sensible people want nothing more to do
with him. He has, in fact, achieved happiness. I understand that such joy, the wallow-
ing well-being of a pig in its sty, is even called
pig's happiness.

"Anyway," said Waverhouse, "do you intend to go to the copper-shop tomorrow?"

"Of course. I've been asked to be there by
nine o'clock, so I'll leave the house at eight."

"What about school?"

"I'll take a day off. That school—who
cares!" retorts my master with almost venomous vigor.

"My, my! What a roaring boy we have
become, and all of a sudden too! But will it
really be all right to take the day off?"

"Of course it'll be all right. My salary's
paid on a monthly basis, so there's no danger
of them deducting a day's wages. It's quite
safe." There is, of course, something unpleasantly sly in these remarks, but the very
frankness of his comments reveals that my
master is more simple than dishonest. Though
he is, alas, both.

"Fine. But do you know how to get there?"

"Why should I know the way to a police
station?" My master is clearly narked. "But
it will presumably be quite easy to get there
by rickshaw."

"Your knowledge of Tokyo seems no better than that of my uncle from the provinces.
I give up."

"You're welcome."

Waverhouse responded to this petty spite-fulness with another burst of laughter. "Don't you realize that the police station you'll be visiting is not in any ordinary district. It's down in Yoshiwara."

"Where?"

"In Yoshiwara."

"You mean in the red-light district?"

"That's right. There's only one Yoshiwara in Tokyo. Well, now do you still want to go?" Waverhouse starts teasing him again.

On realizing that Yoshiwara meant *the* Yoshiwara, my master flinched and seemed to hesitate; but, quickly thinking it over, he decided to put on a quite unnecessarily bold front. "Wherever it may be, red-light district or not, I've said I'll go, so go I will." In circumstances of this kind any fool is like to prove pig-headed.

Waverhouse, unimpressed, coolly re-marked, "It may prove interesting. You really ought to see that place."

The ructions caused by the detective incident died away, and, in the subsequent conversation, Waverhouse displayed his inexhaustible gift for amusing banter. When it began to grow dark, he got up and, explaining that his uncle would be annoyed if he stayed out unduly late, took his departure. After he'd gone, my master downed a hurried dinner and withdrew to the study. There, again with his arms close-folded, he started to muse aloud.

"According to Waverhouse, Singleman

Kidd, whom I admired and whose example I very much wanted to follow, is not in truth a person worthy of imitation. On the contrary, the theory he advocates seems sadly lacking in common sense and, as Waverhouse insists, contains features that strongly suggest lunacy, a suggestion which appears all the more well founded when one remembers that two of Kidd's most enthusiastic disciples are incontrovertibly mad. An extremely dangerous situation. If I become too much involved with him, I myself am liable to be regarded as unbalanced. What's more, that Providence Fair fellow, whose writings really impressed me so much that I believed him to be a great man with enormous depths of knowledge and insight, has turned out to be an unadulterated certified maniac, confined, under his real name of Pelham Flap, in a well-known lunatic asylum. Even allowing for the probability that Waverhouse's portrait of the unfortunate fellow is a distorted caricature, it still seems likely that he's having a high old time in that loony-bin under the impression that he's superintending Heaven. Am I, perhaps, myself a little potty? They say that birds of a feather flock together and that like attracts like. If those old sayings are true, my admiration of a loony's thinking, well, let's say my generous sympathy for his writings, suggest that I myself must be a borderline case at least. Even if I'm not yet clearly certifiable, if I freely choose to live next door to a madman, there's an obvious risk that one fine day I might, perhaps unwittingly, topple across into his demented territory and end up, like my neighbor, completely round the bend. What a terrifying prospect! Now that I come to think of it, I confess that I've been more than a little surprised at the very peculiar way in which my brain has recently been functioning. Perhaps some spoonful of my brain cells has suffered a chemical change. Even if nothing like that has happened, it's still true that, of my own free will, I've been doing and saying immoderate things, things that lack balance. I don't feel, yet, anything queer on my tongue or under my armpits, but what's this maddening smell at the roots of my teeth, these crazy muscular tics? This is no longer a joke. Perhaps I've already gone stark staring mad, and it's only because I've been lucky enough not to have hurt anybody or to have become an obvious public nuisance that I'm still allowed quietly to live on in this district as a private citizen. This is indeed no time to be fooling about with negatives and positives, passive or active training of the mind. First of all, let's check my heart-rate. My pulse seems normal. Is my brow fevered? No, temperature normal; no sign there of any rush of blood to the brain. Even so, I'm still not satisfied there's nothing wrong."

For a little while my master sat in worried silence, straining his wits about what strains his wits could bear. Then, after a few anxious minutes, his mumblings started up again.

"I've been comparing myself solely with

lunatics, concentrating on the similarities between deranged persons and myself. That
way I shall never escape from the atmosphere
of lunacy. Obviously, I've tackled the problem in the wrong way. I've been accepting
lunacy as the norm, and I've been measuring
myself by the wonky standards of insanity.
Inevitably, I've been coming to lunatic conclusions. If, instead, I now start measuring
myself by the normal standards of a healthy
person, perhaps I'll come to happier results.
Let me then start by comparing myself to
those close to me, those whom I know best.
First, what about that old uncle in a frock-
coat who came visiting today? But wasn't it
he who kept demanding where one should
place one's mind? I doubt if he could really
be counted as normal. Secondly then, what
about Coldmoon? He's so mad on polishing
glass beads that, for fear lest lunch should
deprive him of one moment's friction, he
hoiks a lunch-box down to the laboratory.
Hardly normal either. Thirdly, Waverhouse?
That man thinks his only function in life is to
go round rollicking everywhere. Such a mad-
cap must be a completely positive kind of
lunatic. Fourthly, the wife of that man Goldfield. Her disposition is so totally poisonous
as to leave no nook for common sense. I
conclude that she also must be stark staring
mad. Fifthly, Goldfield himself. Though I
haven't had the pleasure of meeting him, it
is obvious that he must be less than normal
because he has achieved conjugal harmony

by conforming with the warped characteristics of so abnormal a woman. Such a degree
of conformity with the abnormal amounts to
lunacy, so he's as bad as she. Who else?
Well, there are those charming little gentlemen from Cloud Descending Hall. Though
they are still mere sprouts, their raving madness could very easily disrupt the entire universe. They're mad as young March hares,
the whole boiling lot of them. Thus, as I re-
view the list of my friends and acquaintances,
most of them emerge as stained with maniac
stigmata of one sort or another. I begin to
feel considerably reassured. The truth may
simply be that human society is no more than
a massing of lunatics. Perhaps our vaunted
social organization is merely a kind of bear-
garden, where lunatics gather together, grap-
ple desperately, bicker and tussle with each
other, call each other filthy names, tumble
and sprawl all over each other in mindless
muckiness. This agglomeration of lunatics
thus becomes a living organism which, like
cells, disintegrates and coalesces, crumbles
again to nothing and again re-integrates. Is
that not the actual nature of our marvelous
human society? And within that organism,
such few cells as are slightly sensible and ex-
hibit symptoms of discretion inevitably prove
a nuisance to the rest. So they find themselves confined in specially constructed lunatic asylums. It would follow that, objectively
speaking, those locked up in mental homes
are sane, while those careering around out-

side the walls are all as mad as hatters. An individual lunatic, so long as he's kept isolated, can be treated as a lunatic; but when lunatics get together and, so massed, acquire the strength of numbers, they also automatically acquire the sanity of numbers. Many lunatics are, by their maniness, healthy persons. It is not uncommon that a powerful lunatic, abusing the authority of his wealth and with myriad minor madmen in his pay, behaves outrageously but is nevertheless honored and praised by all and sundry as a paragon of human virtue. I just don't understand anything any more."

I have not altered a word of my master's sad soliloquies as he sat there, all that evening, deep in twitchless meditation, under the forlorn light of his solitary lamp. If further evidence were needed, his drooling words confirm the dullness of his brain. Though he sports a fine moustache like Kaiser Bill, he is so preternaturally stupid that he can't even distinguish between a madman and a normal person. Not only that, but after he has given himself the heartache and excruciating mental torment of considering lunacy as an intellectual problem, he finishes up by dropping the matter without reaching any conclusion whatever. He lacks the brain-power to think through a problem. Any problem. In any field. He's a poor old blithering mutt. The only thing worth noting about the whole of his evening's performance is that, characteristically, his conclusions are as vague and as elusive as the grayish cigarette smoke leaking from his nostrils.

I am a cat. Some of you may wonder how a mere cat can analyze his master's thoughts with the detailed acumen which I have just displayed. Such a feat is a mere nothing for a cat. Quite apart from the precision of my hearing and the complexity of my mind, I can also read thoughts. Don't ask me how I learnt that skill. My methods are none of your business. The plain fact remains that when, apparently sleeping on a human lap, I gently rub my fur against his tummy, a beam of electricity is thereby generated, and down that beam into my mind's eye every detail of his innermost reflections is reflected. Only the other day, for instance, my master, while gently stroking my head, suddenly permitted himself to entertain the atrocious notion that, if he skinned this snoozing moggy and had its pelt made up into a waistcoat, how warm, how wonderfully warm, that Kittish Warm would be. I at once sensed what he was thinking, and felt an icy chill creep over me. It was quite horrible. Anyway, it is this extrasensory gift which has enabled me to tell you not only what my master said but even what he thought throughout this dreary evening.

But, as you now must know, he's a pretty feeble specimen of his unperceptive kind. When he'd got as far as telling himself that he just doesn't understand anything any more, his energies were exhausted and he dropped off into sleep. Sure as eggs are eggs, when he wakes tomorrow he'll have forgotten everything he's just been thinking, even why he thought it. If the matter of lunacy ever again occurs to him, he'll have to start anew, right from scratch. But if that ever does happen, I cannot guarantee that his thinking will follow the same lines in order to arrive at the conclusion that he just doesn't understand anything any more. However, no matter how often he ponders these problems, no matter how many lines of thought he develops, one thing I can guarantee with absolute assurance. I give you my feline word that he will invariably conclude, just before dropping asleep, with an admission that he just doesn't understand anything any more.

III

"MY DEAR, it's seven already," his wife called out from the other side of the sliding-door. It is difficult to say whether my master is awake or asleep: he lies facing away from me and makes no answer. It is, of course, his habit not to give answers. When he absolutely has to open his mouth, he says, "Hmm." Even this non-committal noise does not easily emerge. When a man becomes so lazy that he finds it a nuisance even to give an answer, he often acquires a certain curiously individual tanginess; a certain personal spice which, however, is never appreciated by women. Even his life-partner, the less-than-fussy Mrs. Sneaze, seems to set low store upon her husband; so one can readily imagine what the rest of the world thinks about him. There's a popular song which asks, "How can a fellow shunned by both his parents and his brothers possibly be loved by some tart who's a perfect stranger?" How, then, can a man found unattractive even by his own wife expect to be favored by ladies in general? There is, of course, no call upon me to go out of my way gratuitously to expose my master as a creature repulsive to females of his own kind; but I cannot just sit by while he cultivates illusions, blurring reality with such nitwitted notions as the happy thought that it is only some unlucky disposition of their stars which preordains his wife's dislike of him. It is thus purely my kind-hearted anxiety to help my master to see the world as it really is, to realize his own reality, which has induced me to provide the foregoing account of his sexual repulsiveness.

Mrs. Sneaze is under strict instructions to rouse him at a set time. Accordingly, when that time arrives, she tells him so. If he chooses to disregard her call, offering not even his normal subhuman Hmm of an acknowledgement, that, she concludes, is his affair. Let him lump the consequences. With an eloquent gesture disclaiming all responsibility if her husband proves late for his appointment, she goes off into the study with her broom in her hand and a dust-cloth slung lightly over her shoulder. Soon I heard sounds of the duster flap-flapping all over the study. The daily housework has begun. Now, since it is not my job to clean rooms, I naturally do not know if doing a room is a form of fun or a means of taking exercise. It's certainly no concern of mine, but I cannot forbear to comment that this woman's method of cleaning is totally pointless—unless, that is, she goes through the motions of cleaning for their own ritualistic sake. Her idea of doing a room is to flip the duster curtly over the paper surfaces of the sliding-doors and let the broom glide once along the floor. With respect to these activities she shows no interest whatever in any possible relation of cause and effect. As a result, the clean places are always clean, while dusty spots and grimy corners remain eternally dusty and begrimed. However, as Confucius pointed out when rebuking a disciple who proposed abandonment of the wasteful and senseless practice of sacrificing a sheep on the first day of every month, a meaningless gesture of courtesy is better than no courtesy at all. It may be that Mrs. Sneaze's style of cleaning a room should be recognized as minimally better than doing nothing at all. At all events, her activities bring my master no benefit. Nevertheless, day after day, she takes the trouble to perform her pointless rite. Which is, alas, the sole redeeming feature. Mrs. Sneaze and room-cleaning are, by the custom of many years, firmly linked in a mechanical association; but their combination has in practice achieved no more actual cleaning than in those old days before she was born and in those even older days before brooms and dusters had been invented. One might indeed say that the relation between Mrs. Sneaze and the cleaning of rooms resembles that of certain terms in formal logic which, totally unrelated in their nature, are nevertheless formally linked.

Unlike my master, I am an early riser, so by this time I was already feeling distinctly

peckish. There is, of course, no question
of a mere cat expecting to get its breakfast before the human members of the household had sat themselves down at the table.
Yet I remain a cat, with all a cat's pure appetites and instincts; and once I had begun to
wonder if there could possibly be a delicious
smell of soup drifting out of that abalone-
shell which serves as my feeding platter, I
was simply unable to remain still. When,
knowing its hopelessness, one yet hopes on
against hope, it is always wisest to concentrate on thinking about that hope and to
discipline oneself into silent immobility. But
it's easier said than done. One cannot help
wanting to check whether one's hope has, or
has not, been fulfilled in reality. Even when
it is absolutely certain that a check must
bring disappointment, one's mind will not
stop fidgeting until it has been fully and finally
disappointed. I could no longer hold myself
in check and accordingly crept out to investi-
gate the kitchen. First, I peep into my aba-
lone-shell in its usual place behind the kitchen
furnace. Sure enough, the shell is empty, just
as it was last night after I'd licked it clean.
This morning, that shell looks singularly
desolate, chillily reflecting the weird glow of
the autumn sunlight filtering down through
the skylight. O-san has already transferred
the boiled rice into the serving container and
is now stirring soup in the saucepan on the
stove. Rice-rich liquid that had boiled over
in the cooking-pot has dried into hard streaks,

some of them looking like stuck-on strips of high-class paper, down the sides of the pot. Since both rice and soup are now ready, I thought my own breakfast should be served at once. It's silly to be backward at such times and, even if I don't succeed in getting what I want, I shan't lose anything by trying. After all, even a hanger-on is as much entitled as anyone else to feel the pangs of hunger; so why shouldn't I call out for my breakfast? First I tried a coaxing kind of mew; an appealing, even a mildly reproachful, noise. O-san does not take the slightest notice. Since she was born polygonal, I am perfectly well aware that her heart is as cold as a clock; but I am counting on my mewing skills to move her rusty sympathies. Next I tried my most pitiable miaowing. I believe this voice of entreaty has a tone so pathetic in its loneliness that it should make a wanderer in a strange land feel that his heart is being torn in pieces. O-san ignores it completely. Can this woman actually be deaf? Hardly. For were she deaf, she'd not be able to hold down her job as a maidservant. Perhaps she is deaf only to cat-voices. I understand that there are persons who are colorblind. Though such persons may think their eyesight perfect, from the medical point of view they are in fact deformed. This O-san creature could be voice-blind; and persons so deformed are no less freaks than their colorblind homologues. For a mere monstrosity, she's a jolly sight too lordly. Take the nights, for instance. However hard I plead with her that I need to go outside, never once has she opened the door. If by some perversion of her character she should once let me out, there's not a wax cat's chance in hell that she'd ever let me in again. Even in summer, the night-dew is bad for one's health, and winter frost is naturally much worse. You can't imagine the agony of staying awake under the eaves and waiting for the sun to rise. The other evening when I chanced to be shut out, some foul stray dog attacked me and only by the skin of my teeth did I manage to escape onto the roof of the tool-shed, there to shiver the whole long night away. All such evil hours are brought upon me by the endless wintriness of that hard woman's heart. I know well enough that from such a person my miaowing performance will evoke no kindness; but just as in the proverb a hungry man will turn to God, a man in want will turn to robbery and a lovelorn loon will take to writing songs, so in my extremity will I try anything once. Accordingly, in a last attempt to catch her attention, my third effort was an especially intricate interweaving of mewls and muted yowling, which, though, at least in my unshakable judgement, a music no less moving than that of Beethoven, produces no effect whatever within that implacable creature's unsociably savage breast. Suddenly O-san sinks down to her knees and, sliding out a removable floorboard, extracts from the cavity below a stick of charcoal roughly four inches long. Rapped sharply against the corner of the stove, the length broke into some three main pieces and the surrounding area was liberally showered with black dust. A plentiful powdering of charcoal seems to have been added to the soup, but O-san is not the kind of woman to be bothered by such trifles. She quickly shoved the three main pieces under the bottom of the saucepan and so into the stove. I see little prospect of her interrupting her sullen chores to give ear to my symphony. Well, that's the way it is.

Dejected, I set off back to the living-room and, as I passed by the bathroom door, I noticed that my master's three small daughters were there busily engaged in washing their faces. Though I say they were washing their faces, the two older girls are still at the kindergarten stage, while the youngest is so tiny that she cannot even trail along with her sisters to their place of schooling. It follows that not one of them can yet properly wash her face or make herself presentable. The baby, having hauled a tangle of damp floor-rags out of the mop-bucket, is happily using it to stroke her face. I would have thought it most unpleasant to wash one's face with floor-rags, but one cannot be surprised at any oddness in this child who regularly responds to earthquakes with outcries of pure joy. Which may, of course, only demonstrate that she is a more enlightened being than Single-man Kidd. Now the eldest girl takes the responsibilities of her seniority with expectedly officious seriousness. Accordingly, she drops her gargling-cup and starts trying to part her baby sister from the latter's precious floor-rags. "Baby-dear," she tells her, "that's for wiping floors."

But Baby-dear, a self-opinionated tot, is not so easily persuaded and, with a piercing shout of "No, babu," she tugs at the floor-cloth which her sister has just grabbed. Nobody knows what "babu" means or how its use originated, but Baby-dear lets fly with it whenever she loses her temper. As the children tug at the ends of that sodden rag, water squeezed from its center portion starts pitilessly dripping down on Baby-dear's twee tooters. Were it only a matter of wetted feet, that were no great shakes; but soon her knees are also sopping wet. Baby-dear is wearing a backhammon. I've been trying to find out the meaning of that word, and it would seem that to the children it signifies any kind of pattern, in this case patterned clothing, of a medium size. Where they got this information, alas, I could not say.

"Baby-dear," the eldest girl is saying, "your backhammon's getting wet. Be a good baby, Baby-dear, and let go of this cloth." This is remarkably intelligent advice, especially from a girl who herself until just recently thought backhammon was a kind of game. Which reminds me that this eldest girl is constantly misusing words and that her malapropisms not infrequently amuse her adult listeners. The other day she remarked that cornflakes were sparking up from the fire and again, when being dosed with castor oil, asked whether the medicine had been squeezed from the brother of bollocks. She once haughtily announced that she was no common plum-child, and it was several days before I discovered that she was in fact bragging that she'd not been born in some back slum. My master sniggers whenever he hears such errors, but I'm prepared to bet that when he's teaching English in his school, he makes in sober earnest far sillier mistakes than ever his daughter does.

Baby-dear, who incidentally always refers to herself as Baby-beer, at last notices that her backhammon is now soaking wet and, bawling out that "Baby-beer's backhammon is got cold," begins to howl her head off. Of course, a cold backhammon is a pretty serious matter, so here comes O-san running from the kitchen. Quickly she dispossesses the squabbling children of their treasured floor-rag and cleans the baby up. Throughout the hullaballoo, the second daughter, Sunko, has remained suspiciously quiet. Standing with her back toward us, she has got hold of a small jar of her mother's cosmetic which has tumbled off its shelf and is now busy plastering white paste on her face. First, having poked her finger into the jar, she drags a broad white line down the length of her nose. Which at least makes it easier to see where her nose is. Next, with her finger liberally re-loaded, she daubs thick blobs on her cheeks and rubs the stuff around till two white lumps are sticking out from her face. Her beautifying self-adornment had reached this interesting stage when O-san bustled up to deal with Baby-dear. Once Baby-dear was set to rights, Sunko too was wiped back into human semblance. She emerged from the white paste looking distinctly peeved.

Leaving this distressing scene behind me, I moved through the living-room to inspect my master's bedroom and so to ascertain whether or not he has at last got up. Stealthily I squinny into the room, but my master's head is nowhere to be seen. Instead, one large and high-arched sole is sticking out from the bottom end of the old-fashioned sleeved bed-quilt. He seems to have burrowed down to avoid the unpleasantness of being woken up. He looks, in fact, like a not too clever tortoise. At this point Mrs. Sneaze, who had finished cleaning the study, returned to the bedroom with her broom and duster shouldered. Halting at the entrance, she called out as before, "Haven't you got up yet?" then stood there for a while, gazing in disgust at the tump of headless bedding. As before, her question brought no answer.

Mrs. Sneaze advanced a short way into the room. Planting her broom upright with a slightly menacing plunk, she pressed again for an answer. "Not yet woken up, dear?"

This time, my master is awake all right. Indeed, it is precisely because he is awake that he is now, head and body tucked well down, entrenched within the bedclothes against the expected onslaught from his wife. He seems to be relying on some silly notion that, so long as he keeps his head concealed, his wife may fail to notice that he's still snugged down in bed. She shows no disposition to let him off so slightly. Her first call, reckoned my master, had come from the threshold, so there should still be a reasonably safe distance, perhaps as much as six feet, between himself and her. He was consequently shaken when the plunk of her grounded broom-haft came from less than three feet off. Worse still, her solicitous "Not yet woken up, dear?" sounded, even under the bedclothes, twice more menacing than before. Seeing no hope for it, my master thereupon surrendered, and his small voice answered, "Hmm."

"You said you'd be there by nine o'clock. Hurry up, or you'll be late."

"You don't have to tell me. I'm getting up," replied my master with his face spectacularly visible through the cuff of one sleeve of the bedclothes. His wife is used to this old trick. Once he has managed to convince her that he's going to get up, he usually goes straight back to sleep again. So she's learnt to keep a sharp eye on his morning gambits and therefore answers his mumbled promises with a curt "Well, get up now." It's annoying, when one's said one's getting up, to be told then to get up. For a selfish man like my master, it is even more than annoying. In one wild angry gesture, he thrusts aside the pile of bedclothes that he's been keeping over his head, and I note that his eyes are staringly wide-open.

"Don't make all that fuss. If I say I'm getting up, then I'm getting up."

"But you always say you're getting up, and then you never do."

"Nonsense! When have I ever told a ridiculous lie like that?"

"Why, always."

"Don't be so silly."

"Who are you calling silly? Answer me that." She looks quite dashingly militant as she stands there beside the bed with her broomstick planted like a spear-shaft. But at this very moment, Yatchan, the child of the rickshawman who lives in the street behind us, suddenly burst out crying with a most tremendous "Waa!" That Yatchan should start crying as soon as my master gets angry is the responsibility of his ghastly mother. For the wife of the rickshawman is paid to make her baby scream every time my master gets into a fury. Which is fine for the money-grubbing mother, but pretty hard on Yatchan. With a mother like that, a child could well have cause to cry the clock around. If my master realized the way things have been rigged and made the little effort needed to control himself, then Yatchan might live longer than seems likely. Even though the victim's mother is being handsomely rewarded by the Goldfields for her torturing of her child, only a person far more dangerously mad than Providence Fair would do such a lunatic thing. Were Yatchan only made to cry on the occasions of my master's anger, he could probably survive; but every time that Goldfield's hireling hooligans come shouting round the house, then too the wretched infant is hurt until he screams. It is taken for granted that the hooligan cat-calls will infuriate my master; so, whether or not my master does flare up, Yatchan catches hell in expectation of my master's anger. Every vulgar yell asserting that my master is a terracotta badger is thus invariably matched by a heart-felt yell from Yatchan. Indeed, it has become difficult to distinguish between Yatchan and my master. It is simple to start my master off by indirect approaches. One only needs to torment Yatchan briefly to produce the same effect on my master as slapping him directly in the face. I understand that years ago in Europe whenever a condemned criminal escaped to a foreign land and could not be recaptured, it was the custom to fashion a simulacrum of the fugitive which was then burnt in his stead. Among these hooligans of Goldfield's there seems to be a tactician well acquainted with such ancient European practices, and I must confess he's certainly worked out some very clever ploys. Both the little louts from Cloud Descending Hall and Yatchan's mother represent real problems for my master who, when all is said and done, is a man of limited abilities. There are many other equally awkward customers to be coped with. One might even say that, from my master's point of view, the entire district is populated with awkward customers; but since these others are not immediately relevant to this story, I'll introduce them later as developments require. For the moment, I will return you to my master quarreling in the bedroom with his wife.

On hearing Yatchan cry and at such an early hour, my master must have felt really angry. He jerked sharply up into a sitting position among the bedclothes, for at times of such stress no years of mental training, not even the presence of Singleman Kidd himself, could exercise the least restraint. Then with both hands he began to scratch his scalp with such vicious violence that nearly every square inch of its skin was clawed away. A month's accumulated dandruff came floating down to settle nastily on his neck and pajama-collar. It is a sight not easily forgotten. Yet another shock greeted my wondering eyes when they fell upon his bristling moustache. Perhaps that ragged growth felt it would be less than seemly to be calm when its owner was so savagely distraught but, whatever the reason, each individual hair has gone completely berserk and, forgetting all sense of co-operation in the frightful vigor of their self-expression, the various hairs are jutting out like the bayonets of ill-trained conscripts in whichever wild direction takes their frantic fancy. This, too, constitutes a sight not easily forgotten. Only yesterday, out of regard for the bathroom mirror and in deference to the German Emperor, these hairs had obediently mustered themselves into disciplined formation, but after no more than a single night's repose all the benefits of their training have been scattered to the winds. Each separate conscript hair has reverted to its aboriginal nature and has resumed that individuality which reduces the moustache to the condition of a rabble. The same sad process of rapid degeneration may be observed in my master. In the space of a single night his mental training loses all effect, and his inborn boorishness comes bristling back into view through every pore in his skin. When one pauses to wonder how such a wildly whiskered tusker has managed to keep his job as a teacher, then for the first time one grasps the varied vastness of Japan. Indeed, only a land of such true enormity could find room for Goldfield and his pack of snooping curs and rabid bitches to pass themselves off as human beings. My master seems to believe that in a society where those monstrosities can indeed pass for human, there is no conceivable reason why his own modest eccentricities should lead to his dismissal. In the last analysis one could always obtain an enlightening explanation of the whole crazy setup by sending a postcard of enquiry to that noble pile which shelters Providence Fair.

At this point my master opened his ancient

eyes, whose drifting cloudiness I have previously described in detail, as wide as they can stretch and, with an unaccustomedly sharp glance, stared at the cupboard in the wall that faced him. This cupboard is about six feet in height, divided horizontally into top and bottom halves, each half having two sliding paper-doors. The bottom end of my master's bedclothes reached almost to the lower part of the cupboard so that, having just sat up, he cannot help but focus, as soon as his lids are lifted, on the picture-painted paper of the cupboard's sliding-doors. Here and there the paper skin has peeled or been torn away, and the curious underlayers, the flattened intestines of the panels, are distinctly visible. These innards are of many different sorts. Some are printed papers, others are handwritten; some have been pasted face-side in, others upside down. The sight of this displayed anatomy of paper stirred in my master a sudden urge to read what there was written. The fact that my master, who until but a moment ago was so frenetically incensed that he could happily have grabbed the wife of the rickshawman and ground her nose against a pine-tree, now suddenly wishes to read old scraps of paper may seem a little strange; but actually such conduct is not all that unusual in an extrovert so easily enired. It is another version of the squalling baby who starts to coo as soon as he is given sweets. Years ago in his student days, when my master lodged in a temple, there were five or six nuns living in the room next to his with nothing but the sliding paper-doors between them. Now, nuns are by nature the cattiest of all cat-natured women. These nuns seem quickly to have perceived the true and inmost character of my master, for they made it their practice to chant, tapping out the rhythm on the rim of their cooking-pot, that jingle parents use to tease a child about its changeable moods:

> The little crow that cried and cried
> Has grown a grin six inches wide.

My master, I've been told, has loathed nuns ever since. They may well be detestable, but their chanting told a truth. For, though none of his moods is lasting, my master contrives to weep, to laugh, to rollick and be downcast more frequently than anyone else in the world. Putting it kindly, one might say he shows a certain lack of tenacity and is inclined to change his mind for insufficient reason. Translated into simple everyday language, that merely means that my master is a shallow stubborn spoilt brat. Now, being a spoilt brat, it's not at all surprising that, full of fighting spirit, he should jerk his torso fiercely up from the bed and then, balanced on his bottom, suddenly change his mind and begin to read the flattened intestines of a damaged cupboard door.

The first thing he noticed was a photograph of Itō Hirobumi standing on his head.

By twisting his neck to study the date associated with this irreverently pasted picture, my master found it to be September 28, 1878. So, even as long as twenty-seven years ago, the present Resident-General in Korea was already doing somersaults. Wondering how the Resident-General might have occupied himself before Korea was available to reside in, my master crooks himself sufficiently to decipher "Finance Minister." This certainly is a great man. Even when he's standing on his head, he's a Finance Minister. A bit to the left of that information, the Minister again appears. This time he is lying down, having a siesta. Which is very understandable. One cannot be expected to stand on one's head for any protracted period. Near the bottom of the exposed area, the two words "You are" can be seen written in large ideographs. My master naturally wanted to read the rest of such an aggressively sized sentence but, alas, nothing more was visible. Of the next line down, all that can be read is "quickly" and, once again, there's no clue to the rest of the text. If my master were a detective of the Metropolitan Police Board, he might have satisfied his curiosity by ripping off the rest of the top layer of paper even though the cupboard door, its skin and its intestines, all belonged to somebody else. Since no detective has been properly educated, such barbarous persons will do anything to sate their lust for facts. Which is a lamentable state of affairs. I wish they would behave with a little more civilized reserve. Matters would be improved if a rule were established that all facts should be withheld from detectives whose conduct lacks reserve. I understand that these disreputable servants of the public sometimes arrest innocent citizens on the basis of false accusations and manufactured evidence. That public servants, employed and paid for by honest citizens, should be given scope to pin crimes on those who pay and employ them is yet another example of the lunatic condition of human society.

My master next studies the center part of the exposed paper where a map of Oita Prefecture has been pasted upside down. Since the Resident-General in Korea is standing on his head, it's not surprising that Oita Prefecture should join him in his somersaults. When my master's eyes had taken in the overthrow of Oita, he clenched both hands and thrust his fists on high toward the ceiling. These mantic gestures foretell a coming yawn. His yawning, too, is signally abnormal: less a human yawn than the yowling of a whale. That performance over, my master pulled some clothes on and lurched off into the bathroom for a wash. His wife, who had been impatiently waiting for this moment, quickly gathered up the quilt, folded it and put the bedclothes in the cupboard. Then, as usual, she began to clean the room. Just as Mrs. Sneaze's cleaning system has become stylized drill, so too over the years her husband has

established a routine pattern for washing his
face. I think I earlier mentioned his noisy
morning gargling, its variations of bass and
treble bubblement, and today he's doing it as
usual. Finally, having made the usual careful
parting in his hair, he appeared in the living-
room with a hand-towel draped across one
shoulder. There, with a lordly air, he sat
himself down beside the oblong brazier.

Mention of that object may lead some of
you to imagine an oblong brazier made from
fine zelkova-wood. Some perhaps may picture a brazier of black persimmon-wood, its
inner sides entirely copper-plated, against the
lip of which a sexy-looking charmer with long
and freshly washed tresses, sitting with one
knee raised, seductively taps out her long slim
tobacco-pipe. But poor old Sneaze's brazier is
sadly less than picturesque. It is, in fact, so
ancient that none but an expert could guess
what wood was used to make it. The fine
point about any such oblong brazier is the
quality and brilliance of the gloss acquired
by years of patient polishing; but this brazier
is not only undetermined as to its material,
which could as well be cherry as zelkova and
paulownia as cherry, but has never once been
polished. It is consequently a gloomy and
most repellent object. Where I wonder, could
he have got it? He would certainly not have
bought it. Could it, then, have been a present? Not that I've ever heard. Which leaves
us with the possibility that he stole it, and at
this point all histories of the brazier become

a little vague. Many years ago, among my master's relatives there was an old, old man. When that ancient died, my master was asked to live in the dead man's house and just look after it. Some years later when my master moved out to occupy his own new house, he simply took along with him, possibly unthinkingly, the oblong brazier which he had used so often that he had come to regard it as his personal property. Usufruct decaying into usucaption. Which sounds a little wicked. Indeed, when one considers the matter, his act was certainly wrong. However, such happenings are common enough. For instance, I understand that bankers grow so accustomed to handling other people's money that they come to regard it as their own. Similarly, public officials are the servants of the people and can reasonably be regarded as agents to whom the people have entrusted certain powers to be exercised on the people's behalf in the running of public affairs. But as these officials grow accustomed to their daily control of affairs, they begin to acquire delusions of grandeur, act as though the authority they exercise was in fact their own and treat the people as though the people had no say in the matter. Since the world is thus demonstrably full of such usurpers, one cannot brand my master as a thief just because of this business with the oblong brazier. However, if you insist that he has a thievish disposition, an evidenced inclination to theft, then the plain fact is that he shares that criminal cant with everyone else in the world.

I had got as far as saying that my master sat down beside the oblong brazier, but I have not yet explained that, in doing so, he was in fact seating himself at the dining-table. Seated around the other three sides and already tucking into their breakfasts were Baby-dear, who cleans her face with floor-rags; Tonko, whose learning includes the starry phenomena of Castor and Bollocks; and sweet little Sunko, who pokes about into make-up jars. My master looks at his three daughters with impartial distaste. Tonko's face is flat and round like the steel guard on some old-fashioned sword. Sunko takes after her elder sister so far as face-shape is concerned, but its color immediately puts me in mind of those round red lacquer trays from Okinawa. Baby-dear's face is the odd one out, and very odd it is: long and square at the corners, with the long sides of the oblong stretching sideways. Of themselves, oblong heads are not uncommon but in such cases the greater length is vertical. An oblong head like Baby-dear's, horizontally long, is, I think, unheard of. However vertiginous the variance of fashion, I cannot believe that a square face squashed out sideways will ever prove the rage. My master suffers random spasms of concern about his growing daughters. Their growth is unpreventable, and they are certainly all growing. Indeed, the speed of their growth reminds one of the sheer blue force of a bamboo-shoot accelerating into sapling size in the garden of some Zen-purveying temple. Every time my master notices an increase in his children's size, he becomes as nervous as if an inexorable pursuer were catching up behind him. Though an inordinately vague person, my master does realize that these three daughters are all females. He also understands that, being females, proper arrangements for their disposition must be made. He understands, yes; but that is all, for he further realizes that he is quite incapable of getting them married off. Therefore, though they are indeed his very own offspring, he finds them more than he cares for. If he's the kind of father who finds his children a bit too much, then he should never have produced them. But such behavior is all too typically human. It is painfully easy to define human beings. They are beings who, for no good reason at all, create their own unnecessary suffering.

But children are terrific. Not even dreaming that their father is thus worried stiff about what to do with them, they go on eating happily. The only unmanageable one is Baby-dear. Baby-dear is now nearly three years old, so her mother, seeking to be kind, has provided for her mealtime use a pair of chopsticks and a rice-bowl, all of size appropriate to her age. But Baby-dear will have none of it. First she grabs her eldest sister's chopsticks, then her rice bowl. Though they are too large for her, she struggles to control these quite unmanageable things. One finds in this sad world that among mean-spirited persons, the greater their incompetence and inefficiency, the sharper their sense of self-importance and the more virulent their ambition to occupy unsuitably high official posts.

This style of character always begins to develop at the stage now reached by Baby-dear; and, since the roots of these defects of character run down so deeply into babyhood, wise persons quickly resign themselves to the wretched truth that no subsequent discipline or education can eradicate such flaws. Baby-dear positively wallows in her tiny tyrannies, refusing to surrender the enormous rice-bowl and the hefty chopsticks which she's looted from her sister. Perhaps, since she is seeking by sheer violence to control objects far too big for her to handle, she has no choice but to play the tyrant. At all events, she begins by clamping both chopsticks tight together in a firm grip applied too far down toward their lower ends. She then rams this wooden wedge into the bottom of the rice-bowl, which is about four-fifths full of rice topped up to its brim with bean-paste soup. The rice-bowl had managed, somewhat precariously, to retain its balance throughout Baby-dear's initial raid but, as soon as it felt the force of her chopstick battering-ram, it tilted some thirty degrees out of the true and poured a sluice of still-hot soup all down the front of its assailant. But Baby-dear is not to be daunted by

such a petty set-back. For Baby-dear's a tyrant. Accordingly, she yanks the chopsticks
savagely out of the bowl, shoves her rosebud
mouth right up against the rice-bowl's lip
and then proceeds to shovel masses of soggy
rice into her slurping maw. Grains that escape her wild style of engulfment joined the
soup in its bid for freedom and, with a happy
shout, alighted variously on her nose-tip, on
her cheeks and on her chin. Those, and they
were many, that missed their human target
finished up on different parts of the floor.
This is a most reckless manner in which to
eat rice. I respectfully advise all persons in
positions of power, including that infamous
Goldfield fellow, that if they persist in treat-
ing people with the same crude violence which
Baby-dear applies to the rice-bowl and the
chopsticks, they too will finish up with only
a spattering of rice-grains in their mouths.
The only grains that will, in fact, land up in
their gullets will not be those on whom pressure has been applied but merely those that
have lost all sense of direction. I do most
earnestly entreat all persons of influence to
reflect deeply upon this matter. Men who are
truly wise in this world never act so stupidly.

The eldest girl, her bowl and chopsticks
snitched by the baby, has been obliged to
make do with Baby-dear's dwarf versions;
but the baby's bowl can hold so little rice
that three quick mouthfuls empty it. Forced
into frequent replenishments, she has already
downed her fourth helping and is apparently

going to take a fifth. She lifts the lid of the
rice-container and, holding the broad rice-scoop momentarily poised, stares at the bunkered grains as though undecided whether or not to help herself to more. In the end she plumps for another bowlful and carefully scoops out a dollop of rice that looks unburnt. So far, so good. However, as she brought the laden scoop up toward the rim of her bowl, she accidentally banged the two together, with the result that a largish lump of rice fell down onto the floor. Looking not the least put out, she began to pick it up again with almost finicking care. Naturally, I wondered what she was going to do with it. She put it all, every single grain, back into the container. Which seems a dirty thing to do. The conclusion of this ugly business came at the same moment as the climax of Baby-dear's performance with the shoveling chopsticks. And an eldest sister can hardly be expected to overlook a face a foully spattered with rice as Baby-dear's.

"Baby-dear, you look terrible with your face all covered in rice." She begins to clean up the mess. First, she disengaged the rice-grain sticking on the baby's nose but, instead of throwing it away, popped it, much to my surprised disgust, into her own mouth. Next she tackles the cheeks. Here the grains, some twenty altogether, are clotted in scattered groups. One by one, her eldest sister picked the kernels off the baby's cheeks, and one by one she ate them.

At this point, the middle sister, Sunko, who hitherto has demurely busied herself with crunching pickled radish, suddenly scooped from her brimming soup-bowl a broken gobbet of sweet potato and slung that wretched object straight into her widely opened mouth. As my readers are no doubt aware, nothing can sear the mouth more painfully than sweet potato cooked in bean-paste soup. Unless very careful, even a hardened adult can give himself a truly nasty burn. It is thus understandable that a mere beginner in the art of eating such sweet potatoes should feel scorched, as certainly did Sunko, out of her tiny mind. With a fearful squawking "Waa," she spat the burning gobbet out upon the table. This slightly mangled object skidded across the table surface, coming at last to rest within convenient grabbing-distance of Baby-dear. Now Baby-dear, as tough-mouthed as a carthorse, just dotes on sweet potatoes. Seeing her favorite goody skid to a steaming halt only a hand's stretch from her rice-stripped face, she pitched away her chopsticks, snatched the sweet potato and gobbled it gladly down.

My master, a fully conscious witness of all these ghastly happenings, watches them as dispassionately as if they were occurring on some other planet. Without saying a word, he has quietly got on with eating his own rice and soup, and is now engaged in probing his jaws with a toothpick. He seems to be following a policy of complete non-intervention, even of masterly inactivity, in the rearing of his daughters. One fine day in the not too distant future this trio of bright college girls may be fated to find themselves wild lovers with whom, for the sake of passion, they'll run away from home. If that in fact should happen, I expect that, calmly continuing to eat his rice and soup, my master will just watch them as they go upon their ways. He is certainly a man of little resource; but I've noticed that those who are nowadays regarded as most admirably resourceful know nothing in fact except how to deceive their fellows with lies, how to sneak up upon the unwary, how to jump queues, how to create a sensation by bluffing and by what tricks to ensnare the simple-minded. Even boys at the middle school level, influenced by such conduct, get the idea that only by such means can they expect to make their way in the world. Indeed they seem to think that they can only become fine gentlemen by the successful perpetration of acts of which they ought, in truth, to be thoroughly ashamed. Of course, these imitative loutlings do not display resource, and are in fact no more than hooligans. Being a Japanese cat, I have a certain amount of patriotic sentiment and, every time I see these allegedly resourceful creatures I wish I had the chance to give them a right good hiding. Each new creature of that type weakens the nation to the degree of his presence. Such students are a disgrace to their school, and such adults a disgrace to their country. Nonetheless, disgraceful as they are, there are lots of them about. Which is really inexplicable. The human beings in Japan, shamefully enough, seem less mettlesome than the cats. One must admit that, compared with hooligans, my master is a very superior model of humankind. He is superior because he is weakminded. His very uselessness makes him their superior. He is their clear superior because he is not smart.

Having thus uneventfully, and with a show of no resource whatever, finished his breakfast, my master put on his suit, climbed into a rickshaw and left to keep his appointment with the police. As he climbed aboard, he'd asked the rickshawman if he knew the location of Nihon-zutsumi. The rickshawman just grinned. I thought it rather silly of my master to make a point of reminding the rickshawman that his destination lay in the brothel quarter.

After my master's unusual departure—unusual, that is, because he left in a rickshaw—Mrs. Sneaze had her own breakfast and then started nagging at the children. "Hurry up," she says, "or you'll be late for school."

But the children pay no heed. "There isn't," they answer back, "any school today"; and they make no effort to get themselves ready.

"Of course there is," she snaps in a lecturing tone of voice. "Hurry and get ready."

"But yesterday the teacher said, 'We have no school tomorrow,' " the eldest girl persists.

It was probably at this point that Mrs.
Sneaze began to suspect that the children
might be right. She went to the cupboard,
lifted out a calendar and checked the date.
Today is marked in red, the sign of a national
holiday. I fancy that my master was unaware
of this fact when he sent a note to his school
advising them of his absence. I fancy, too,
that Mrs. Sneaze was similarly unaware when
she put his note in the post. As for Waverhouse, I can't make up my mind whether he
too was unaware or whether he simply found
it diverting to keep quiet.

Mrs. Sneaze, surprised and softened by this
discovery, told the children to go out and
play. "But please," she bade them, "just behave yourselves." She then settled down, as
she daily does, to getting on with her sewing.

For the next half hour peace reigned
throughout the house, and nothing happened worth my bother to record. Then, out
of the blue, an unexpected visitor arrived: a
young girl-student aged, I would guess, perhaps seventeen or eighteen. The heels of her
shoes had worn crooked and her long purple
skirt trailed along the ground. Her hair was
quaintly dressed in two big bulges above the
ears, so that her head resembled an abacus
bead. Unannounced, she walked in through
the kitchen entrance. This apparition is my
master's niece. They say she is a student.
She's always liable to drop in on a Sunday,
and she usually contrives to have some kind
of row with her uncle. This young lady pos-

sesses the unusually beautiful name of Yukie but, far from reminding its viewers of a snowy river, her ruddy features are of that dull normality which you can see in any street if you take the trouble to walk a hundred yards.

"Hullo, Auntie!" she casually remarked as, marching straight into the living-room, she plonked herself down beside the sewing-box.

"My dear, how early you are. . . ."

"Because today's a national holiday. I thought I'd come and see you in the morning, so I left home in a hurry about half past eight."

"Oh? For anything special?"

"No, but I haven't seen you for such a long time, and I just wanted to say hullo."

"Well then, don't just say hullo but stay for a bit. Your uncle will soon be back."

"Has Uncle gone out already? That's unusual!"

"Yes, and today he's gone to rather an unusual place. In fact, to a police station. Isn't that odd?"

"Whatever for?"

"They've caught the man who burgled us last spring."

"And Uncle's got to give evidence? What a bore."

"Not altogether. We're going to get our things back. The stolen articles have turned up and we've been asked to go and collect them. A policeman came round yesterday especially to tell us."

"I see. Otherwise Uncle wouldn't have gone out as early as this. Normally he'd still be snoring."

"There's no one quite such a lie-abed as your uncle, and if one wakes him up he gets extremely cross. This morning, for instance, because he'd asked me to wake him up at seven, that's when I woke him up. And d'you know, he promptly crept inside the bed-clothes and didn't even answer. Naturally I was worried about his appointment with the police, but when I tried to wake him up for the second time, he said something rather unkind through a sleeve of the padded bed-clothes. Really, he's the limit."

"I wonder why he's always so sleepy. Perhaps," said his niece in almost pleasured tones, "his nerves are shot to pieces."

"I don't know, I'm sure."

"He does lose his temper far too easily. It surprises me that they keep him on as a teacher at that school."

"Well, I'm told he's awfully gentle at the school."

"Which only makes things worse. A blow-hard in the house and all thistledown at school."

"What d'you mean, dear?" asks my mistress.

"Well, don't you think it's bad that he should act round here like the King of Hell and then appear at school like some quaking jelly?"

"And of course it's not just that he's so

terribly bad tempered. He's also an ornery man. When one says right, he immediately says left; if one says left, then he says right. And he never, but never, does anything that he's been asked to do. He's as stubborn and crank-minded as a mule."

"Cantankerous, I call it. Being plain contrary is his whole-time hobby. For myself, if I ever want him to do something, I just ask him to do the opposite. And it always works. For instance, the other day I wanted him to buy me an umbrella. So I purposely kept on telling him that I didn't want one. 'Of course you want an umbrella,' he exploded and promptly went and bought me one."

Mrs. Sneaze broke out in a womanly series of giggles and titters. "Oh, how clever you are," she said, "I'll do the same in future."

"You certainly should. You'll never get anything out of that old skinflint if you don't."

"The other day an insurance man called round and he tried hard to persuade your uncle to take out an insurance policy. He pointed out this and that advantage and did his very best for about an hour to talk your uncle round. But your obstinate old uncle was not to be persuaded, even though we have three children and no savings. If only he would take out even the most modest insurance, we'd naturally all feel very much more secure. But a fat lot he cares for things like that."

"Quite so. If anything should happen, you

could be very awkwardly placed." This girl doesn't sound teen-aged at all, but more, and most unbecomingly, like an experience-hardened housewife.

"It was really rather amusing to hear your uncle arguing with that wretched salesman. Your uncle said, 'All right, perhaps I can concede the necessity of insurance. Indeed, I deduce that it is by reason of that necessity that insurance companies exist.' Nevertheless he persisted in maintaining that 'nobody needs to get insured unless he's going to die.' "

"Did he actually say that?"

"He did indeed. Inevitably, the salesman answered, 'Of course, if nobody ever died, there'd be no need for insurance companies. But human life, however durable it may sometimes seem, is in fact a fragile and precarious thing. No man can ever know what hidden dangers menace his tenuous existence.' To which your uncle retorted, 'I've decided not to die, so have no worry on my account.' Can you imagine anyone actually saying such an idiotic thing?"

"How extremely silly! One dies even if one decides not to. Why, I myself was absolutely determined to pass my exams, but in fact I failed."

"The insurance man said the same thing. 'Life,' he said, 'can't be controlled. If people could prolong their lives by strength of resolution, nobody anywhere would ever leave this earth.' "

"The insurance man makes sense to me."

"I certainly agree. But your uncle cannot see it. He swears he'll never die. 'I've made a vow,' he told that salesman with all the pride of a nincompoop, 'never, never to die.' "

"How very odd."

"Of course he's odd, very odd indeed. He looks entirely unconcerned as he announces that, rather than paying premiums for insurance, he prefers to hold his savings in a bank."

"Has he got any savings?"

"Of course not. He just doesn't give a damn what happens after his death."

"That's very worrisome for you. I wonder what makes him so peculiar. There's no one like him among his friends who come here, is there?"

"Of course there's not. He's unique."

"You should ask someone like Suzuki to give him a talking-to. If only he were as mild and manageable as Suzuki, he would be so much easier to cope with."

"I understand what you mean, but Mr. Suzuki is not well thought of in this house."

"Everything here seems upside-down. Well, if that's no good, what about that other person, that person of such singular self-possession?"

"Singleman Kidd?"

"Yes, him."

"Your uncle recognizes Singleman's superiority, but only yesterday we had Waverhouse round here with some dreadful tales to tell of Singleman's behavior and past history. In the circumstances, I don't think Singleman could be much help."

"But surely he could do it. He's so generously self-possessed, such a winning personality. The other day he gave a lecture at my school."

"Singleman did?"

"Yes."

"Does he teach at your school?"

"No, he's not one of our teachers, but we invited him to give a lecture to our Women's Society for the Protection of Female Virtue."

"Was it interesting?"

"Well, not all that interesting. But he has such a long face and he sports such a spiritual goatee, so everyone who hears him is naturally much impressed."

"What sort of things did he talk about?" Mrs. Sneaze had barely finished her sentence when the three children, presumably drawn by the sound of Yukie's voice, came bursting noisily across the veranda and into the living-room. I imagine they had been playing outside in the open space just beyond the bamboo fence.

"Hurray, it's Yukie," shouted the two elder girls with boisterous pleasure.

"Don't get so excited, children," said Mrs. Sneaze. "Come and sit down quietly. Yukie is going to tell us an interesting story." So saying, she shoved her sewing things away into a corner of the room.

"A story from Yukie?" says the eldest. "Oh, I do love stories."

"Will you be telling us again that tale of

Click-Clack Mountain?" asks the second daughter.

"Baby-beer a story!" shouts the baby as she rams her knee forward between her squatting sisters. This does not mean that she wants to listen to a story. On the contrary, it means she wants to tell one.

"What! Baby-dear's story yet again!" scream her laughing sisters.

"Baby-dear, you shall tell us your story afterward," says Mrs. Sneaze cajolingly, "after Yukie has finished."

But Baby-dear is in no mood for sops or compromises. "No," she bellows, "now!" And to establish that she's totally in earnest, she adds her gnomic warning of a tantrum. "Babu," she thundered.

"All right, all right. Baby-dear shall start," says Yukie placatingly. "What's your story called?"

" 'Bōtan, Bōtan, where you going?' "

"Very good, and what next?"

"I go rice-field, I cut rice"

"Aren't you a clever one!"

"If you tum there, rice go rotten"

"Hey, it's not 'tum there'; it's 'if you *come* there.' " One of the girls butts in with a correction. The baby responds with her threatening roar of "Babu," and her interrupting sister immediately subsides. But the interruption has broken the baby's train of remembrance so that, stuck for words, she sits there in a glowering silence.

"Baby-dear, is that all?" asks Yukie at her sweetest.

The baby pondered for a moment and then exclaimed, "Don't want fart-fart, that not nice."

There was a burst of unseemly laughter. "What a dreadful thing to say! Whoever's been teaching you that?"

"O-san," says the treacherous brat with an undisarming smirk.

"How naughty of O-san to say such things," says Mrs. Sneaze with a forced smile. Quickly ending the matter, she turned to her niece. "Now, it's time for Yukie's story. You'll listen to her, won't you, Baby-dear? Yes?" Tyrant though she is, the baby now seems to be satisfied, for she remained quiet.

"Professor Singleman's lecture went like this," Yukie began at last. "Once upon a time a big stone image of the guardian god of children stood smack in the middle of the place where two roads crossed. Unfortunately, it was a very busy place with lots of carts and horses moving along the roads. So this big stone Jizō, interfering with the flow of traffic, was really an awful nuisance. The people who lived in that district therefore got together and decided that the best thing to do would be to move the big stone image to one corner of the cross-roads."

"Is this a story of something that actually happened?" asks Mrs. Sneaze.

"I don't know. The Professor did not mention whether the tale was real or not. Anyway, it seems that the people then began to discuss how the statue could in fact be moved. The strongest man amongst them told them not to worry, for he could easily do the job. So off he went to the cross-roads, stripped himself to the waist and pushed and pulled at the big stone image till the sweat poured down his body. But the Jizō did not move."

"It must have been made of terribly heavy stone."

"Indeed it was. So terribly heavy that in the end that strongest man of them all was totally exhausted and trudged back home to sleep. So the people had another meeting and talked it over again. This time it was the smartest man amongst them who said, 'Let me have a go at it,' so they let him have a go. He filled a box with sweet dumplings and put it down on the ground a little way in front of the Jizō. 'Jizō,' he said, pointing to the dumpling-box, 'come along here.' For he reckoned that the big stone fellow would be greedy enough to be lured forward in order to get at the goodies. But the Jizō did not move. Though the clever man could see no flaw in his style of approach, he calculated that he must have misjudged the appetites of Jizō. So he went away and filled a gourd with *saké* and then came back to the cross-roads with the drink-filled gourd in one hand and a *saké*-cup in the other. For about three hours he tried to tease the Jizō into moving. 'Don't you want this lovely *saké*?' he kept shouting. 'If you want it, come and get it! Come and drink this lovely *saké*. Just a step and the gourd's all yours.' But the Jizō did not move."

"Yukie," asks the eldest daughter, "doesn't Mr. Jizō ever get hungry?"

"I'd do almost anything," observed her younger sister, "for a boxful of sweet dumplings."

"For the second time the clever man got nowhere. So he went away again and made hundreds and hundreds of imitation banknotes. Standing in front of the big stone god, he flashed his fancy money in and out of his pocket. 'I'll bet you'd like a fistful of these bank-notes,' he remarked, 'so why not come and get them?' But even the flashing of banknotes did no good. The Jizō did not move. He must, I think, have been quite an obstinate Jizō."

"Rather like your uncle," said Mrs. Sneaze with a sniff.

"Indeed so, the very image of my uncle. Well, in the end the clever man also gave up in disgust. At which point along came a braggart who assured the people that their problem was the simplest thing in the world and that he would certainly settle it for them."

"So what did the braggart do?"

"Well, it was all very amusing. First, he rigged himself out in a policeman's uniform and a false moustache. Then he marched up to the big stone image and addressed it in a loud and pompous voice. 'You there,' he bellowed, 'move along now quietly. If you don't move on, you'll find yourself in trouble. The authorities will certainly pursue the matter with the utmost rigor.' This must all have happened long ago," said Yukie by way of comment, "for I doubt whether nowadays you could impress anyone by pretending to be a policeman."

"Quite. But did that old-time Jizō move?"

"Of course it didn't. It was just like Uncle."

"But your uncle stands very much in awe of the police."

"Really? Well, if the Jizō wasn't scared by the braggart's threatenings, they couldn't have been particularly frightening. Anyway, the Jizō was unimpressed and stayed where it was. The braggart then grew deucedly angry. He stormed off home, took off his copper's uniform, pitched his false moustache into a rubbish-bin and re-appeared at the cross-roads got up to look like an extremely wealthy man. Indeed, he contorted his face to resemble the features of Baron Iwasaki. Can you imagine anything quite so potty?"

"What sort of face is Baron Iwasaki's?"

"Well, probably very proud. Toffee-nosed, you know. Anyway, saying nothing more, but puffing a vast cigar, the braggart took no further action but to walk round and round the Jizō."

"Whatever for?"

"The idea was to make the Jizō dizzy with tobacco smoke."

"It all sounds like some story-teller's joke! Did he succeed in dizzying the Jizō?"

"No, the idea didn't work. After all, he

was puffing against stone. Then, instead of just abandoning his pantomimes, he next appeared disguised as a prince. What about that?"

"As a prince? Did they have princes even in those days?"

"They must have, for Professor Kidd said so. He said that, blasphemous as it was, this braggart actually appeared in the trappings of a prince. I really think such conduct most irreverent. And the man nothing but a boastful twerp!"

"You say he appeared as a prince, but as which prince?"

"I don't know. Whichever prince it was, the act remains irreverent."

"How right you are."

"Well, even princely power proved useless. So, finally stumped, the braggart threw his hand in and admitted he could do nothing with the Jizō."

"Served him right!"

"Yes indeed; and, what's more, he ought to have been jailed for his impudence. Anyway, the people in the town were now really worried, but though they got together for a further pow-wow, no one could be persuaded to take another crack at the problem."

"Is that how it all finished?"

"No, there's more to come. In the end, they paid whole gangs of rickshawmen and other riffraff to mill around the Jizō with as much hullaballoo as possible. The idea was to make things so unbearably unpleasant that the Jizō would move on. So, taking it in turns, they managed to keep up an incredible din by day and night."

"What a painful business!"

"But even such desperate measures brought no joy, for the Jizō, too, was stubborn."

"So what happened?" asks Tonko eagerly.

"Well, by now everyone was getting pretty fed up because, though they kept the racket going for days and nights on end, the din had no effect. Only the riffraff and the rickshaw-men enjoyed the row they made, and they of course were happy because they were getting wages for making themselves a nuisance."

"What," asked Sunko, "are wages?"

"Wages are money."

"What would they do with money?"

Yukie was flummoxed. "Well, when they have money . . ." she began and then dodged the question first by a loud false laugh and then by telling Sunko how naughty she was. "Anyway," she continued, "the people just went on making their silly noises all through the day and all through the night. Now it so happened that at that time there was an idiot boy in the district whom they all called Daft Bamboo. He was, as the saying goes, simple. He knew nothing, and nobody had anything to do with him. Eventually even this simple-ton noticed the terrible racket. 'Why,' he asked 'are you making all that noise?' When someone explained the situation, the idiot boy remarked, 'What idiots you are, trying

for all these years to shift a single Jizō with
such idiotic tricks.' "

"A remarkable speech from an idiot.' "

"He was indeed a rather remarkable fool.
Of course nobody thought he could do any
good but, since no one else had done better,
why not, they said, why not let him have a
go at it? So Daft Bamboo was asked to help.
He immediately agreed. 'Stop that horrible
noise,' he said, 'and just keep quiet.' The
riffraff and the rickshawmen were packed off
somewhere out of sight, and Daft Bamboo,
as vacuous as ever, then walked up to the
Jizō with utter aimlessness."

"Was Utter Aimlessness a special friend of
Daft Bamboo?"

Mrs. Sneaze and Yukie burst into laughter
at Tonko's curious question.

"No, not a friend."

"Then, what?"

"Well, utter aimlessness is . . . impossible
to describe."

" 'Utter aimlessness' means 'impossible to
describe'?"

"No, that's not it. Utter aimlessness
means . . ."

"Yes?"

"You know Mr. Sampei, don't you?"

"Yes, he's the one who gave us yams."

"Well, utter aimlessness means someone
like Mr. Sampei."

"Is Mr. Sampei an utter aimlessness?"

"Yes, more or less. . . . Now, Daft Bamboo

ambled up to the Jizō with his hands in his pockets and said, 'Mr. Jizō, the people in this town would like you to move. Would you be so kind as to do so?' And the Jizō promptly replied, 'Of course I'll do so. Why ever didn't they come and ask before?' With that he slowly moved away to a corner of the cross-roads."

"What a peculiar statue!"

"Then the lecture started."

"Oh! Is there more to come?"

"Most certainly. Professor Kidd went on to say that he had opened his address to the women's meeting with that particular story because it illustrated a point he had in mind. 'If I may take the liberty of saying so,' he said, 'whenever women do something, they are prone to tackle it in a roundabout way instead of coming straight to the point. Admittedly, it is not solely women who beat about the bush. In these so-called enlightened days, debilitated by the poisons of Western civilization, even men have become somewhat effeminate. There are, alas, all too many now devoting their time and effort to an imitation of Western customs in the totally mistaken conviction that aping foreigners is the proper occupation of a gentleman. Such persons are, of course, deformed, for, by their efforts to conform with alien ways, they deform themselves. They deserve no further comment. However, I would wish you ladies to reflect upon the tale I've told today so that, as occasion may arise, you too will act with the same clear-hearted honesty as was shown by Daft Bamboo. For if all ladies did so act, there can be no doubt that one-third of the abominable discords between husbands and wives and between wives and their mothers-in-law would simply disappear. Human beings are, alas, so made that the more they indulge in secret schemes, schemes whose very secrecy breeds evil, the deeper they drive the well-springs of their own unhappiness. And the specific reason why so many ladies are so much less happy than the average man is precisely because ladies overindulge themselves in secret schemes. Please,' he begged us as his lecture ended, 'turn yourselves into Daft Bamboos.' "

"Did he, indeed! Well, Yukie, are you planning to follow his advice?"

"No fear! Turn myself into a Daft Bamboo! That's the last thing I would do. Miss Goldfield, too, she was very angry. She said the lecture was damned rude."

"Miss Goldfield? The girl who lives just round the corner?"

"Yes. Little Miss Popinjay in person."

"Does she go to the same school as you, Yukie?"

"No, she just came to hear the lecture because it was a Women's Society meeting. She certainly dresses up to the nines. Really astonishing."

"They say she's very good-looking. Is it true?"

"She's nothing special, in my opinion.

Certainly not the knock-out that she fancies herself. Almost any girl would look good under that much make-up."

"So if you, Yukie, daubed on the same amount of make-up, you'd look twice as pretty as she does? Right?"

"What a thing to say! But truly, Auntie, she puts on far too much. Rich she may be, but really she overdoes it."

"Well, it's pleasant to be rich, even if one does consequently overdo the paints and powder. Wouldn't you agree?"

"Yes, perhaps you're right. But if anyone needs to take lessons from Daft Bamboo, that Goldfield girl's the one. She is so terribly stuck-up. Only the other day she was swanking to all the other girls that some poet or other had just dedicated to her a collection of his new-style poetry."

"That was probably Mr. Beauchamp."

"Really? He must be a bit flighty."

"Oh no, Mr. Beauchamp is very soberminded man. He would think such a gesture the most natural thing in the world."

"A man like that shouldn't be allowed to. . . . Actually there is another amusing thing. It seems that somebody recently sent her a love-letter."

"How disgusting! Whoever did such a thing?"

"Apparently nobody knows who sent it."

"Wasn't there a name?"

"It was signed, but with a name that no one's ever heard of. And it was a very, very long letter, about a yard long, full of the weirdest things. For instance, it said, 'I love you in the same way that a saintly man loves God.' It said, 'Gladly for your sake would I die like a lamb sacrificed on the altar; for me, so to be slaughtered would be the greatest of all honors.' It said, 'My heart is shaped like a triangle in the center of which, like a bull's-eye pierced by a blowgun-dart, is Cupid's arrow stuck'!"

"Is all that meant to be serious?"

"It would seem to be. Three of my own friends have actually seen the letter."

"I do think she's awful to go round showing people such a letter. Since she intends to marry Mr. Coldmoon, she could get into trouble if that sort of story begins to get around."

"On the contrary, she'd be terribly pleased if everyone should know about it. I'm sure she'd say you'd be welcome to pass the news to Mr. Coldmoon when next he pays a visit. I don't suppose he's heard about it yet. Or do you think he has?"

"Probably not, since he spends his entire time polishing little glass beads at the university."

"I wonder if Mr. Coldmoon really intends to marry that girl. Poor man!"

"Why? With all her money she'll be of real help to him on some rainy day in the future. So why should you think he's doing badly?"

"Auntie, you are so vulgar, always talking about money, money, money. Surely love is more important than money. Without love no real relation between husband and wife is possible."

"Indeed? Then tell me, Yukie, what sort of man do you intend to marry?"

"How should I know? I've no one in mind."

Though she had hardly understood a word of what was being said, my master's eldest daughter had listened attentively while her mother and Cousin Yukie launched out upon their earnest discussion of the question of marriage. But suddenly, out of the blue, the little girl opened her mouth. "I," she announced, "would also like to get married." Though Yukie is herself so brimming with youthful ardor that she could well be expected to sympathize with Tonko's feelings, she was in fact struck dumb by such reckless lust. Mrs. Sneaze, however, took it all in her stride and, smiling at her daughter, simply asked, "To whom?"

"Well, shall I tell you? I want to marry Yasukuni Shrine. But I don't like crossing Suidō Bridge, so I'm wondering what do do."

Both Mrs. Sneaze and Yukie were distinctly taken aback by this unexpected declaration of an ambition to marry the shrine dedicated to the departed spirits of those who'd fallen in war for the sake of the fatherland. Words failed them, and all they could do was shake with laughter. They were still laughing when the second daughter said to her eldest sister. "So you'd like to marry Yasukuni Shrine? Well, so would I. I'd love it. Let's both do just that. Come on. No? All right then, if you won't join me, I'll take a rickshaw and go get married by myself."

"Babu go too," piped up the smallest of my master's daughters. Indeed, such a triple marrying-off would suit him very well.

At that moment there came the sound of a rickshaw stopping in front of the house, followed by the lively voice of a rickshawman announcing the arrival of my master. It would seem he has got back safely from the police station. Leaving the rickshawman to hand over a large parcel to the maid, my master came into the living-room with an air of perfect composure. Greeting his niece with a friendly "Ah, so there you are," he flung down beside the family's famous oblong brazier some bottle-shaped object he'd brought back. An object of that shape is not necessarily a bottle, and it certainly doesn't look much like a vase. Being so odd a specimen of earthenware, for the time being I'll content myself with calling it a bottle-shaped object.

"What a peculiar bottle! Did you bring it back from the police station?" asks Yukie, as she stands it up on its base.

Glancing at his niece, my master proudly comments, "Isn't it a beautiful shape?"

"A beautiful shape? That thing? I don't think it beautiful at all. What ever made you bring home such an awful oil-jar?"

"How could this treasure possibly be an oil-jar! What a vulgar comment! You're hopeless."

"What is it then?"

"A vase."

"For a vase, its mouth is too small and its body far too wide."

"That's exactly why it's so remarkable. You have absolutely no artistic taste. Almost as bad as your aunt." Holding the oil-jar up toward the paper-window, he stands and gazes at it.

"So, I have no artistic sense. I see. I certainly wouldn't come home from a police station bearing an oil-jar as a present. Auntie, what do you think?"

Her aunt is far too engrossed to be bothered. She has opened the parcel and is now frantically checking the goods.

"Gracious me! Burglars seem to be making progress. All these things have been washed and ironed. Just look, dear," she says.

"Who said I was given an oil-jar at the police station? The fact is that I got so bored with waiting that I went out for a walk and, while I was walking, I saw this splendid vessel in a shop and picked it up for a song. You, of course, wouldn't see it, but it's a rare object."

"It's too rare. And tell me, where was it that you walked about?"

"Where? Around Nihon-zutsumi, of course. I also visited Yoshiwara. It's quite a lively

I bet you haven't."

"Nothing would ever induce me to go and
look at it. I have no cause to traipse around
a brothel area like Yoshiwara. How could
you, a teacher, go to such a place? I am
deeply shocked. What d'you say, Auntie?
Auntie!"

"Yes, dear. I rather think there's something
missing. Is this the lot?"

"The only item missing is the yams. They
instructed me to be there by nine o'clock and
then they kept me waiting till eleven. It's outrageous. The Japanese police are plainly no
good at all."

"The Japanese police may be no good, but
trotting about in Yoshiwara is very decidedly
worse. If you're found out, you'll get the
sack. Won't he, Auntie?"

"Yes, probably. My dear," she went on
turning to her husband, "the lining of my
obi is gone. I knew there was something
missing."

"What's so serious about an obi-lining?
Just forget it. Think about me. For three long
hours they kept me waiting. A whole half-
day of my precious time completely wasted."
My master has now changed into Japanese
clothes and, leaning against the brazier, sits
and gawps entrancedly at his ghastly oil-jar.
His wife, recovering rapidly from her loss,
replaces the returned articles in a cupboard
and comes back to her seat.

"Auntie," says the persistent Yukie, "he

says this oil-jar is a rare object. Don't you think it dirty?"

"You bought that thing in Yoshiwara? Really!"

"What do you mean by 'Really!'? As if you understand anything!"

"But surely, a jar like that! You could find one anywhere without cavorting off to Yoshiwara."

"That's just where you're wrong. This isn't an object you could find any old where."

"Uncle does take after that stone Jizō, doesn't he?"

"None of your cheek, now. The trouble with college girls today is their far too saucy tongues. You'd do better to spend time reading the *Proper Conduct of a Woman*."

"Uncle, it's a fact, isn't it, that you don't like insurance policies? But tell me, which do you dislike more, college girls or insurance policies?"

"I do not dislike insurance policies. Insurance is a necessary thing. Anyone who gives even half a thought to the future is bound to take out a policy. But college girls are good-for-nothings."

"I don't care if I am a good-for-nothing. But you can talk! You aren't even insured!"

"As of next month, I shall be."

"Are you sure?"

"Of course I'm sure."

"Oh, you shouldn't. It's silly to get insured. It would be much better to spend the premium-money on something else. Don't you agree, Auntie?"

Mrs. Sneaze grins, but my master, looking serious, retorts, "You only say such irresponsible things because you imagine you're going to go on living until you're a hundred years old. Even two hundred. But when you've grown a little more mature, you'll come to realize the necessity of insurance. From next month, I shall definitely insure myself."

"Oh, well. Can't be helped then. Actually, if you can afford to throw away cash on an umbrella as you did the other day, you might as well waste your wealth on insuring yourself. You bought it for me even though I kept saying I didn't want it."

"You didn't really want it?"

"No. I most certainly did not want any umbrella."

"Then you can give it back to me. Tonko needs one badly, so I'll give it to her. Have you brought it with you today?"

"But that's really mean. How could you! It's terrible to make me give it back after you've bought it for me."

"I asked you to return it only because you clearly stated that you didn't want it. There's nothing terrible about that."

"It's true I don't need it. But you're still terrible."

"What nonsense you do talk. You say you don't want it, so I ask you to return it. Why should that be terrible?"

"But . . ."

"But what?"

"But that's terrible."

I Am a Cat (III)

"You're making no sense at all, just repeating the same irrational assertion."

"Uncle, you too are repeating the same thing."

"I can't help that if you initiate the repetitions. You did definitely say you didn't want it."

"Yes, I did say that. And it's true that I don't need it. But I don't like to return it."

"Well, I am surprised. You're not only irrational and unreasonable but downright obstinate. A truly hopeless case. Don't they teach you logic at your school?"

"Oh, I don't care. I am uneducated anyway. Say anything you like about me! But to ask me to return my own thing. . . . Even a stranger wouldn't make such a heartless request. You could learn a thing or two from poor old Daft Bamboo."

"From whom?"

"I mean you should be more honest and frank."

"You're a very stupid girl and uncommonly obstinate. That's why you fail to pass your exams."

"Even if I do fail, I shan't ask you to pay my school fees. So there!" At this point Yukie appeared to be shaken by uncontrollable emotions. Tears gushed out of her eyes and, pouring down her cheeks, fell to stain her purple dress.

My master sat there stupefied. As though he believed it might help him understand what mental processes could produce such copious tears, he sat and blankly stared, sometimes at the top of her skirt, sometimes at her down-turned face. Just then, O-san appeared at the door where, squatting with her hands spread out on the matting, she announced, "There is a visitor, Sir."

"Who is it?" asks my master.

"A student from your school," answers O-san, casting a sharp sidelong glance at Yukie's tear-stained face.

My master took himself off to the drawing-room. In pursuit of further material for this book, in particular as it might bear upon my study of the human animal, I sneaked out after him by way of the veranda. If one is to make a worthwhile study of mankind, it is vital to seize upon eventful moments. At ordinary times, most human beings are wearisomely ordinary; depressingly banal in appearance and deadly boring in their conversation. However, at certain moments, by some peculiar, almost supernatural, process, their normal triviality can be transformed into something so weird and wonderful that no feline scholar of their species can afford to miss any occasion when that transformation seems likely to take place. Yukie's sudden deluge of tears was a very good example of this phenomenon. Though Yukie possesses an incomprehensible and unfathomable mind, she gave no evidence of it in her chattering with Mrs. Sneaze. However, as soon as my master appeared and flung his filthy oil-jar into the situation, Yukie was instantly trans-

figured. Like some sleeping dragon startled
into its draconian reality by torrents of water
pumped upon it by some idiotic fire-engine,
unbelievably Yukie suddenly revealed the
depths of her wonderfully devious, wonderfully beautiful, wonderfully wondrous character in all its exquisite subtlety. Such
wonderful characteristics are, in fact, common among women throughout the world;
and it is regrettable that women so seldom
make them manifest. On reflection, it would
perhaps be more accurate to say that, while
these characteristics do continuously manifest
themselves, they rarely appear in such unin-
hibited form, so purely, openly and uncon-
strainedly, as they did in Yukie's outburst.
No doubt I owe it to my master—that com-
mendably crotchety crank who harbors no
ill-heartedness when he strokes my fur in the
wrong direction—that I have been privileged
to witness such a revelation of the female
soul. As I tag along through life behind him,
wherever we go he provokes more drama
than any of the protagonists ever realize. I
am fortunate to be the cat of such a man,
for, thanks to him, my short cat's life is
crammed with incident. Now, who, I wonder, is the visitor awaiting us?

It proved to be a schoolboy of about the
same age as Yukie, perhaps sixteen or seventeen. His hair is cropped so short that the
skin of his skull, a truly massive skull, shines
through it. With a dumpy nose in the middle
of his face, he sits despondently waiting in a

corner of the room. Apart from his enormous skull, there is nothing remarkable in his features. However, since that head looks huge in its virtually hairless state, it will certainly catch the eye when he lets his hair grow long as does my master. It is one of my master's private theories that heads so vast are always addled. He may, of course, be right, but heads of such Napoleonic grandeur remain indeed impressive. The lad's kimono, like that of any houseboy, is made out of common dark blue cotton with patterns splashed in white. I cannot identify the style of the pattern, possibly Satsuma, possibly Kurume, even perhaps plain Iyo; but he is undoubtedly wearing a lined kimono of dark blue cotton patterned with splotches of white. Its sleeves seem somewhat short, and he would appear to be wearing neither a shirt nor any underwear. I understand that it is currently considered very stylish, positively dandified, to go about in a lined kimono without underwear and even without socks; but this particular young man, far from seeming stylish, gives a strong impression of extreme shabbiness. In particular I notice that, barefooted like our recent burglar, he has marked the matting with three dirty footprints and now, doing his best to look respectful and certainly looking ill at ease, sits uncomfortably upon the fourth of them. It is in no way extraordinary to see respectable persons behaving respectfully; but when some wild young hooligan with his skinhead hairstyle and his too-small clothing seats himself in a reverent posture, the effect is distinctly incongruous. Creatures who have the effrontery even to be proud of their insolent refusal to bow to their teachers when they meet them in the street must find it very painful to sit up properly like anyone else, even for so little as half an hour. Moreover, since this particular yahoo is actually trying to behave as if he were a gentleman by birth, a man of natural modesty and of cultivated virtue, the comic incompetence of his performance must surely add to his sufferings. I marvel at the agonizing self-control by which a lout so boisterous both in the classroom and on the playground can bring himself to endure such a laughable charade. It is pitiful but, at the same time, funny. In confrontations of this sort, however stupid my master may be, he still seems to carry rather more weight than any individual pupil. Indeed, my master must be feeling pretty pleased with himself.

The saying goes that even motes of dust, if enough of them pile up, will make a mountain. One solitary schoolboy may well be insignificant, but schoolboys ganged together can be a formidable force, capable of agitating for the expulsion of a teacher, even of going on strike. Just as cowards grow aggressive under the spur of grog, so may students emboldened by mere numbers into stirring up a riot be regarded as having lost their senses by becoming intoxicated with people. How else can one explain how my master, who, however antiquated and decrepit he may be, is nevertheless a teacher, could in his own schoolroom have been reduced to an object of derision by this scruffy little runt now making himself small, dejected perhaps rather than truly humbled, in a corner of our room? Even so, I find it hard to credit that so miserable a snivelard could ever have dared to rag or mock my master.

That noble figure, shoving a cushion toward the drooping crophead, bade him sit on it; but the latter, though he managed to mumble a nervous "thank you," made no move at all. It's quaint to see a living being, even this bighead, sitting blankly with a partly faded cushion rammed up against his knees. The cushion, of course, says nothing, not even, "Sit on me." But cushions are for sitting on. Mrs. Sneaze didn't go to a market-stall and buy this particular cushion in order that it should be looked at. It follows that anyone who declines to sit on the cushion is, in effect, casting a slur on its cushionly good name. Indeed, when my master has specifically offered the cushion for sitting upon, a refusal to do so extends the insult to the cushion into a slight upon my master. This crophead glaring at the cushion and thereby slighting my master does not, of course, have any personal dislike for the cushion itself. As a matter of fact, the only other occasion in his life when he sat in a civilized manner was during the memorial rites for his grand-father, so his present sally into decorum is bringing on pins and needles in his feet while his toes, excruciated by the pressures of propriety, have long been signaling blue murder. Nevertheless, the clot won't sit on the cushion. He will not do so, though the cushion, clearly embarrassed by the situation, yearns to be sat on. Even though my master requests he use the cushion, still this oaf declines it. He is a very wearisome young man. If he can be so overweeningly modest on a visit, he ought to trot out a little more of his precious modesty when roistering around with his cronies in the schoolroom and at his lodgings. He positively reeks of decorous reserve when it's totally uncalled for; yet, when just a touch of self-depreciation would hardly come amiss, he's raucous, coarse and cocky. What an irksome cross-grained crophead this young rascal is.

At that moment the sliding-door behind him quietly slid open and Yukie came in formally to place a cup of tea before the silent youth. In normal circumstances, he would have greeted the appearance of such refreshment with jeering catcalls about poor old Savage Tea, but today, already wilting under my master's immediate presence, he suffers further agony as a prissily conducted young lady serves him tea with all that affected ceremoniality which has only recently been drilled into her at school. As Yukie closed the sliding-door she allowed herself, safe behind the young man's back, to break into a broad grain. Which shows that a female is remarkably more self-possessed than a male of the same age. Indeed, Yukie very evidently has far more spirit to her than this cushion-shunning twit. Her bare-faced grin is all the more remarkable when one remembers that, only a few minutes ago, tears of resentment were pouring down her cheeks.

After Yukie had left, a long silence fell. Eventually my master, feeling that the interview was in danger of becoming some kind of dour religious exercise, took the initiative and opened his mouth.

"Your name . . . what did you say it was?"

"Yore."

"Yore? Yore and what else? What's your first name?"

"Lancelot."

"Lancelot Yore. . . . I see. Quite a resounding name. Certainly not modern, a somewhat old-fashioned name. You are in your fourth year, aren't you?"

"No."

"Your third year?"

"No, my second year."

"And in Class A?"

"In Class B."

"In B? Then, you're in my class. I see." My master appeared impressed. He had taken note of this particularly monstrous head since its bearer first joined the school, and had recognized it immediately. In fact, that head has so long and so deeply impressed my master that, every so often, he actually dreams about it. However, being of a totally impractical nature, he had never connected that extraordinary head with that odd old-fashioned name; and had somehow failed to connect either with his own second-year Class B. Consequently, when he realized that the impressive head that haunted his dreams actually belonged to one of his own pupils, he was genuinely startled. All the more so since he cannot imagine why this big-headed and oddly named member of his own class should now have come to see him. My master is unpopular, and hardly a single schoolboy ever comes near him, even at the New Year. As a matter of fact, this Lancelot Yore is the very first such visitor, and my master is understandably puzzled by his call. It is inconceivable that the visit could be purely social, for how could my master be of the faintest interest to any of his pupils? It seems equally inconceivable that a boy of this kind could need advice about his personal affairs. Of course, it is just conceivable that Lancelot Yore might come around to urge my master into resigning; but in such a case one would expect him to be, if not blatantly aggressive, at least defiant. My master, unable to make head or tail of the situation, is at a complete loss and, to judge by his appearance, it would seem that Lancelot Yore is himself by no means certain why he has made his visit. In the end my master was driven to asking pointblank questions.

"Have you come here for a chat?"

"No, not for that."

"Then you have something to tell me?"

"Yes."

"About school?"

"Yes, I wanted to tell you something about . . ."

"What is it? Tell me."

"Right, then."

Lancelot lowers his eyes and says nothing. Normally, considered as a second-year student at middle school, Lancelot is talkative. Though his brain is undeveloped in comparison with his skull, he expresses himself rather more effectively than most of his fellow-students in Class B. In fact, it was he who recently made my master look rather a fool by asking him how to translate "Columbus" into Japanese. That such a tricky questioner should be as reluctant to start speaking as some stammering princess suggests that something very weird must be involved. Hesitation so prolonged and so entirely out of character cannot possibly be due to modesty. Even my simple master thought the matter really rather odd.

"If you have something to say, go ahead and say it. Why do you hesitate?"

"It's a bit difficult to explain . . ."

"Difficult?" says my master peering across to study Lancelot's face. But his visitor still sits with his eyes lowered, and my master finds it impossible to read anything from their expression. Changing his tone of voice, he added, "Don't worry. Tell me anything you like. Nobody else is listening, and I won't pass on a single word to anyone."

"Could I really tell you?" Lancelot is still wavering.

"Why not?" says my master, taking a sort of plunge.

"All right, I'll tell you." Abruptly lifting up his close-cropped head the boy glanced diffidently at my master. His eyes are triangular in shape. My master puffed out his cheeks with cigarette smoke and, slowly expelling it, looked at his visitor sideways.

"Well, actually . . . things have become awkward . . ."

"What things?"

"Well, it's all terribly awkward, and that's why I've come."

"Yes, but what is it that you find so awkward?"

"I really didn't mean to do such a thing, but as Hamada urged and begged me to lend it . . ."

"When you say Hamada, do you mean Hamada Heisuke?"

"Yes."

"Did you lend him money for board and lodging?"

"Oh, no, I didn't lend him that."

"Then, what did you lend him?"

"I lent him my name."

"Whatever was he doing borrowing your name?"

"He sent a love-letter."

"He sent what?"

"I explained I'd rather do the posting than the lending of my name."

"You're not making much sense. Who did what anyway?"

"A love-letter was sent."

"A love-letter? To whom?"

"As I said, it's so difficult to tell you."

"You mean you've sent a love-letter to some woman? Is that it?"

"No, it wasn't me."

"Hamada sent it?"

"It wasn't Hamada either."

"Then who did send it?"

"That's not known."

"None of this makes sense. Did no one send it?"

"Only the name is mine."

"Only the name is yours? I still don't understand. You'll have to explain what's happened clearly and logically. In the first place, who actually received the love-letter?"

"A girl named Goldfield who lives just round the corner."

"Goldfield? The businessman?"

"Yes, his daughter."

"And what do you mean when you say you lent only your name?"

"Because that girl is such a dolled-up and conceited pinhead, we decided to send her a love-letter. Hamada said it had to be signed; but when I told him to sign it himself, he argued that his name wasn't sufficiently interesting, that Lancelot Yore would be very much more impressive. So I ended up by lending my name."

"And do you know the girl? Are you friends?"

"Friends? Of course not. I've never set eyes on her."

"How very imprudent! Fancy sending a love-letter to someone you've never even seen! What made you do such a thing?"

"Well, everyone said she was stuck-up and pompous, so we thought we'd make a fool of her."

"That's even more rash! So you sent the letter clearly signed with your name?"

"Yes. The letter itself was written by Hamada. I lent my name, and Endō took it round to her house at night and stuck it in the letter-box."

"Then all three of you are jointly responsible?"

"Yes, but afterward, when I thought about being found out and possibly expelled from school, I got so worried that I haven't been able to sleep for the last two or three nights. That's why I'm not my usual self."

"It's a quite unbelievably stupid thing you've done. Tell me, when you signed that letter did you give the school's address?"

"No, of course I made no mention of the school."

"Well, that's something. If you had and it ever came out, the good name of our school would be disgraced."

"Do you think I'll be expelled?"

"Well, I don't know . . ."

"My father is very strict and my mother is only a stepmother, so if anything happened like being expelled, I'd really be in the soup. Do you reckon I'll get expelled?"

"You must understand, you shouldn't have done a thing like that."

"I didn't mean to really, but somehow I just did. Couldn't you save me from being expelled?" With the tears running down his face, the pathetic Lancelot implores my master's help.

For quite some time behind the sliding-door Mrs. Sneaze and her niece have been convulsed with silent giggles. My master, doggedly maintaining an air of importance, keeps on repeating his "Well, I don't know." Altogether a fascinating experience.

It is possible that some of you human beings might, and very reasonably, ask me what I find so fascinating about it. For every living being, man or animal, the most important thing in this world is to know one's own self. Other things being equal, a human being that truly knows himself is more to be respected than a similarly enlightened cat. Should the humans of my acquaintance ever achieve such self-awareness, I would immediately abandon, as unjustifiedly heartless, this somewhat snide account of their species as I know them. However, just as few human beings actually know the size of their own noses, even fewer know the nature of their own selves, for if they did, they would not need to pose such a question to a mere cat whom they normally regard, even disregard, with contempt. Thus, though human beings are always enormously pleased with themselves, they usually lack that self-perception which, and which alone, might justify their seeing themselves, and their boasting of it wherever they go, as the lords of all creation. To top things off, they display a brazenly calm conviction in their role which is positively laughable. For there they are, making a great nuisance of themselves with their fussing entreaties to be taught where to find their own fool noses, while at the same time strutting around with placards on their backs declaring their claim to be lords of creation. Would common logic or even common sense lead any such patently loony human being to resign his claim to universal lordship? Not on your life! Every idiot specimen would sooner die than surrender his share in the fantasy of human importance. Any creature that behaves with such blatant inconsistency and yet contrives never to recognize the least minim of self-contradiction in its behavior is, of course, funny. But since the human animal is indeed funny, it follows that the creature is a fool.

The foregoing events occurred precisely as I have recorded them and, as external realities, they left their quaint little ripples on the stream of time; but in this particular case it was not their manifested conduct which made my master, Yukie and Yore strike me as amusing. What tickled me was the differing quality of reaction in their inmost hearts which the same external events evoked in these several persons. First of all, my master's heart is rather cold, and so was his reaction to these happenings. However strictly Yore's harsh father may treat the boy, however hurtfully his stepmother may pick on him, my master's heart would not be moved. How could it be? Yore's possible expulsion from school does not raise any of the issues that would be involved if my master were dismissed. Of course, if all the pupils, nearly a thousand of them, were simultaneously expelled, then the teachers might find it hard to earn a living: but whatever fate befalls this wretched single pupil, the daily course of my master's own life will be totally unaffected. Obviously, where there is no self-interest there is not going to be much sympathy. It is just not natural to knit one's brows, to blow one's nose or to draw great sighs over the misfortunes of complete strangers. I simply do not believe the human animal is capable of showing such understanding and compassion. People sometimes squeeze out a few tears or try looking sorry as a kind of social obligation, a sort of tax-payment due in acknowledgement of having been born into a community. But such gestures are never heart-felt, and their effective performance, like any other act of chicanery, does in fact demand a high degree of skill. Persons who perform these trickeries most artfully are regarded as men of strong artistic feelings and earn the deepest respect of their less-gifted fellows. It follows, of course, that those who are most highly esteemed are those most morally dubious, an axiom which can easily be proved by putting it to the test. My master, being extremely ham-handed in matters of this kind, commands not the least respect and, having no hope of winning respect by crafty misrepresentation of his true feelings, is quite open in expressing his inner cold-heartedness. The sincerity of his indifference emerges very clearly from the way in which he fobs off poor young Yore's repeated pleas for help with repetitions of the same old formulae: "Well, I don't know" and "Hmm, I wonder." I hasten to comment that I trust my readers will not begin to dislike so good a man as my master just because he happens to be cold-hearted. Coldness is the inborn natural condition of the human heart, and the man who does not hide that fact is honest. If in circumstances such as I've described you really are expecting something more than cold-heartedness, then I can only say that you have sadly overestimated the worth of humankind. When even mere honesty is in notably short supply, it would be absolutely ridiculous to expect displays of magnanimity. Or do you seriously believe that the Eight Good Men have stepped out of the pages of Bakin's silly novel in order to take up residence in our neighborhood?

So much for my master. Let us now consider his womenfolk tittering away together in the living-room. They, in fact, have gone a stage beyond the pure indifference of my master and, naturally adapted as they are to the comic and the grotesque, are thoroughly enjoying themselves. These females regard the matter of the love-letter, a matter of excruciating concern to that miserable crophead, as a gift from a kindly heaven. There is no particular reason why they regard it as a blessing. It just seems like one to them. However, if one analyzes their mirth, the simple fact is that they are glad that Yore's in trouble. Ask any female whether she finds it amusing, even a cause for outright laughter, when other people are in trouble, and she will either call you mad or affect to have been deliberately insulted by a question so demeaning to the dignity of her sex. It may well be true that she feels she's been insulted, but it is also true that she laughs at people in trouble. The reality of this ladylike position is that, inasmuch as the lady intends to do something that would impugn her character, no decent person should draw attention to the fact. Correspondingly, the gentleman's position is to acknowledge that he steals but to insist that nobody should call him immoral because an accusation of immorality would involve a stain on his character, an insult to his good name. Women are quite clever: they think logically. If one has the ill luck to be born a human being, one must prepare oneself not to be distressed that other people will not so much as turn to look when you are being kicked and beaten up. And not just that. One must learn to think it a pleasure to be spat upon, shat upon and then held up to be laughed at. If one cannot learn these simple lessons, there is no chance of becoming a friend of such clever creatures as women. By an understandable error of judgement the luckless Lancelot Yore has made a sad mistake and is now greatly humiliated. He might possibly feel that it is uncivilized to snigger at him behind his back when he is thus humiliated; but any such feeling on his part would simply be a demonstration of pure childishness. I understand that women call it narrow-mindedness if one gets angry with persons who commit a breach of etiquette. So, unless young Yore is prepared to acquire that further humiliation, he'd best belt up.

Finally, I will offer a brief analysis of Yore's own inward feelings. That infantile suppliant is a living lump of quivering anxiety. Just as Napoleon's massive head was bulgy with ambitions, so Yore's gurt skull is bursting with anxiety. The occasional puppy-like quivering of his pudgy nose betrays that this inner distress has forced a connection with his nasal nerves so that, by the nastiest of reflex actions, he twitches without knowing it. Now for several days he has been at the end of his tether, going around with a lump in his stomach as though he'd swallowed a cannon-ball. Finally, at his wits' end and in the extremity of his desperation, he

has come to humble his head before a teacher
he most cordially dislikes. I imagine the addled thinking behind this desperate act was
that, since teachers are supposed to look after
their pupils, perhaps even the loathed Sneaze
might somehow help him. Lost in the miasma
of his inner agony is any recollection of his
habitual ragging of my master; forgotten,
too, is the fact that he spent his witless days
in egging on his fellow-hooligans to hoot and
mock old Savage Tea. He seems to believe
that, however much he's made a nuisance of
himself, he's actually entitled to his teacher's
help for the single reason that he happens to
be a member of that teacher's class. He is indeed a very simple soul. My master did not
choose the class he teaches: he was directed
to that work by order of the headmaster. I
am reminded of that bowler-hat of Waverhouse's uncle. It was no more than a bowler-
hat in name. The idea of my master as a
teacher who is also the mentor of his pupils
is equally unreal. Teacher, smeacher. A name
means nothing. If it did, any marriage-broker
would by now have been able to interest some
aspiring bachelor in a girl with a name as
beautiful as that snow-river name of Yukie's.
The dismal Yore is not only daftly egocentric
but, daftly overestimating human kindliness,
assumes that his fellow-creatures are under
some form of obligation to be nice to him.
I'm sure he has never dreamt that he might
be laughed at, so at least he's learning some
useful home truths about his species from his

吾輩は猫である

visit to the home of the "person in charge." As a result, he will himself become more truly human. His heart, benignly chilled, will grow indifferent to other people's troubles and, in time, he'll even learn to jeer at the distressed. The world will come to swarm with little Yores, all doing their best to stretch themselves into full-blown Goldfields. For the lad's sake, I do hope he learns his lesson quickly and grows up soon into his full humanity. Otherwise, no matter how hard he worries, no matter how bitterly he repents, no matter how fervently his heart may yearn to be reformed, he can never so much as hope to be able to achieve the spectacular success of that model of humanity, the highly respected Goldfield. On the contrary, he will be banished from human society. Compared with that, expulsion from some piddling middle school would be as nothing.

I was idly amusing myself with these reflections when the sliding-door from the hall was roughly jerked aside and half a face suddenly appeared at the opening. My master was mumbling, "Well, I really don't know," when this half-face called his name. He wrenched his head around to find a shining segment of Avalon Coldmoon beaming down upon him.

"Why, hello," says my master making no move to get up, "come along in."

"Aren't you busy with a visitor?" the visible half of Coldmoon asks politely.

"Never mind about that. Come on in."

"Actually, I've called to ask you to come out with me."

"Where to? Akasaka once again? I've had enough of that district. You made me walk so much the other day that my legs are still quite stiff."

"It will be all right today. Come on out and give those legs a stretch."

"Where would we go? Look, don't just stand there. Come along in."

"My idea is that we should go to the zoo and hear their tiger roar."

"How dreary. I say, old man, do come in if only for a few minutes."

Coldmoon evidently came to the conclusion that he would not succeed by negotiating from a distance so, reluctantly removing his shoes, he slouched into the room. As usual, he is wearing gray trousers with patches on the seat. These patches, he is always telling us, are not there either because the trousers are old or because his bottom is too heavy. The reason is that he has just started to learn how to ride a bicycle, and the patches are needed to resist the extra friction involved. Greeting Yore with a nod and a brief hello, he sits down on the veranda side of the room. He has, of course, no least idea that he is now sitting down with a direct rival in the lists of love, with the very person who has sent a love-letter to that damsel now regarded by all and sundry as the future Mrs. Coldmoon.

"There's nothing particularly interesting about a tiger's roar," observed my master.

"Well, not just at this exact moment. But my idea is that we should walk about for a bit and then go on to the zoo around eleven."

"So?"

"By then, the old trees in the park will be darkly frightening like a silent forest."

"Well, possibly. Certainly, it will be a little more deserted than by daytime."

"We'll follow a path as thickly wooded as possible, one where even in daytime few people pass. Then, before you know what, we'll find ourselves thinking we're far away from the dusty city and a feeling, I'm sure, will grow within us that we've somehow wandered away into far-off mountains."

"What does one do with a feeling like that?"

"Feeling like that, we'll just stand there, silent and motionless for a little while. Then, suddenly, the roar of a tiger will burst upon us."

"Is the tiger trained to roar precisely at that moment?"

"I guarantee he'll roar. Even in broad day that fearsome sound can be heard all the way over at the Science University. So, after dark, in the very dead of night, when not a soul's about in the deep-hushed loneliness, when death can be felt in the air and one breathes the reek of evil mountain-spirits. . . ."

"Breathing the reek of evil mountain-spirits? Whatever does that mean?"

"I understand it's an expression used to signify a condition of extreme terror."

"Is it indeed. Not an expression in common use. I don't believe I've ever heard it before. Anyway, what then?"

"Then the tiger roars. A savage shattering roar that seems to strip each shaking leaf from the ancient cedar-trees. Really, it's terrifying."

"I can well believe it is."

"Well then, how about joining me for such an adventure? I'm sure we'll enjoy it. An experience to be treasured. Everyone, sometime, that's how I see it, really ought to hear a tiger roar from the depths of night."

"Well," says my master, "I don't know. . . ." He drops on Coldmoon's enthusiastic proposal for an expedition the same wet blanket of indifference with which he has muzzled Yore's agonized entreaties.

Up till this moment that dim nincompoop has been listening, enviously and in silence, to the talk about the tiger; but as a hypnotist's key phrase will bring his subject to his senses, my master's repetition of his indifference snapped Yore smartly back into remembrance of his own dilemma. "Revered teacher," he muttered from his broken trance, "I'm worried sick. What, what, shall I do?"

Coldmoon, puzzled, stares at that enormous head. As for me, I feel suddenly moved, for no particular reason but the feeling, to leave this trio to themselves. Accordingly, I excuse myself from their company and sidle round to the living-room.

There I find Mrs. Sneaze with the giggles.

She has poured tea into a cheap china cup and, placing that cup on a nasty antimony saucer, says to her niece, "Would you please take this to our guest?"

"I'd rather not."

"Why not?" The mistress sounds surprised and her giggling stops abruptly.

"I'd just rather not," says Yukie. She suddenly adopts a peculiarly supercilious expression and, firmly seating herself on the matting, bends forward and low to study some rag of a daily newspaper.

Mrs. Sneaze immediately resumes negotiations. "What a funny person you are. It's only Mr. Coldmoon. There's no reason to act up."

"It's simply that I really would prefer not to." The girl's eyes remain fixed on the newspaper, but it's obvious that she's too het up to be able to read a word of it. What's more, if anyone points out that she isn't reading, there'll be another flood of maidenly tears.

"Why are you being so shy?" This time, laughing, Mrs. Sneaze deliberately pushes the cup and saucer right onto the newspaper as it lies there flat on the floor.

"What a nasty thing to do!" Yukie tries to yank the paper out from under the tea-things, knocks them flying and the spilt tea shoots all over the paper and the living-room matting.

"There, now!" says the mistress.

With a cry expressing a curious mixture of anger, shock and embarrassment, Yukie scrambles to her feet and runs out into the

kitchen. I imagine she's gone to fetch a mop.
I find this little drama rather amusing.

Mr. Coldmoon, totally unaware of the female flurry which his visit appears to have stirred up in the living-room, continues, somewhat oddly, his conversation with my master.

"I notice," he says, "that you've had new paper fixed on that sliding-door. Who did it, if I may ask?"

"The women. Quite a good job they made of it, don't you think?"

"Yes, very professional. You say 'the women.' Does that include that college girl who sometimes comes here visiting?"

"Yes, she lent a hand. In fact she was boasting that, since she can make such an obviously splendid job of papering a sliding-door, she is also obviously well qualified to get married."

"I see," says Coldmoon still studying the door. "Down the left side, there," he eventually continued, "the paper has been fixed on taut and smooth; but along the right-hand edge it seems to have been inadequately stretched. Hence those wrinkles."

"That was where they started the job, before they'd really got the hang of it."

"I see. It's certainly less well done. The surface forms an exponential curve irrelatable to any ordinary function." From the abyss of his scientific training Coldmoon dredges up monstrosities.

"I dare say," says my master, indifferent as ever.

That dispassionate comment, it would

seem, at last brings home to our hooligan scribe the complete hopelessness of hoping that even the most searing of his supplications could ever melt my master's chilly disconcern. Suddenly lowering his huge skull to the matting, Yore in total silence made his farewell salutation.

"Ah," said my master, "you're leaving?"

Yore's crestfallen appearance provided his only answer. We heard him dragging his heavy cedarn clogs even after he'd gone out through the gate. A pitiable case. If someone doesn't come to his rescue, he could well compose one of those rock-top suicide-poems and then fling his stupid body over the lip of Kegon Falls. Come what may, the root-cause of all this trouble is the flibbertigibbet self-conceit of that insufferable Miss Goldfield. If Yore does do himself in, it is to be hoped that his ghost will find the time to scare that girl to death. No man need regret it if a girl like that, even a brace or more of them, were removed from this already sufficiently troubled world. It seems to me that Coldmoon would be well advised to marry some more ladylike young person.

"Was that, then, one of your pupils?"

"Yes."

"What an enormous head. Is he good at his work?"

"Rather poor for that size of head. But every now and again he asks original questions. The other day he caught me off balance by asking for a translation of the meaning of Columbus."

"Maybe the improbable size of his brain-case leads him to pose such an improbable question. Whatever did you answer?"

"Oh, something or other off the cuff."

"So you actually did translate it. That's remarkable."

"Children lose faith in a language teacher who fails to provide them, on demand, with a translation of anything they may ask."

"You've become quite a politician. But to judge by that lad's look, he must be terribly run down. He seemed ashamed to be bothering you."

"He's just managed to get himself into something of a mess. Silly young ass!"

"What's it all about? The mere sight of him moves one's sympathy. What's he done?"

"Rather a stupid thing. He's sent a love-letter to Goldfield's daughter."

"What? That great numbskull? Students nowadays seem to stop at nothing. Quite astonishing! Really, I am surprised."

"I hope this news has not upset you?"

"Not in the very least. On the contrary, I find it most diverting. I do assure you, it's quite all right by me however many love-letters may come pouring in upon her."

"If you feel that self-assured perhaps it doesn't matter . . ."

"Of course it doesn't matter. I really don't mind at all. But isn't it rather remarkable that that great muttonhead should take to writing love-letters?"

"Well, actually, it all started as a kind of joke. Because that girl was so stuck-up and conceited, my precious trio got together and . . ."

"You mean that three boys sent one love-letter to Miss Goldfield? This business grows more whacky by the minute. Such a joint letter sounds rather like three people settling down to share one portion of a Western-style dinner. Don't you agree?"

"Well, they did divide the functions up between them. One wrote the letter, another posted it, and the third loaned his name for its signature. That young blockhead whom you saw just now, quite the silliest of them all, he's the one who lent his name. Yet he actually told me that he's never even set eyes on the girl. I simply can't imagine how anyone could do such a ludicrous thing."

"Well, I think it's spectacular, a wonder of our times, a real masterpiece of the modern spirit! That that oaf should have it in him to fire off a love-letter to some unknown woman. . . . Really, it's most amusing!"

"It could lead to some very awkward misunderstandings."

"What would it matter if it did? It would be skin off nobody's nose but the Goldfields'."

"But this daughter of theirs is the very girl you may be marrying."

"True, but I only may be marrying her. Don't be so concerned. Really, I do not mind in the least about the Goldfields."

"You may not mind but . . ."

"Oh, I'm quite sure the Goldfields wouldn't mind. Honest!"

"All right, then, if you say so. Anyway, after the deed was done and the letter delivered, that boy suddenly began to get qualms of conscience. More precisely, he became scared of being found out and therefore came sheepishly round here to ask me for advice."

"Really? Was that why he looked so very down in the mouth? He must, at heart, be a very timid boy. You gave him some advice, I suppose?"

"He's scared silly of being expelled from school. That's his chief worry."

"Why should he be expelled from school?"

"Because he has done such a wicked and immoral thing."

"You can't call sending a love-letter, even in joke, either wicked or immoral. It's just not that important. In fact, I'd expect the Goldfields to take it as an honor and to go around boasting about it."

"Oh, surely not!"

"Anyway, even if it was wrong to do such a thing, it's hardly fair to let that poor boy worry himself sick about it. You could be sending him to his death. Though his head is grotesque, his features are not evil. He was twitching his nose, you know. Rather sweet, really."

"You're becoming as irresponsible as Waverhouse in the breezy things you say."

"Well, that's no more than the current style. It's a bit old-fashioned to take things quite as seriously as you do."

"It's hardly a question of being up-to-date

or out-of-fashion. Surely, at any time, any-where, only a complete fool could think it funny to send a love-letter to an unknown person. It flies in the face of common sense."

"Come now. The vast majority of all jokes depends on the reversal of ordinary common sense. Ease up on the lad. If only in common charity, do what you can to help him. From what I saw he was already on his way to Kegon Falls."

"Perhaps I should."

"Indeed you should. After all, the world is stiff with full-grown men, men with older and presumably wiser heads, who neverthe-less spend all their lives in practical jokes which risk disaster for their fellowmen. Would you punish an idiot schoolboy for signing a love-letter when men whose jokes could wreck the world go totally unpenalized? If you ex-pel him from school, you can do no less than banish them from civilized society."

"Well, perhaps you're right."

"Good. Then that's settled. Now, how about going out and listening to a tiger?"

"Ah, the tiger."

"Yes. Do come out. As a matter of fact, I've got to leave Tokyo in a few day's time and go back home to attend to some busi-ness. Since it will be quite a while before we'll be able again to go out anywhere together, I called today in the express hope we could make some little expedition this evening."

"So you're going home. And on business?"

"Yes, something I myself must cope with. Anyway, let's go out."

"All right, I'll come."

"Splendid. Today, dinner's on me. If, after that, we walk across to the zoo, we should arrive at exactly the right time." Coldmoon's enthusiasm is infectious and, by the time they bustled out together, my master himself was scarcely less excited.

Mrs. Sneaze and Yukie, ever, eternally feminine, just went on with their chit-chat and their sniggering.

IN FRONT OF the alcove, Waverhouse and Singleman sit facing each other with a board for playing *go* set down between them.

"Damned if I'm playing for nothing," says Waverhouse forcefully. "The loser stands a dinner. Right?"

Singleman tugs at his daft goatee. "In my experience," he murmurs, "to play for gain, for food or filthy lucre, cheapens this noble pastime. It maims the mind to burden its cells with thoughts of loss or profit. Betting's a scruffy business. I feel, don't you, that the true value of a game-encounter is only really appreciated in an atmosphere of leisurely calm where, all considerations of success or failure set aside, one lets things run their own sweet natural course. Then, and only then, can the finer points of the game be properly savored by its connoisseurs."

"There you go again. Harping away on the same old metaphysical drivel. It's really quite impossible to have any sort of sensible game with a man who carries on as if he'd stepped from the pages of some ancient Chinese tome recording the maunderings of the scholar-hermits of remote antiquity."

"If I harp at all," says Singleman with quite surprising spirit, "it is, as Yüan Ming so neatly put it, that I play on a harp that has no strings."

"Ah," says Waverhouse dryly, "like wiring messages on wire-less sets, I suppose."

"Now then, Waverhouse, you can do better than that. But please don't try. Let's get on with the game."

"Will you be Black or White?"

"Suit yourself. Either."

"As one might expect of a hermit, you are transcendentally generous. If you'll take White, I'm necessarily Black. Right. Let's get cracking. Now then, off you go. Place your first piece anywhere you like."

"The rule is that Black starts."

"Really? Is that so? Very well, being a modest fellow, my opening gambit shall be a Black piece somewhere round here."

"You can't do that."

"Why not?"

"It's against the rules."

"Never mind them. It's a brand new opening gambit, one I've just invented."

Since I know so little of the world outside my master's house, it was only recently that I first clapped eyes on a *go* board. It's a weird contraption, something no sensible cat would ever think up. It's a smallish square divided into a myriad smaller squares on which the players position black and white stones in so

higgledy-piggledy a human fashion that one's
eyes go skew to watch them. Thereafter the
devotees of this strange cult work themselves
up into a muck-sweat, excitedly shouting that
this or that ridiculous little object is in danger, has escaped, has been captured, killed,
rescued or whatever. And all this over a bare
square foot of board where the mildest tap
with my right front paw would wreak irre-
parable havoc. As Singleman might quote
from his compendium of Zen sermons, one
gathers grasses and with their thatch creates
a hermitage only to find the same old field
when the thatch is blown away. You set the
pieces out and then you take them off. A
silly occupation. Why don't the players keep
their hands in the folds of their kimonos and
simply stare at an empty board? In the earlier
stages of the game, with only thirty or forty
pieces in place, one could not honestly describe the effect as an eyesore; but as things
move to a climax, the scrimmage of black
and white becomes an offense to the civilized
mind. The black and white pieces are so
crammed together that they squeak and grate
in a jostle of stones. The ones at the edges
seem bound to be pushed clean off the board.
No piece can get its neighbors to make room.
None has the right to order those in front to
offer gangway to the crush behind. All they
can do is to crouch down where they are
and, without stirring, resign themselves to
their fate. *Go* is a product of the mind of
man and, just as human taste is accurately

mirrored in this ever-more-restrictive game,
so one may see in the cramping of the pieces
an image of the human urge to be jammed
up tight together. In that ugly crowding one
may fairly read man's mean antipathy to
openness, his deliberate squeezing and di-
minishment of the very universe, his passion
for territorial limitation within such dwarfish
boundaries that he rarely steps beyond his
own immediate shadow. He wallows in the
rigors of constriction, in the painful inhibitions of his choice. He is, in short, a mas-
ochist.

Heaven knows why the flippant-minded
Waverhouse and his Zen-besotted friend have
chosen today for their game, but chosen it
they have. They dug the board out from some
dusty cupboard, found the necessary playing-
stones and eventually settled down to the
crass fatuity of *go*. As might be expected of
them, they began by playing almost skittishly,
plonking down their Blacks and Whites in a
random scatter across the board. But the
board has only just so many squares and it
wasn't long before flippancy and other-world-
liness found themselves in conflict. As the
pressure increased, so did the verbal exchanges, spiced, as is their wont, with scarcely
relevant quotations from the minor Chinese
classics.

"Waverhouse, your play is simply awful.
Can't you see it's crazy to place your piece
there? Take it away and try it somewhere
else."

"A mere Zen zealot may choose to think it crazy, but I learnt that ploy from studying the practice of the great *go* master Hon'imbō. You must learn to live with greatness."

"But the piece will be slaughtered."

"Did not the noble Hankai accept not only death for the sake of his lord but even pork on a poignard? Consider me no less sporting. Fair enough? Right then, that's my move."

"So that's your decision. All right. It soothes my troubled brow. As the poet said, 'A balmy breeze has blown in from the south and the palace grows a shade more cool.' Now," says Singleman, "if I link my chain of pieces with another piece, just here, lo and behold, I'm safe."

"Aha, so you've linked them. My, what a clever old thing you are. I never thought you'd see that one. But there you go, quick as a flash, bang, bang, and you think I'm dead. I'd hoped you'd be guided by the good old folk-song 'Don't Bang Bells at the Hachiman Shrine.' So what do I do now?" Waverhouse sought to look crafty. "I'll tell you what I'll do. I'll put one here. And what will poor Pussy do next?"

"Poor Pussy will next do something both simple and daring, like this. Which blocks your line like 'a sword that points up sharply at the sky.' "

"Steady on, old man. If you do that, I've had it. Hang on a moment, now. Really, that's not funny."

"I warned you not to make that move."

"I offer my abject apologies. You were
quite right, and I'll take that move back. So,
while I ponder, take your White off, will
you?"

"What! Is this another of your sorry-I-
wasn't-really-ready gambits?"

"And while you're about it, you might remove the piece right next to it too."

"You've got a damn nerve."

"You couldn't be suggesting that I'm cheat-
ing, eh? Oh, come on, Singleman, what's a
stone or two between friends? Don't act so
stuffy. Just be a good chap and take the
damn things off. It could hardly matter to a
lofty soul like you, but to me it's a matter of
life and death. Like that moment of supreme
crisis in Kabuki plays when some character
comes bounding on stage with shouts of
'Hang on, hold it.' "

"I fail to see the similarity."

"Never mind what you see or don't see.
Just be a decent fellow and take those pieces
off the board."

"This is the sixth time you've asked to
have your move back."

"What a remarkable memory you have.
When we play next, I'll double it up to a
good round dozen. Anyway, all I'm asking
now is that you should remove a couple of
miserable stones, and I must say you're being pretty stubborn about it. I would have
thought that, with all your years of contem-
plating your navel, you'd have learnt by now
to show a bit more give."

"But if I let you off, that daring risk I took just now will stack the odds against me."

"I thought I heard you prating that you pay no heed to such mundane considerations as winning or losing."

"I certainly don't mind losing, but I don't want you to win."

"Singleman, you dazzle me with the sophistication of your spiritual enlightenment. I positively gawp at this further manifestation of your gift for cutting through lightning by flashing your sword at the winds of spring."

"You've got that wrong. It should be the other way round—cutting through the spring winds with a sword-flash sharp as lightning."

"Indeed, indeed, a laughable mistake. Only I somehow feel my version sounds the better of the two. I see myself as the last of the great diaskenasts. But let that pass. 'That passed,' the poet said, 'so may this too.' Since I see you've still got all your wits about you, it looks as though I'm done for on this part of the board, so I'd best give up the ghost."

"We have it from the patriarchs that, sharply different as they are, in ultimate reality there's little to differentiate the quick from the dead. I think you're dead, and you'd be wise to be quick to accept it."

"Amen," says Waverhouse, slapping down with a savage clack the piece in his hand on a different part of the board.

While Waverhouse and Singleman are thus slugging it out in front of the alcove, Coldmoon and Beauchamp are sitting side by side

near the entrance to the room. My wretched
master with his yellow face sits with them.
Neatly lined up on the matting of the floor,
just in front of Coldmoon and eyeing him
fishily, three dried bonitos present an extraordinary spectacle. He'd brought them round
in the breast of his kimono and, though now
exposed in all their nakedness, they still look
warm from their walk. Beauchamp and my
master were sitting staring at them with a
finely balanced mixture of repulsion and
curiosity when Coldmoon finally opened his
mouth. "As a matter of fact, I got back to
Tokyo from my visit home about four days
ago, but I've been so rushed off my feet with
this and that that I couldn't call round
sooner."

"There was no need to hurry here," observes my master with his usual lack of any
social grace.

"I wouldn't have hurried, but for my anxiety to give you these fish as quickly as
possible."

"But, they're properly dried, aren't they?"

"Oh yes indeed! Dried bonitos are the
speciality of my hometown."

"A speciality?" says my master. "But I
fancy one may find excellent dried bonito
right here in Tokyo." He lifts the largest fish
and, bending slightly, sniffs it.

"One cannot judge the quality of a dried
bonito by smelling it."

"Are they special because they're that much
bigger?"

"Eat one and see."

"Certainly I shall eat one. But this one here seems to have an edge chipped off."

"That's precisely why I was in a hurry to get them to you."

"I don't understand."

"Well, actually it was slightly gnawed by rats."

"But that's dangerous! Anyone eating that could blacken with the plague."

"Not at all, it's perfectly safe. Such modest gnawings, mere nips and nibbles, never hurt anyone."

"How on earth did the rats get at it?"

"On board ship."

"Ship? What ship? How?"

"I took passage here from home and, having nothing in which to carry your dried bonitos, I popped them into my violin's cloth carrier-bag. And it was there, that night, that the damage was done. Frankly, I'd not have cared if the rats had kept to the fish but unfortunately, perhaps mistaking it for another dried bonito, they also gnawed away at the frame of my precious instrument."

"What idiotic creatures! Perhaps the life at sea blunts their sense of taste. All that salt, you know: the coarseness of the sea-gone soul." Having delivered himself of these odd remarks, my master sat and stared, fish-eyed and ictrine, at Coldmoon's wrinkled gift.

"It's in the nature of rats, wherever they may happen to be living, not to discriminate in their rapacity. Hence, even when I'd got the dried fish to my Tokyo lodgings, I worried for their safety. It kept me awake at night. So in the end I took them into my bed and slept with them."

"How revolting. Surely a danger to health?"

"Yes, I agree. You'd better wash them thoroughly before you eat them."

"I doubt if just washing will do."

"Perhaps you should soak them in lye and then, for good measure and to restore the color, polish them up a bit."

"Aside from sleeping with ratty fish, did you also take your violin to bed?"

"The violin's too bulky to sleep with in one's arms and . . ."

At this point the conversation was interrupted from the other side of the room by delighted shouts from Waverhouse. "Do you mean you've been to bed with a violin? How truly romantic! I recall a little poem from the past:

> The spring is passing. Arms can feel
> The weight of the lute
> Becoming real.

That, of course, is just an old-fashioned *haiku*. If he wants to outdo the ancients, the bright young man of today has no choice but to sleep with a violin in his arms. Beauchamp, lend me your ears. How about this for a modern variation on the theme?

Beneath this quilted coverlet,
Warm to one's skin,
Night-long held safe, frets free from
    fret:
My treasured violin.

Of course violins don't have frets, but what
of that? One can't expect a nitpicking accu-
racy of detail in such a splendid example of
new-style poetry."

Beauchamp, poor fellow, is a literal-minded
youth and his serious mold of character cannot accomodate itself to the verve and shim-
mers of frivolity. "I'm afraid," he says, "that,
unlike *haiku,* new-style poems cannot be constructed off the cuff. They need deep thought,
deep feeling, arduous fabrication. But once
they're properly composed, their exquisite
tonation, working on the inmost soul, can
call up spirits from the vasty deep."

"Can they really? Well, I never," says
Waverhouse at his falsely ingenuous best.
"I'd always thought that only the smoke of
hemp-stalks, correctly burnt at the Feast of
the Hungry Dead, could lure souls back to
earth. Do you mean to say that new-style
poetry is equally efficacious?" Letting his
game go hang, he concentrates on teasing
Beauchamp.

"You'll get trounced again if you keep on
babbling rubbish," my master warns him.

But Waverhouse takes no notice. "I myself am quite indifferent to winning or losing; but it just so happens that my opponent

is now immobilized, squashed up tight like
an octopus in a saucepan. And it's only to
while away the tedium of waiting for him to
decide upon his next wee wriggle of a move
that I am forced to join you in your con-
course of violins."

Singleman snorts in his exasperation. "For
goodness' sake, Waverhouse, it's your move
now. I'm the one who's being kept waiting."

"Ah? So you've made a move?"

"Of course I have—ages ago."

"Where?"

"I've extended this diagonal of Whites."

"So you have.

> Diagonal and white
> His hand extends
> The line that in disaster ends.

Well, in that case my response shall be . . .
shall be. . . . I know not what, but it shall be
the terror of this earth.

> As I was saying, 'I plan, I plan,'
> Daylight darkened
> And the night began.

I tell you what. Out of the extreme kindness
of my heart I shall grant you an extra move.
Place a stone anywhere you like."

"You can't play *go* like that."

"You refuse my generosity? Then you leave
me no choice but to . . . what? Suppose I set
a piece down here, over in this relatively un-

settled territory, right in the corner. Incidentally, Coldmoon, your fiddle can't be up to much if even the rats don't like it. Why don't you splash out on a better one? Shall I get one of those antique models, at least three hundred years old, from Italy?"

"I could never thank you enough—especially if you were also so kind as to foot the bill."

"How could anything as old as that be any use whatever?" His ignorance does not stop my master from speaking his mind.

"I think, Sneaze, you're comparing antique fiddles with antiquated men. They're not the same, you know. Yet even among men, some of the older models—Goldfield for example—become more valuable with age. And when it comes to violins it's invariably a case of the older the better. . . . Now, Singleman, will you please get a move on. Being myself no windbag, indeed a man succinct if not actually terse in speech, I will not waste time on a full quotation from the relevant Kabuki play, but have we not been warned by Keimasa that autumn days draw swiftly to their close?"

"It's pure agony playing *go* with a feckless galloper like you. There's never time to think. Well, if you insist on headlong play, that's the way of it. I shall place one here."

"What a pity! You've escaped my clutches after all. I had so hoped you wouldn't make that move, and I've been racking my brains to think up enough rubbish to distract you. All, I fear, in vain."

"Naturally. Some of us concentrate on the game, not on trying to cheat."

"Sir, I never cheat. I may pay less regard to the game than to gamesmanship, but that is precisely the teaching of the school of Hon'imbō, of the Goldfield School and of the School of Modern Gentlemen. I say, Sneaze, you remember those sharpish pickles that Singleman gobbled down at Kamakura? They seem, after all, to have done him good. He's not much use at *go,* but nothing now seems able to perturb him. I take my hat off to his pickled nerves. They're steady as steel."

"Then why," says my master with his back still turned toward Waverhouse, "doesn't an inconsequential fidget like yourself make the effort to imitate his steadiness and sense?"

Waverhouse, unusually, said nothing but just stuck out a large red tongue.

Singleman, seemingly unconcerned by these exchanges, tries once again to interest Waverhouse in their game. "It's you to go," he says.

As Waverhouse takes back his tongue and looks down at the board, Beauchamp turns to Coldmoon. "Tell me, when did you start playing the violin? I'd very much like to learn, but they say it's terribly difficult."

"Anyone can learn to play a little."

"It's always been my sneaking hope that, given the similar nature of all arts, persons with an aptitude for poetry ought to be quick at mastering music. Do you think there's anything in it?"

"Perhaps. I'm sure you'd do all right: indeed, very well."

"When did you start your own study of the art?"

"In high school. Have I ever told you," said Coldmoon turning to my master, "how I first came to learn the violin?"

"No, not yet."

"Was it perhaps," asks Beauchamp, "that you had some high school music teacher who encouraged you to learn?"

"No, no teacher; in fact no human encouragement at all. I simply taught myself."

"Quite a genius."

"Being self-taught doesn't necessarily mean that one's a genius," says Coldmoon looking sour. He is, I think, the only being who'd resent being called a genius.

"The point's irrelevant. Just tell us how you taught yourself. It would be useful to know."

"And I'd be happy to tell you. Sir," he addresses my master, "have I your permission to do so?"

"Of course. Please carry on."

"The streets these days are chock-a-block with bright young men walking along with violin-cases in their hands. But when I was a high school lad, very few of us could play any Western instrument whatever. My own particular school was way out in the sticks

where, since life was lived in accordance with
a strong tradition of extreme simplicity, nary
a student played the violin."

"An interesting story seems to have started
over there, Singleman, so let's pack up this
game right now."

"There are still a few points left undecided."

"Forget them all. I'm only too happy to
make you a present of the lot."

"But I can't accept that."

"What a meticulous man you are, totally
insensitive to that broad approach one expects from a scholar of Zen. All right then,
we'll finish it off in double quick time. Coldmoon, my dear fellow, I'm fascinated by your
account of that high school. Am I right in
thinking yours must be that one where all
the students went barefoot?"

"It's true I attended the school about which
so many such lying yarns have been told."

"But I've heard you drilled without shoes
and that, from a thousand about-turns, the
soles of your feet grew inches thick."

"Absolute nonsense! Whoever stuffed you
up with such a ludicrous canard?"

"Never mind who. But they also said that
every student brings in for his lunch an
enormous rice-ball, big as a summer orange,
hanging from his hip on a string. Is that a
canard too? It's further said that the students
gobble the rice like mad, unsalted though it
is, in order to get at the pickled plum allegedly buried inside. They certainly sound an

extremely vigorous and hardy group of youngsters. Are you listening, Singleman? This is exactly the sort of story that appeals to you."

"I'm not at all sure that I get the story's point, but I do indeed approve of simplicity and sturdiness."

"As to simplicity, there's yet another characteristic of that area which should earn your praise. It is, in fact, so simple that they've not yet heard of making ash-trays by sectioning bamboo. A friend of mine who was once on the staff of Coldmoon's school tried to buy such an ash-tray, even one of the roughest hew, and the shopkeeper simply told him that, since anyone could go and cut himself an ash-tray in the forest, there was no point in trying to make them as objects for sale. Now that's what I call true simplicity. True sturdiness as well. Singleman, you agree?"

"Yes, yes, of course I do. But if you're going to secure your position, Waverhouse, you must immediately put down a reinforcing piece."

"Right. I'll make assurance doubly doubly sure. A stone placed there should finish the game. You know, Coldmoon, when I heard your account of your early struggles I was frankly amazed. It's quite astonishing that in such a backward place you should, unaided, have taught yourself to play the violin. More than two thousand years ago, in the high days of the Han, that marvelous man

Ch'ü Yüan was writing poems, still un-
matched, about the wonders of a life
withdrawn from the madding crowd. It could
be, Coldmoon, you were born to be our new
Ch'ü Yüan."

"That I should very much dislike."

"Well than, how about being the Werther of
our times? What's that, Singleman? You want
me to pick up my stones and count them?
What a pernickety bore you are! There's no
need for counting. It's perfectly obvious that
I've lost."

"But one cannot leave things hanging in
the air. One wants to know the score."

"All right, then. Be so good as to do my
counting for me. I really can't be bothered
with such a dull accountant's chore when it
is my solemn aesthetic duty to learn how the
most gifted Werther of our day started learning to play the violin. Would you have me
shunned by my ancestors? Therefore," says
Waverhouse, "you must excuse me." Sliding
his cushion away from the game-board,
Waverhouse moved to sit near Coldmoon.
Singleman stayed where he was, methodically
gathering stones and marshaling them in little
armies to be counted. Coldmoon resumes the
telling of his story.

"It was not only that the land was rugged;
its inhabitants were philistine and coarse.
They considered that any student with even
the mildest interest in the arts would get them
all laughed at for effeminacy by the students

of other prefectures, so their persecution of anyone guilty of refinement was unremittingly merciless."

"It's a sad fact," says Waverhouse, "but the students in Coldmoon's part of the country really are uncouth. Why, for instance, are they always dressed in those dark blue skirted trousers? The color itself is odd enough, but it looks unpleasantly worse against their near-black skin which is, presumably, occasioned by the high degree of sea-salt in the local air. Of course, it doesn't greatly matter how dark the men become, but, if their women-folk are similarly blighted, it must affect their marriage prospects." As usual, when Waverhouse joins in a conversation, its original drift is soon diverted into new and unlikely channels.

"The women there are no less black than the men."

"Do the men show any wish to marry them?"

"Since they're all as black as each other, no one seems to notice."

"What a ghastly state of affairs. One's heart bleeds, doesn't it, Sneaze, for all those muddy women."

"Well, if you're asking me, my opinion of women is that the blacker they are the better. A light-skinned female tends to grow more and more conceited every time she sees herself in a mirror. And all women, all the time, are incorrigible, so anything," says my master with a heavy sigh, "that makes them less delighted with themselves is very much to be wished for."

"But if the entire population is dark-skinned, won't black become beautiful and the blackest most fair?" Beauchamp puts his finger on a tricky point.

"The world would be a better place if we were only rid of them all." My master puts his view in a nutshell.

"If you go round saying things like that," laughs Waverhouse, "your wife will give you what-for later on."

"No danger of that."

"She's out?"

"Yes, she went out quite some while ago with the children."

"No wonder it's been quiet. Where's she gone?"

"I haven't the faintest idea. She goes out where and when she likes."

"And she comes home as she likes?"

"More or less. You two don't know how lucky you are to be single. I envy you both from the bottom of my heart."

Beauchamp looks slightly uncomfortable, but Coldmoon keeps on grinning.

"All married men grow to feel like that," says Waverhouse. "What about you, Single-man? Does your wife drive you crazy?"

"Eh? Hang on a tick. Six fours are twenty-four, plus one and one and one makes twenty-seven. Waverhouse, you managed to do better than it looked from the lay-out on the

吾輩は猫である

board. The margin in my favor is no more than a measly eighteen stones. Now then, what was that you asked?"

"I asked if you too were driven crazy by a troublesome wife."

"You must be joking again. But, to answer your question, I'm not particularly troubled by my wife; perhaps because she loves me."

"Oh, I do beg your pardon. How typical of Singleman to have a loving wife."

"Singleman's no singleton. The world is full of loving wives." Coldmoon, a somewhat unlikely champion of the ladies, pipes up sturdily in their defense.

"Coldmoon's right," says Beauchamp. "As I see it, there are only two roads by which a man may come to perfect bliss: by the road of love, and by the road of art. Of all the forms of love, married love is perhaps the noblest. It therefore seems to me that to remain unmarried is to flout the will of Heaven. And what," asks Beauchamp, bending upon Waverhouse his sad and serious gaze, "do you, sir, think of that?"

"I think you have stated an unanswerable case. I fear that this old bachelor will never enter the sphere of perfect bliss."

"If you get yourself a wife, you'll have made it doubly sure that bliss will not be yours." My master croaks from the bottom of the grim well of experience.

"Be that as it may," says Beauchamp, "we young bachelors will never grasp the meaning of life unless we open our hearts and minds to the elevating spirituality of the arts.

That is why, in the hope that I might learn to improve myself by playing the violin, I am so particularly interested to hear more of Coldmoon's interrupted account of his actual experience."

"Ah, yes," says Waverhouse, "we were going to hear the tale of our own young Werther's fiddling. Please tell us now. I promise, no more interruptions." With this belated acknowledgement of his habitual failing, Waverhouse at last shut up.

But the spirit of Waverhouse, like the monstrous Hydra itself, is not easily suppressed. Cut off one head, and in its place grow two. Silence Waverhouse, and Singleman gives tongue. "No man ever," he waffled, "became a better man by virtue of a violin. It would be intolerable if universal truth were accessible through self-abandonment to mere fun. Truly to lose the Self and thus to achieve the ultimate reality of the identity of Self and Non-self, a man must be willing to hang by his nails from a cliff, to let go and to fall to that death in which his spirit may be re-born." With these pomposities Singleman sought to reprove Beauchamp's frivolous materialism; but he might as well have saved his breath, for Beauchamp knows nothing of Zen and, as his next dry words revealed, has no desire to do so.

"Really?" he comments. "You may be right, but I remain convinced that art is the clearest expression of the highest human aspirations, and I am not to be shaken in that conviction."

"Good for you," says Coldmoon. "I shall be glad to speak of my artistic experience to so congenial a soul. Well, as I was saying, I had great difficulties to contend with before I could even start learning the violin. Can you imagine, Mr. Sneaze, the agonies I suffered merely to buy a violin?"

"Well, I assume that in a place so generally God-forsaken as not to have even hemp-soled sandals for sale, it can't have been easy to find a shop that offered violins."

"Oh, there was shop, alright. And I'd saved up cash enough for a purchase. But it wasn't as simple as that."

"Why not?"

"Because if I bought a fiddle in a dorp that small, everyone would know, and its brute inhabitants would immediately have made my life unbearable. Believe you me, anyone out there who was thought to be the least bit arty had a very thin time."

"Genius is always persecuted," sighed Beauchamp with deep sympathy.

"There you go again. I do wish you'd stop calling me a genius. It's an embarrassment. Anyway, every day as I passed that shop where the fiddles were displayed, I'd say to myself, 'Ah, how wonderful it would be just to hold one in my arms, to be the owner of a fiddle. Oh how I wish and wish that one of them were mine.' "

"Quite understandable," commented Waverhouse.

"But it's distinctly odd," my master mused in a voice where his usual bilious perversity was overlaid with genuine wonder, "that some otherwise sensible lad should wander about a back-woods hamlet drooling over a violin."

"It simply proves what I've just been saying. Drooling's a sign of genius."

Only Singleman held aloof, vouchsafing nothing and twisting his foolish beard.

"Perhaps you're wondering how there came to be violins available in such a graceless place, but the explanation's quite simple. There was, you see, a ladies' academy in the neighborhood, and, since the curriculum included daily violin-practice, the local shopkeepers were quick to exploit such a captive market. Of course, the violins were of poor quality; more rustic gues than genuine violins. And the shop-folk treated them very roughly, hanging them up at the shop-entrance in bunches of two or three, like so many vegetables. Yet, as one passed the shop, one could hear them humming in the wind or, in response to some shopboy's casual finger, quivering into sound. Their singular timbre, every time I heard it, thrilled my heart to such a pitch of excitement that I felt it could but burst."

"That sounds dangerous. There are, of course, many varieties of epilepsy, such as that brought on by the sight of water and that provoked by the presence of crowds. But our young Werther," says Waverhouse —never one to miss an opportunity to wallow in the absurd—"seems unique in suffering seizures at the thrumming of fiddle-strings."

But the plodding Beauchamp, prosaic even in his passion for the poetic, wouldn't recognize a flight of fancy if it landed on his nose. "It's not a matter for mockery," he snaps. "No man can truly be an artist unless he has sensitivities as keen as Coldmoon's. I say again, Coldmoon is a genius."

Coldmoon still looks restless to have such greatness thrust upon him. "No, no," he says, "maybe it really is some epileptic variant; but the fact remains that the timbre of those sounds moved me to the core. I've played and heard the violin time and again since then, but nothing ever has matched the beauty of that random music. There are no words to convey the faintest echo of its magic. . . ."

Nobody paid the slightest attention to Singleman when, rather aptly as it seemed to me, he quoted from an obscure Taoist text: "Only from gems, the jewels in its hilt, could such sweet sounds have issued from the sword." I felt sorry, not only for Singleman but for Chuang-tzu too, that the words were left to die.

"Day after day for many months, I walked past that shop, but I heard that marvelous music only thrice. On the third occasion I decided that, come what might, I would have to buy a violin. Reproof from the people of my own district, sneers from the slobs in neighboring prefectures, thumpings organized by my fellow-students, fist-lynchers to a man, not even formal expulsion from the school could budge me from my resolution. I had no choice but to satisfy my all-consuming need. I would buy a violin."

"How characteristic of genius. That drive, that total concentration upon fulfillment of an inner need. Ah, Coldmoon, how I envy you! How I have longed, lifelong and always in vain, to experience feelings of such vehemence. I go to concerts and I strain my ears till they ache in an effort to be carried away; but for all my full-hearted striving, nothing seems to happen. How you must pity," said Beauchamp in tones that mixed black sadness and green envy, "us earth-bound clods."

"Count yourself lucky," Coldmoon answers. "I can speak of my enthrallment now with relative calm. But then it was pure agony. Excruciating agony. Anyway, my masters, in the end I took the plunge and bought a violin."

"Say on."

"It was the eve of the Emperor's birthday, in November. Everyone in my lodgings had gone off to some hot spring for the night, and the place was empty. I'd reported sick that day and, absenting myself from school, had stayed in bed, where, all day long, I nursed the single thought: this evening I'll go out and get that violin."

"You mean you played truant by shamming illness?"

"That's right."

"Talent indeed," says Waverhouse lost in wonder. "Perhaps he really is a genius."

"As I lay with my head sticking out of the bedclothes, I grew impatient for the nightfall. To break the tension, I ducked beneath the covers and, with my eyes tight-closed, entreated sleep. Which did not come. So I pulled my head back out, only to find the fierce autumn sun still fully ablaze on the paper-window six feet long. Which niggled me. I then noticed, high up on the paper-window, a long stringy shadow which, every so often, wavered in the autumn wind."

"What was that long stringy shadow?"

"Peeled astringent persimmons strung like beads on raffia cords suspended from the eaves."

"Hmm. What happened next?"

"Next, having nothing else to do, I got up from bed, opened the paper-window and went out onto the veranda. There I detached one of the persimmons that had dried to sweetness, and ate it."

"Did it taste good?" My master can be trusted, whatever the subject, to find some childish question to be asked.

"Excellent. Persimmons down there really

are superb. You will not taste their like anywhere in Tokyo."

"Never mind the persimmons. What did
you do next?" This time it was Beauchamp
who was pressing for clarification.

"Next, I ducked back into bed again, closed
my eyes and breathed a silent prayer to all the
gods and Buddhas for nightfall to come soon.
It then seemed that three, perhaps four, long
hours had passed; so thinking the evening
must have come, I brought my head out from
under the bed-clothes. To my surprise, the
fierce autumn sun was still fully ablaze on
the six-foot paper-window, and, on its upper
part, those long and stringy shadows were
still swaying."

"We've heard all that."

"The same sequence happened again and
again. At all events, I got up from bed,
opened the paper-window, ate one persimmon that had dried to sweetness, went back
to bed and breathed a silent prayer to all the
gods and Buddhas for nightfall to come
soon."

"We don't seem to be making much progress with that promised story about learning
to play the violin."

"Don't rush me. Just listen, please. Well,
having endured the next three, or perhaps
four, hours in my bed until, I thought, surely
it must now be evening, I popped my head
up out of the covers only to find the fierce
autumn sun still fully ablaze on the paper-

window while, on its upper part, the long stringy shadows were asway."

"You're getting us nowhere."

"Then, I got up from bed, opened the paper-window, went out onto the veranda, ate one persimmon dried to sweetness and . . ."

"So you ate another one? Is there no end to your dreary guzzle of persimmons dried to sweetness?"

"Well, my impatience grew worse."

"*Your* impatience! What about ours?"

"You want everything so rushed along that I find it hard to continue my story."

If Coldmoon finds it hard, so does his audience; and even the devoted Beauchamp makes little whimpers of complaint.

"If you all find listening too hard, I have no choice but to bring my story abruptly to its end. In short, I repeated this oscillation between eating persimmons and ducking into bed till all the fruit were gone."

"By the time you'd guzzled that lot the sun must surely have gone down."

"As a matter of fact, it hadn't. After I'd eaten the last persimmon I ducked back into bed and in due course popped my head out yet again, only to find the fierce autumn sun still fully ablaze upon that six-foot paper-window . . ."

"I've had enough of this. It just goes on and on."

"Me too. I'm bored stiff with the way you tell your tiresome story."

"But it isn't easy on me, you know."

"With the degree of perseverance you have already proven you possess, no enterprise whatever could be too difficult. If we had sat here uncomplaining, your autumn sun would have gone on blazing till tomorrow morning. Tell me this: do you, and if so when, intend to buy that violin?" Even the indefatiguable Waverhouse is showing signs of wear. Singleman alone seems unaffected by the slow unrolling (or rather the slow unrolling and re-rolling) of Coldmoon's quaint account. For all he cared, Coldmoon's autumn sun could go on blazing all through the night; even, perhaps, till the day, or days, beyond tomorrow.

Coldmoon too shows no least sign of strain. Calm and composed, he drones on with his story. "Someone has asked me when I intend to buy my violin. The answer is that I intend to go out and buy it just as soon as the sun has set. It is hardly my fault that, whenever I peer out from the bedclothes, the autumn sun is still so brilliantly ablaze. Oh, how I suffered! It was far far worse, that deep impatience in my soul, than this superficial irritation which seems, so pettily, to irk you all. After I'd eaten the last of the hanging persimmons and saw the day still bright, I could not help but perish into tears. Beauchamp, my dear fellow, I felt so reft of hope that I wept, I wept."

"I'm not at all surprised. Your weeping does you credit. All artists are essentially emotional and their tears are distillations of the truth of things. Nevertheless, one does rather wish that you could speed things up a bit." Beauchamp's a decent-hearted creature and, even when he's knee-deep in absurdities, maintains his earnest manner.

"Much as I'd like to speed it up, that laggard sun won't set. Its hang-up is most hard to bear."

"Your endlessly unsetting sun is no less hard on us, your tanned and sweating audience. So, let's forget the whole interminable tale before its lentor kills us. Scrub it, Coldmoon," says my master who is now quite clearly nearing the end of his tether.

"You'd find it harder still if we stopped at this point. For we are now coming to the really interesting part of the story."

"All right then. We're prepared to listen, but only on condition that the sun goes down."

"That's a pretty tall order, but all things yield to my revered teacher, and lo the sun has set."

"How extraordinarily convenient." Singleman uttered his toneless comment with so much nonchalance that everyone broke into laughter.

"So night, at last, had fallen. You can perhaps imagine my relief. With great stealth I slipped out of my lodgings into the quietness of Saddletree, for so that huddle of poor dwellings had been named. My nature shrinks from noisy places so that, despite the obvious conveniences of a city life, I had at that time chosen to withdraw from the whirl of the world and to live secluded in a snail-shell of a dwelling, a farmhouse miles from anywhere in a corner of the countryside scarce trodden by the foot of man."

"That 'scarce trodden by the foot of man' seems to be piling it on a bit," objects my master.

"And that touch about the 'snail-shell dwelling,'" adds Waverhouse, "is insufferably bombastic. Why don't you say, 'in a tiny room too small even to have an alcove'? That would sound much better, if only because a great deal less affected."

But Beauchamp, as he immediately makes clear, finds the description praiseworthy. "Whatever the facts of the room's dimensions, Coldmoon's phrasing is poetic. I find it very pleasing."

The meticulous Singleman chips in with a serious enquiry. "It must have been an exhausting business trudging there and back to school from such a remote shack. How many miles, roughly, would you say?"

"Perhaps five hundred yards. You see, the school itself was in the remote village . . ."

"In that case, many of its students would have been boarded in near-by lodgings. Is that correct?" asks Singleman in relentless tones which suggest the far-off baying of bloodhounds.

"Yes. Most of the farm dwellings had one or two student-lodgers."

"Yet, did you not describe the place as scarcely trodden by the foot of man?" Singleman moves in for the kill.

"I did indeed. But for the school the place would have been virtually uninhabited. Now, let me tell you how I was dressed as I slipped out into lonely Saddletree in that deepening dusk. Over a padded hand-woven cotton kimono, I wore the brass-buttoned overcoat of my school uniform. With the overcoat's hood pulled well down over my head to make sure I'd not be recognized, I drifted along the road in such a way as not to attract attention. Being November, the road from my lodgings to the Southern Highway was thick with fallen persimmon-leaves. Every step I took set the dead leaves scurrying, and their rustle behind me seemed proof that I was being followed. When I turned and looked back, the dense mass of the Tōrei Temple, blacker even than its surrounding forest, loomed up black above me. As you may know, that temple is the family shrine of the Matsudaira Clan. An extremely quiet and little-visited building, it lies at the foot of Mount Kōshin not more than a hundred yards from where I was then living. Above the forest trees the sky's vast hollow glittered with moonlit stars, while the Milky Way, slicing across the River of Long Rapids, stretched east and ever east toward . . . now let me see, toward . . . well yes, Hawaii."

"Hawaii? That's quite startling," said a startled Waverhouse.

"I walked some two hundred yards along the Southern Highway, entered the township from Eagle Lane, turned into Old Castle

First Street, Second Street and Third Street,
all running off Main Street which itself runs
parallel to the Road of the Cost of Food.
From there I took Owari Street, Nagoya
Street and the Street of the Magic Dolphin
into Fishball Lane and thence . . ."

"You can spare us the topography. What
we want to know," my master rudely inter-
rupts, "is whether or not you bought a
violin."

"The man who sells musical instruments is
Kaneko Zenbei so, using parts of his own
name, he calls his shop Kane-zen. But to
reach the shop, sir, we've still some way to
go."

"Forget the distance. Just go and buy a
violin. And do it quickly."

"Your wish, sir, is, as always, my command. Well, when I got to Kane-zen, the
shop was ablaze with lantern-light and . . ."

"Ablaze? Oh no. Not that again. How
often this time are you going to scorch us
with the blazing repetition?" On this occasion it was Waverhouse who raised the fire-
alarm.

"Friends, have no fear. It's only a passing
kind of blaze that lights your immediate
horizon. It will, I do assure you, flicker and
die down. Well, as I peer through the light-
blaze from the shop, I can see a faint reflection of that glare shining from the polished
body of a violin while the roundness of its
pinched-in waist gleams almost coldly. So

falls the lantern's light across its tightly drawn strings that only a section of the fiddle's stringing flings out at me its glistening darts of silver."

"Now that," says Beauchamp almost moaning in his pleasure at the words, "is a truly masterly piece of description."

"That's the one, I thought; that's the one for me. The blood began pounding in my head and my legs so weakened they could barely hold me up."

Behind a scornful smile, Singleman grunted.

"Instinctively and with no further thought I rushed into the shop, yanked out my purse, pulled from it a couple of five-yen notes and . . ."

"So in the end you bought it?" asked my master.

"I was certainly going to do so, but then I thought to myself, 'Wait. This is the moment of crisis. If I act rashly I may bungle things. Should I not pause for deeper reflection?' So, at the eleventh hour, I reined myself in."

"Sweet heaven," groaned my master, "d'you mean to say that even now, after we've slogged along behind you across such veritable Australias of balderdash, you've still not bought your fiddle. You really do drag things out. And all for some piddling contraption of cheap wood and catgut."

"It is not, sir, my intention to drag things out. I can't help being unable to buy it."

"Why can't you?"

"Why can't I? Because it's still too early in
the evening. There were still too many people passing by."

"What does it matter if there are two or
even three hundred people in the streets?
Coldmoon, you really are an extraordinary
man," my master shouted in his anger and
frustration.

"If they were just people," says Coldmoon,
"even a thousand, even two thousand of them,
of course it wouldn't matter. But many of
them were in fact my fellow-students; prowling about with their sleeves rolled up and
with bludgeons in their hands. There's a particular group, the Dregs, who pride themselves on being permanently at the bottom of
the class. I had to be careful because louts of
that kind are invariably good at judo, and I
dared not take the risk of any kind of tangle
with them. For who knows where even the
most trivial brush with violence may end? Of
course, I yearned to have that violin, but I
was also fairly anxious to remain alive. I pre-
ferred to go on breathing without playing a
violin to lying dead for having played it."

"Then am I right in thinking that you
didn't buy a fiddle?" My master struggles
on in search of certainties.

"Oh, but I did make a purchase."

"Coldmoon, you're driving me mad. If
you're going to buy a fiddle, buy it; if you
don't want to buy one, don't. But for the sake
of my sanity, please settle the matter one
way or the other."

Coldmoon grinned. "Things settle themselves," he said, "and all too rarely in the way one had most hoped." With careless care he lit a cigarette and blew out smoke at the ceiling.

I think it was the smoke which finally snapped my master's patience. At all events it was at this point that he abruptly rose to his feet, went off into his study and, returning with a musty-looking foreign book, lay down flat on his stomach and began to read. Singleman had earlier slipped away unremarked, and is now sitting in front of the alcove playing *go* by himself. The plain fact is that Coldmoon's story has proved so boringly long that, one by one, his listeners have abandoned him. Only two of them are still sticking it out: Beauchamp with his unquenchable faith in art and Waverhouse to whom longeur is second nature. Coldmoon somewhat crudely blew out a last long stream of smoke and resumed telling his story at the same leisurely pace.

"Having decided that an immediate purchase of that violin would be ill timed, I now had to decide upon a suitable timing. The early part of the evening had already been found too dangerous and the shop would of course be closed if I came too late. Clearly the ideal time would be somewhere before closing-time but after the prowling students had all retired to their lairs. Yet to identify the precise best moment of purchase was not, as I'm sure you, Beauchamp, will appreciate, at all easy."

"I can see it would be difficult."

"Eventually I fixed upon ten o'clock as the best time for action. But what should I do until then? I didn't much like the idea of going back to my lodgings only to sneak out again; while visiting some friend for a time-wasting chat struck me as too selfish. I accordingly decided to pass the waiting period in a simple stroll around town: two or three hours, I thought, could always be quickly and congenially consumed in such a leisured ramble. But on this particular evening so leadenly the time dragged by that I understood as deeply in my heart as if I myself had coined that ancient line which says, 'A single day seems long as a thousand autumns.' " Coldmoon twisted his features into a pattern which he presumably considered expressive of the agonies of waiting and, confident of some suitable reaction from Waverhouse, turned the full glare of his faked distress upon that subtle aesthete.

Nor was he disappointed. Waverhouse would interrupt the announcement of his own death-sentence for the sake of hearing himself babble, and Coldmoon's look of open invitation was utterly irresistible. "As I recall," he immediately responded, "the old song tells us not only that it is painful to be kept waiting by the beloved but also, as one might of course expect, that the waiter feels more pain than the awaited. So perhaps that eaves-strung violin actually experienced more bitter pains of waiting than did you on your aimless and dispirited wandering around town like some clueless detective. 'Dispirited' is a splendid word. Isn't it the Chinese who say, 'dispirited as an unfed dog in a house of mourning?' Indeed, there's nothing more dismal than the whining of a homeless dog."

"A dog? That's cruel. I've never before been likened to a dog."

"As I listen to your story I feel as though I were reading the biography of some ancient master-artist, and my heart brims with sympathy for your sufferings. Our tame comedian Waverhouse was only trying to be funny when he compared you with a dog. Take no notice of his nonsense but pray continue with your story." Beauchamp pours oil on potentially troubled waters, but Coldmoon in truth needs neither encouragement nor consolation. Come what may, he's going to tell his story.

"Well," he continues, "I wandered up Infantry Road and, along the Street of a Hundred Houses and thence, through Money-changers' Alley, into the Street of the Falconers. There I counted first the withered willows in front of the prefectural office and then the lighted windows in the side-wall of the hospital. I smoked two cigarettes on Dyer's Bridge and then I looked at my watch . . ."

"Was it yet ten o'clock?"

"Not yet, I'm sorry to say. I drifted across Dyer's Bridge and as I walked eastward along the river path I passed a home-bound group of three masseurs. Somewhere in the distance dogs were howling at the moon."

"To hear, on an autumn night by the riverside, the distant barking of dogs. . . . That sounds like some scene-setting speech from a Kabuki play. You, Coldmoon, are cast as the fugitive hero."

"Have I done anything wrong?"

"You are about to do something frightful."

"That's a bit much. All I'm going to do is to buy a violin. If that's to be considered criminal, every student at every school of music must be guilty of crime."

"Criminality is not determined by any absolute standard of good or evil. The acts of a criminal may actually be good in absolute terms but, since they have not been recognized as good by the consensus of public opinion enshrined in the law, they will be treated, and punished, as crimes. It is extremely difficult to establish what, in truth, is a crime. For what is truth? Christ himself in the context of his society was a criminal and was punished as a criminal. Of the bloodline from King David, he was accused by his fellow-Jews of wishing to be a king. He did not deny the charge, which naturally was very serious to the Roman governor of that conquered province, and the plaque on his crucifix, 'The King of the Jews,' identified his crime. Now, does our handsome Coldmoon deny being an artist in a society where artists are regarded as offensive? Of lusting after a violin in a community where such a filthy emotion is virtually criminal?"

"All right," says Coldmoon. "I acknowledge my guilt. But what worries me is how to pass the time till ten o'clock finally deigns to arrive."

"Nonsense," replies Waverhouse. "You can run through, yet again, that time-consuming naming of the names of streets. If that doesn't work, you can haul up your dear old autumn sun for a few more bouts of blazing. And what about those persimmons, sun-dried, of course, to sweetness? I'm sure you could eat at least another three dozen. That sort of stuff will keep you going till ten, and I'm prepared to listen for as long as you like."

Coldmoon had the grace to break into a broad grin. "Since you've taken the very words from my mouth, I won't insist on using them myself. So, by an artistic distortion of the truth, all of a sudden it's ten o'clock. Right on that appointed hour I returned to Kane-zen. The streets were deserted, and the sound of my wooden clogs was desperately lonely. The big outer shutters had already been hoisted into place across the front of the shop and only the paper sliding-door of its small side-entrance was still available for use. As I slid that light door open, I was again assailed by a vaguely uneasy feeling that some sneaky dog was still slinking along behind me."

At this point, my master glanced up from his grubby-looking book and asked, "Have you bought that violin yet?"

"He's just going to buy it now," said Beauchamp.

"What! He still hasn't bought it after all this time? Buying fiddles must be an arduous business," my master mutters to himself and turns back to his reading. Singleman, who has by now practically covered the whole board with black and white pieces, maintains his disinterested silence.

"Summoning up my courage, I dived into the shop and, with my head buried in my hood, said that I wanted a violin. Several shop-boys and young assistants who were sitting chattering around a brazier looked up in surprise and stared at my half-hidden face. Automatically, with my right hand, I tugged the hood still lower. When I had asked for a second time to be shown a violin, the boy sitting nearest me, who'd been trying to peer up under my hood, got to his feet and, with a half-hearted 'Certainly, sir,' slouched off to the front of the shop and came back with a tied cluster of some four or five. In response to my question, he said a violin cost five yen and twenty sen.

" 'As cheap as that? These must be only toys. Are they all the same price?'

" 'Yes,' he answered, 'all the same price.

All exactly the same and all strongly and carefully constructed.'

"I took out my purse and extracted from it one five-yen note and a twenty-sen silver coin. Then I wrapped the violin in a big cloth I'd specially brought for that purpose. Apart from myself and the inquisitive shop-boy, no one in the shop had spoken a word since I entered. They just sat there watching me. Since my face was well concealed, I knew there was no risk of being recognized; but I still felt nervous and anxious to get back out to the street as quickly as possible. At long last, with my cloth-wrapped treasure tucked inside my overcoat, I left the shop. 'Thank you, sir,' they chorused as I did so, and my blood ran cold. Outside, I glanced quickly up and down the street. It was pretty well empty; except that, perhaps a hundred yards away, I could hear some two or three voices quoting Chinese poems at each other in accents so loud as to waken the whole town. Edgy as ever and fearing lest the loudness of the voices forewarned of a troublesome incident with argumentative drunks, I slipped away westward round the corner of the shop, hurried along beside the moat till I came out on to Drug King's Temple Road. Then, passing through Alder Village to the foot of Mount Kōshin, I at last got back to my lodgings. And the time was ten to two."

"Then you've been walking practically the whole night long," exclaimed Beauchamp with his usual admiring sympathy.

"So! At long long last it's over," says Waverhouse with impolitely obvious relief. "The way it went on and on, it was like traveler's backgammon."

"But it's only now," protests Coldmoon, "that we come to the really interesting part. So far it's only prelude."

"More to come? But that's terrible. You can't expect the patience of your audience to last out through a full recital after such an exhausting prelude."

"I only hope that, for their own sakes, my audience will bear with me. To break off now would be, as the saying has it, to have plowed a field and then to forget to sow the seed. I shall therefore press on."

"My dear chap," says Waverhouse, "what you decide to say is entirely up to you. For my part, I shall simply sit and hear whatever it is I'll hear."

"What about you, my revered master? Will you consent to be so gracious as to hearken to my stumbling tale? May I mention, sir, that I have already bought a violin."

"So what are you now proposing? To sell it? I see no reason to listen to an odyssey of sale."

"I am far from selling it."

"In that case there's even less need to listen."

"Your decision grieves me. Well then, Beauchamp, it seems that only you have the kindness and discriminating taste to hear me out. I confess it's all a bit discouraging.

But never mind. I'll do my best to be brief."

"You needn't be brief. Take your time. I find your story fascinating."

"Well now, where was I? Ah yes, back safely in my lodgings, the proud possesser after so many vicissitudes of my precious violin. But my troubles were not over. First, I didn't know where to keep it. All sorts of visitors were accustomed to dropping in on me, so I couldn't just leave it about the place where they would immediately spot it. If I dug a hole and buried it, it would have been tiresome to dig it up whenever I wanted to play."

"Quite so. Could you perhaps hide it up in the ceiling?"

"I was lodged in a farmhouse, so the ceilings had no boards."

"That was hard. Where did you put it then?"

"Where do you think I put it?"

"I've no idea. In the space where the storm-boards for the windows can be slid away?"

"No."

"Wrapped up in your bed-clothes and tucked away in the bedding-cupboard?"

"No."

While Beauchamp and Coldmoon continue with their guessing-game, my master and Waverhouse become engrossed in a totally separate conversation. "How do you read these lines?" my master asked.

"Which lines?"

"These two lines here."

"What's this then? *Quid aliud est mulier nisi amicitiæ inimica.* . . . But it's Latin."

"I know it's Latin. But how do you read it?"

"Come off it, Sneaze," says Waverhouse evasively as his sensitive nose scents danger, "you're always bragging about your knowledge of dead languages. Can't you read it yourself?"

"Of course I can. Quite easily. But I'm asking you for your reading of this particular text."

"You know how to read it, and yet you ask me what it means. That's a bit thick, you know."

"Never mind if it's thick or thin. Just translate the Latin into English."

"Tut-tut. Such giving of orders, such military ways. D'you take me for your batman or something?"

"Don't slide away from the question behind a military smoke-screen. Just be so good as to let me hear your version of these two lines."

"Let's leave your Latin problems for the moment. I'm keen—aren't you?—to keep up with developments in Coldmoon's extraordinary story. He's just coming to a crisis point, trembling between discovery and the successful cacheing of his treasure. Am I not right, Coldmoon? Well, how then did you cope with your dilemma?" Waverhouse evinces a sudden new enthusiasm for Coldmoon's fantasy on a violin and moves over to rejoin the

fiddle group. My wretched master, I regret to
say, is left alone with his text.

Encouraged by this unexpected attention,
Coldmoon proceeded to explain where he'd
hidden his violin. "I ended up," he said, "by
smuggling it away into the old varnished
wicker-box that my grandmother had given
me for storing clothes when first I'd left
home. It was her parting gift to me; and she
herself, I seem to remember, brought it into
the family as part of her own bridal gear."

"Such an antique would hardly seem to
sort with a brand-new violin. What do you
think, Beauchamp?"

"I agree they sound a poor match."

"But you yourself suggested the ceiling,
and that," said Coldmoon, squashing Beauchamp, "is hardly a good match either."

"Despite the oddity of Coldmoon's hidey-
hole, his decision strikes me as the very stuff
of *haiku*. So let's not start a squabble. How
about this?

In an ancient wicker-box a hidden violin:
A feeling of utter lonesomeness
As the autumn closes in."

"Today you're fairly oozing with little
squibs."

"Not just today. Day in, day out, they well
up in my mind. My knowledge of the art is
so profound that even the late, great Masaoka
Shiki was struck dumb by its depth."

"Goodness, did you know Shiki?" asked the honest-hearted Beauchamp. His voice rose in serious enquiry and he sounded thrilled actually to know someone who had known the late, great master-poet.

"We were never physically close," said Waverhouse, "but we were always directly in warm contact by a kind of spiritual telepathy." Shocked, even disgusted, by this ridiculous answer, Beauchamp fell silent.

Coldmoon merely smiled and went on with his own improbable story. "Having decided on how to hide it, my next problem was how to make use of it. I foresaw no trouble about taking it out from its wicker-box and looking at it, but such mere gloating would hardly suffice. I needed to be able actually to play it. But the resulting sounds would scarcely pass unnoticed. Therein lay a particular danger because the leading bully-boy of those damnable Dregs happened to lodge in the boarding-house immediately south of mine: the two buildings were, in fact, separated only by a scrawny hedge consisting of a single row of Roses of Sharon."

"That was stinking luck," Beauchamp chimes in sympathetically.

"Stinking luck indeed. For one cannot mask a tell-tale sound. As we all well know, the whereabouts of the luckless Lady Kogō were betrayed to the vengeful Taira by the sound of her harp. If," says Waverhouse, "you were merely guzzling stolen food or faking paper money, that could be managed; but one cannot scrape a fiddle and keep one's presence hidden."

"If only my fiddle made no sound, I could have got away with it . . ."

"You speak as though sound were the only betrayer; but there are soundless things which still can not be hidden. I remember that years ago, when we were self-catering students lodging in a temple over in Koishikawa, one of our gang, a certain Suzuki Tō, was passionately fond of sweetened cooking *saké*. He used to keep it in a beer bottle, never offered it around but swigged it all by himself. One day, when Suzuki was out for a walk, the otherwise decent Sneaze, very unwisely, nicked Suzuki's bottle, took a couple of gulps and then . . ."

"That's a flat lie. I never touched Suzuki's stuff. It was always you who were knocking it back," exclaimed my master suddenly and in a loud voice.

"Oh, so you're still with us, are you? I'd thought you were so busy in your book that I could safely tell these terrible truths without fear of interruption by the guilty party. But all the time you were listening. Which just shows what a sneaky *saké*-sneaking sort of fellow you are. One talks of people who are equally skilled in thought and action. Thought and faction are more your style. I don't deny that, now and again, I took a modest nip from Suzuki's bottle. But you were the villain who got found out. And how did you come

to be caught? Just listen to this, you two.
We all know, don't we, that our miserable
host is anyway incapable of serious drinking.
Alcohol! He just can't take it. But just because that cooking *sake* belonged to someone else, he slugged it down as though his
life depended on it. Imagine what inevitably
followed. His face swelled up and turned a
ghastly red. It was a most fearsome sight."

"Pipe down, Waverhouse! You can't even
read Latin."

"That's a laugh! You want a laugh? Then
listen to the sequel. When Suzuki got back,
he made a bee-line for his grog, lifted the
bottle, shook it and immediately discovered
it was more than half-empty. Sneaze had
really given it a hammering. Of course Suzuki realized that someone had been at it and,
when he looked around, there was Sneaze flat
out in a corner, as stiff and dully scarlet as
some crude clay doll."

Remembering that ludicrous incident,
Waverhouse exploded into raucous laughter
and the others joined in. Even my master
chuckled into his book. Only Singleman
seems proof against low comedy. He's probably overstrained his Zen-besotted mind with
all those bits of stone. At all events, slumped
down across the board, he's fallen fast asleep.

When his guffaws had ended, Waverhouse
began again, "I remember another occasion
when a noiseless action nevertheless betrayed
itself. I'd gone," he said, "to a hot spring
inn at Ubako where I found myself sharing

a room with some old man who was, I believe, a retired draper from Tokyo. Since he
was no more to me than a temporary room-
mate, it hardly matters whether he was a
retired draper or a practicing second-hand
clothes dealer; but I thought you'd like a bit
of background detail. At all events, he got
me into trouble. That is to say, after some
three days at the inn I ran out of cigarettes.
Ubako is an out-of-the-way place, miles up
in the mountains with only a single inn and
absolutely nothing else. One can eat and one
can bathe in the hot springs. But that's all.
Imagine what it's like to run out of fags in
Ubako. It put me under strain. When one is
deprived of something, one begins to crave
for it as never before. Though I'm not much
of a smoker, the moment I realized I was out
of cigarettes I found myself aching for a puff.
What made it worse was that the old man
had brought with him a big stock of cigarettes carefully bundled up in a carrying-cloth,
from which he would take out several at a
time, squat down right in front of me and
chain-smoke like a sooted chimney. If he'd
smoked in an ordinary decently human sort
of way, I would not have hated him so passionately. But he flaunted his tobacco wealth.
He made smoke-rings, blew the fumes out
forward, sideways, straight up at the ceiling,
in and out of his nostrils and almost out of
his ears until I could have killed him. Some
men are born show-offs. This man was a
smoke-off."

"What d'you mean, a smoke-off?"

"If you flaunt your clothes or jewelry, you're a show-off; if you flaunt your fags, you're a smoke-off."

"If it put you through such agony, why didn't you simply ask him to let you have a few of his cigarettes?"

"There are things a man can't do. To beg I am ashamed."

"So it's wrong to ask for a cigarette?"

"Perhaps not actually sinful, but I could never beg."

"Then what did you do?"

"As a matter of fact, I stole."

"Oh, dear!"

"When the old man, clutching his personal hand-towel, tottered off for a hot spring bath, I knew my chance had come. I looted his hoard and I smoked and smoked and smoked as fast as I could go. Just as I was smirking to myself, partly with the pleasure of smoking, partly with the even greater self-satisfaction of the successful thief, the door opened and there he was again."

"What happened to his bath?"

"Oh, he was certainly planning to take it, but when he'd gone some way down the corridor he suddenly remembered he'd left his purse behind so he came back to get it. Damn cheek! As if I'd steal someone's purse . . ."

"Well, wouldn't you? You seem to have been pretty quick with his cigarettes."

"You must be joking. That's not the same at all. Anyway, apart from his disgraceful be-

298
-
I Am a Cat (III)

havior in that matter of the purse, the old man proved a person of real feeling. When he opened the door, the room was thick with at least two days' worth of cigarette-smoke. Ill news travels fast, they say. It didn't take him long to read the situation."

"Did he say anything?"

"He hadn't lived all those years without growing more shrewd than that. Saying nothing, he wrapped some fifty or sixty cigarettes in a piece of paper; then, turning to me, he courteously observed, 'Do please forgive their miserable quality, but if these cigarettes could be of any use to you, I'd be honored if you'd accept them.' Then he went off down to the bath."

"Perhaps that's what's meant by 'the Tokyo style.'"

"I don't know if it's Tokyo style or draper's style; but anyway, after that incident, the old man and I became firm friends and we spent a most enjoyable two weeks together."

"With free fags for a fortnight?"

"Since you ask me, yes."

My master finds it difficult to give in gracefully, but he sometimes tries. He accordingly closed his book, rolled off his stomach and said, as he sat up, "Have you finished with that violin?"

"Not yet. We're just coming to the interesting part, so do please listen. As for that person flaked out on the *go* board—what was his name?—What? Singleman? Well, I'd like him to listen too. It's bad for him to sleep so much. Surely it's time we woke him up."

"Hey, Singleman, wake up. Wake up. This is an interesting story. Do wake up. They say it's bad for you to sleep so much. Your wife is getting anxious."

"Eh?" Singleman lifted up his face. Slobber had dribbled down his goatee to leave a long shining line as if a slug had trailed its slime across him. "I was sleeping," he managed to get out, "like a white cloud on the mountain-top. I've had a delightful nap."

"We've all seen how delightfully you sleep. Suppose you wake up now."

"I expect it's time I woke. Has anyone had anything to say worth hearing?"

"Coldmoon's been telling us about his violin. He's just about to. . . . What was it he was going to do? Come on, Sneaze. What was it?"

"I haven't the foggiest idea."

Coldmoon intervened. "I am," he said, "just about to play it."

"He's going to play his violin at last. Come over here and join us as we listen."

"Still that violin? Bother."

"You've no cause to be bothered because you're one of those people who only play on stringless harps; but Coldmoon here has every reason to be bothered out of his tiny skull because his screeching squawks are heard all over the neighborhood."

"Ah yes? Coldmoon, don't you yet know

how to play a violin without being heard by
your neighbors?"

"No, I don't. If there is such a way, I'd
very much like to learn about it."

"There's really nothing to learn. Just concentrate, as all the Zen masters advise, on
the pure white cow which stands there in the
alley. Desire will drop away from you and,
as enlightenment occurs, you'll find you already know how soundless music can be
played. And because you'll already know,
you'll have no need to learn." Singleman's
distorted messages from the Gateless Gate,
even when he's wide awake, are usually incomprehensible.

But Coldmoon simply assumed that the
man babbled like that because his brains
were still floating about somewhere in the
land of Nod. So he deliberately ignored him
and continued with his story. "After long
thought I devised a plan. The next day, being
the Emperor's Birthday, was a national holiday and I proposed to spend it in bed. But I
felt restless all day long and I kept getting up,
first to lift and then to replace the lid of my
wicker-box. When, in due course, the daylight faded and the crickets in the bottom of
my grandmother's parting gift began to chir-
rup, I took my courage in both hands and
lifted the violin and its bow from their
hiding place."

"At wonderful last," chirruped Beauchamp, "Coldmoon's going to play."

"Gently, gently, Coldmoon. Don't do anything hasty. Let caution rule your twilight."

"First I took out the bow and examined it
from its tip to its guard . . ."

"You sound like some half-witted seller of
swords," chaffed Waverhouse.

"If you can take a bow in your hands and
feel that it is your own soul that you're holding, then you will have achieved that same
spiritual condition which transfuses a *samurai*
when he unsheathes his white-honed blade
and dotes upon it in the failing light of autumn. Holding that bow in my hands I trembled like a leaf."

"Ah, what a genius!" sighs Beauchamp.

"Ah, what an epileptic," adds Waverhouse
tartly.

"Please," said my master, "please get on
with playing it. And right away. Now."

Singleman makes a wry face as though
acknowledging the pointlessness of trying to
bring light to the invincibly ignorant.

"Happily the bow proved in perfect condition. Next I took the violin and, holding it
close under the lamp, examined its front and
back. All these preparations had taken about
five minutes. Please now try to picture the
scene. Tirelessly, from the bottom of their
box, the crickets are still chirruping . . ."

"We'll imagine anything you like. Set your
mind at rest, take up your precious instrument and play."

"No, not yet. Now I have checked it over
and, like its bow, the violin is flawless. All is
wonderfully well. I spring to my feet . . ."

"Are you going out?"

"Oh, do keep quiet and listen. I cannot tell
this story if you keep interrupting every single
phrase . . ."

"Gentlemen! We are to be silent. Hush!"
calls Waverhouse commandingly.

"It's you yourself who do the interrupting."

"Oh, I see. I beg your pardon. Pray carry
on."

"With the violin beneath my arm, soft-
soled sandals on my feet, I had taken some
few steps beyond the outer glass-door of my
lodgings when . . ."

"I knew it. I knew it. I knew in my bones
there was going to be a breakdown. Coldmoon cannot walk two steps or breathe two
minutes without a hitch or hang-up."

"I suppose you do realize," said my master
at his most sarcastic, "that there are no more
dried persimmons hanging from the eaves.
Even if you're now very hungry there's no
point in turning home for them."

"It is highly regrettable that two such scholars as you and you"—Coldmoon nodded at
Waverhouse and Sneaze—"should persist in
behaving like common hecklers. I shall have
to address my further remarks to Mr. Beauchamp only. Now, Beauchamp, as I was saying, though I had left my lodgings, I was
obliged to turn back for something I should
need. Thereafter, having draped around my

head a scarlet blanket (for which I'd paid three yen and twenty sen in my own home-town before I left it years before), I blew out the lamp. Unfortunately, in the consequent pitch darkness I could not find my sandals."

"But why did you want to go out? Where were you off to?"

"Patience, patience. I shall come to that. At long last, outside in my scarlet blanket, my violin beneath my coat, I again found myself, as on the previous night, ankle-deep in fallen leaves under a star-lit sky. I turned away to the right and, as I came to the foot of Mount Kōshin, the boom of the temple-bell on Eastern Peak struck through my blanket-shrouded ears and penetrated to my inmost head. Beauchamp, can you guess what time it was?"

"This is your story, Coldmoon. I've no idea what the time was."

"Beauchamp, it is nine. Nine and the even-ing chill. I am now climbing through the early autumn darkness along a mountain path which rises nearly three thousand feet to a sort of terrace-plateau which the locals call Big Flat. Timid as I am, at any other time I'd have been scared clean out of my wits, but it's one of those strange things that, when the mind is truly concentrated upon one spe-cific aim, all sense of being frightened or not frightened is wiped from one's heart. Odd as it must sound, I had become a lion-heart by virtue of my single-minded lust to play a fid-dle. This place, Big Flat, is a famous beauty-spot on the south flank of Mount Kōshin. Looking down from there on a fine day, one can see through the red pines the whole lay-out of the castle-town below. I'd guess the level area must cover some four hundred square yards and, smack in the middle of it, a large flat rock protrudes to form a low fif-teen-square-yard platform. On the north side of Big Flat there's a swampy pond called Cormorant's Marsh, and around the pond there's nothing but a thick stand of quite enormous camphor-trees, each one no less than three arm-spans around. The place is deep in the mountains and the only sign of man is a small hut used by the camphor-gath-erers. Even by day the pond oppresses the visitor with its air of sodden gloom. Remote as it is, Big Flat is not too hard to visit be-cause, on some long-ago maneuvres, the Corps of Engineers cut a pathway up the mountainside. When I finally reached the flat rock, I spread out my scarlet blanket and sat down on it. I'd never climbed up here before on a night so cold and, as my pulse steadied, I began to feel the surrounding loneliness encroach upon me as a kind of cramp creep-ing ever deeper into my belly. When one is thus alone in the mountains the sheer inten-sity of that loneliness can fill the mind with a feeling of terror; but if that feeling can be emptied away, all that remains in the mind is an extraordinary sense of icy crystalline clarity. For some twenty minutes I sat there on my scarlet rug completely abstracted from my normal self and feeling as though I were totally alone in a palace of pure crystal. It was as though every bit of me, my body, even my soul, had become transparent, as if made of some kind of quartz; and I could no longer tell whether I was inside that palace of crystal or that freezing palace was within my belly."

Not quite sure how to react to Coldmoon's strange account, Waverhouse contented himself with a style of teasing more demure than his mocking wont. "How terrible," he said. Singleman, however, was genuinely impressed by Coldmoon's personal report of a state of consciousness not unknown to many meditation sects. "Quite extraordinary," he observed. "Most interesting."

"Had my condition of cold translucency persisted, I might well have stayed frozen on that rock until I melted in the morning sun. Then I should never have played my violin."

"Have there been any earlier reports," Beauchamp asked, "to suggest that Big Flat might be haunted? You know, by foxes, badgers or any other such shape-changing creatures?"

"As I was saying, I couldn't even tell whether I was my own self or not, and I scarcely knew if I were alive or dead when suddenly I heard a harsh screaming cry from the far end of the old marsh."

"Aha," says Waverhouse, "things are happening."

"This awful cry, like a blast of autumn wind tossing the treetops, echoed away far and deep across the entire mountain; and at its sound, I came to myself with a jerk."

"What a relief!" sighed Waverhouse, heaving a grotesquely simulated sigh.

"As the masters say, 'One must perish into life.' Isn't that so, Coldmoon?" Even Singleman, who winked as he offered his observation, now seems disposed to treat his friend's spiritual experience in the spirit of light farce. However, his Zen reference was completely lost on Coldmoon.

"Having been thus startled back into my usual self, I looked around me. The whole vast mountain was now dead quiet: nothing, not even the drip of a raindrop, could be heard. What then was that ghastly cry? Too piercing to have been human, too loud for any bird. Could it have been a monkey? But around there there aren't any monkeys. What on earth could it have been? Once that question had entered my head and I began to search around for its answer, all the demons of misgiving who had hitherto lain quiet in the crannies of my mind erupted into pandemonium. You remember how the city-crowds went wild, people running here and there and even all over each other in a lunacy of welcome, when Prince Arthur of Connaught came to Tokyo in February 1906? Well, inside my head it was worse than that. And then things suddenly came to a crisis. I felt my very pores gape open and through their yawn my body's flightiest visitors—Courage, Pluck, Prudence and Composure—departed

from me. Like cheap alcohol blown in a
spray on hairy shins to cool them, my visitors
evaporated. Under my ribs my heart began
to hammer. It leapt and danced like a red
frog. My legs trembled like the humming
strings of a kite. And my nerve broke. In
mindless panic I grabbed my scarlet blanket
round my head and, with the violin clutched
beneath one arm, I scrambled down from
the low flat rock and helter-skelter fled away
down the rough mountain-path. When, scam-
pering like a rat through the layers of dead
leaves, I came at last to my lodgings, I crept
in quietly and hid myself in my bed. I had
been so exhausted by terror that I fell immediately asleep. D'you know, Beauchamp,
that was the most terrifying experience of my
whole life."

"And then?"

"That's it. There isn't any more."

"No playing of the violin?"

"How could I possibly have played? If you
had heard that eldritch cry, I bet my boots
the last thing you'd have thought about would
be playing a violin."

"I find your story less than satisfactory."

"Perhaps so, but it was the truth." Coldmoon, vastly pleased with himself, surveyed
his audience. "Well," he said, "and what did
you think of it?"

"Excellent. A point well taken," laughed
Waverhouse. "You really must have gone
through great travail to bring your story to
that remarkable conclusion. In fact, I've been

307
・
吾輩は猫である

following your account with the closest attention, for it seemed increasingly clear to me
that, in the person of yourself, these Eastern
climes have perhaps been visited by a male
re-incarnation of Sandra Belloni." Waverhouse paused in the obvious hope that someone would give him an opportunity to air his
knowledge of Meredith's heroine by asking
for clarification of this obscure reference. But
all the members of his audience, having been
caught that way before, held their peace; so
Waverhouse, regrettably un-cued, simply rattled on. "Just as Sandra Belloni's harp-play-
ing and Italian song in a moonlit forest called
down the goddess of that silver orb, so Coldmoon's near-performance with a violin upon
the ledges of Mount Kōshin called up some
phantom-badger from a fen. There is, of
course, a difference of degree but the principle's the same. What I find peculiarly interesting is that such a slight difference in degree
should produce so vast a difference in result:
in Sandra's case a manifestation of ethereal
beauty, but in Coldmoon's nothing but crude
and earthy farce. That must have been a
painful disappointment to you."

"No disappointment at all," said Coldmoon who seemed genuinely uninterested,
perhaps not in his own weird experience, but
certainly in Waverhouse's question.

"Trying to play a violin on a mountain-
top! What effete behavior! It serves you right
that you got scared silly." My master's scath-
ing comment showed his usual lack of sym-

Singleman piped in:

> How more than pitiful it is to find
> That one must live one's human life
> confined
> Within a world of an inhuman kind.

None of Singleman's mangled quotations from the works of deluded medieval metaphysicians ever makes the least sense to Coldmoon. Or to anyone else. Perhaps not even to Singleman. His words were left to float away into the nothingness of a long silence.

After a while, Waverhouse changed the subject by asking, "Incidentally, Coldmoon, are you still haunting the university in order to polish your little glass balls?"

"No. My visit home rather interrupted things. Indeed, I doubt if I'll ever resume that line of research. It was always, if you'll pardon the joke, something of a grind, and lately I've been finding it a real bore."

"But without your polished beads, you won't get your doctorate," says my master, looking slightly worried.

Coldmoon seems no more concerned about his doctorate than he was with his failure to become a Japanese version of Sandra Belloni. "Oh that," he says with a careless laugh. "I've no longer any need for a degree."

"But then the marriage will be canceled and both sides will be upset."

"Marriage? Whose marriage?"

"Yours."

"To whom am I supposed to be getting married?"

"To the Goldfield girl."

"Really?"

"But surely you've already plighted your troth?"

"I've never plighted anything. I had no part in the spread of that particular rumor."

"That's a bit thick," says my master. "I say, Waverhouse, you too remember that incident, don't you?"

"Incident? You mean that business when the Nose came shoving herself in here? If so, it's not just you and I who've heard about the engagement, but the world and his wife have long been in on the secret. As a matter of fact, I'm constantly being pestered by some quite respectable newspapers who want me to let them know when they may have the honor of printing photographs of Coldmoon and his blushing Opula in their Happy Couples column. What's more, Beauchamp there finished his epic epithalamium, 'A Song of Lovebirds,' at least three months ago and has since been waiting anxiously to learn the right date for its publication. You don't want your masterpiece to rot in the ground like buried treasure just because Coldmoon's grown bored with buffing up his little glass beads, do you, Beauchamp, eh?"

"There's no question of pushing for early publication. Of course, my very heart and

soul have gone into that poem, but I am happily convinced that it will remain suitable for
publication at any appropriate time."

"There, you see: the question of whether
or not you take your degree has wide and
potentially painful repercussions. So, pull
yourself together. Get those beads rubbed
spherical. Polish the whole thing off."

"I like the joke in your phrasing, and I'm
truly sorry if I've given any of you cause to
worry. But I really do not any longer need a
doctorate."

"Why not?"

"Because I have already got my own wife."

"I say, that's grand! When did this secret
marriage take place? Life is certainly full of
surprises. Well, Sneaze, as you've just heard,
Coldmoon has apparently acquired a wife
and children."

"No children yet. It would be terrible if a
child were born after less than a month of
marriage."

"But when and where did you ever get
married?" demanded my master as though
he were the presiding judge at some official
court of inquiry.

"As a matter of fact, during my recent trip
home. She was there waiting for me. Those
dried bonitos were one of the wedding pres-
ents from her relatives."

"Three miserable dried bonitos! That was
rather a stingy gift."

"No, no. There were scads of them. I only
brought you three."

"So your bride is from your own home-district? Does it then follow that she's on the dark-skinned side?"

"Yes, she's dark-complexioned. Exactly right for me."

"And what are you going to do about the Goldfields?"

"Nothing."

"But you can't just leave things, poof, like that," my master bleated. "What do you think, Waverhouse?"

"I think he can. The girl will marry someone else. After all, marriage is little more than two people bumping against each other in the dark. If they cannot manage such bumping by themselves, other people contrive their blind collision. It doesn't much matter who bumps whom. In my opinion, the only person deserving our tears and pity is the unfortunate author of 'A Song of Lovebirds.' "

"Thank you, but please don't worry. My epithalamium, as it stands, is perfectly suitable for dedication to Coldmoon on the already achieved occasion of his marriage. I can easily write another when Opula gets wed."

"Ah, that marvelous heartless professionalism of the true poet," sighed Waverhouse, "whipping out a masterpiece at the drop of a hat. Easy as wink an eye. One's heart is cramped with jealousy."

"Have you notified the Goldfields?" My master is still touchingly concerned about the feelings of that granite clan.

"No, and why should I? I never proposed to the girl or asked her father for her hand in marriage. I have no reason whatever to say a single word to either of them. Moreover, I'm sure they've already learnt the last least detail from those dozens of detectives they employ."

My master's face, as the word "detectives" entered his ear, immediately turned sour. "You're right, Coldmoon, tell such people nothing," and he proceeded to offer the following comments on detectives as though they were all weighty arguments against observing the proprieties in handling a broken engagement. "Persons who snatch property from the unwary in the streets are called pickpockets; those who snitch the thoughts of the unwary are called detectives. Those who jimmy open your doors and windows are called thieves; those who use leading questions to lever out one's private thoughts are called detectives. Those who threateningly jab their swords into one's floor-matting as a way of forcing the surrender of money are called armed burglars; those who by the jabbing menace of their words force one into admissions against one's will are called detectives. To my way of thinking, it inexorably follows that pickpockets, thieves, armed burglars and detectives are all spawn of the same subhuman origin, things unfit to be treated even as men. Their every endeavor should be thwarted and they themselves quite mercilessly put down."

"Don't work yourself into such a lather. I'm not frightened by detectives, even though they should appear by the battalion. Let all be warned with whom they will be dealing. Am I not the King of the Glass-Ball Polishers, Avalon Coldmoon B.Sc.?"

"Bravo! Well spoken! That's the stuff to give 'em! Just the spirited words one would expect from a newly married bachelor of science. However, Sneaze," Waverhouse continued, "if you categorize detectives with such grubs as pickpockets, thieves and common robbers, where do you place a creature such as Goldfield who gives employment to such vermin?"

"Perhaps a modern version of that long-departed villain, Kumasaka Chōhan."

"Oh yes, I like that. Chōhan, as I recall it, was said to have disappeared when he was sliced in half. But our modern version over the way, squatting on a fortune made by blatant usury, is so intensely alive in his meanness and sharp greediness that, cut in a million pieces, he'd reappear as a million Chōhan-clones. It would be a life-long source of trouble if such a blood-sucking creature ever came to believe he had a bone to pick with you. So be careful, Coldmoon."

"To hell with that! I shall face him down with the sort of speech you hear from heros of the Hōshō style of Noh play. You know what I mean. 'Pretentious thief, though well aware of my fearsome reputation, you yet dare break into my house.' That should stop him short." Coldmoon, unwisely careless of the real dangers he might have to cope with from a vengeful Goldfield, strikes a series of dramatic poses.

"Talking of detectives, I wonder why it is that nearly everyone nowadays tends to behave as detectives do." In strict accordance with his usual style, Singleman begins his observations by reference to the matters under discussion and then veers off into complete irrelevance.

"Perhaps," says Coldmoon kindly, "it's because of the high cost of living."

Beauchamp mounts his hobby-horse. "I myself believe it's because we have lost our feeling for art."

"It's because the horns of modern civilization are sprouting from the human head and the irritations of that growth, like nettles in one's underwear, are driving us mad." It's a pity that Waverhouse, who is both well-read and intelligent, still should strive to be merely clever.

When it came to my master's turn, he opened the following lecture with an air of enormous self-importance. "I have, of late, devoted considerable thought to this topic and I have concluded that the current marked trend toward detective-mindedness is entirely caused by the individual permitting himself too strong a realization of the self. By that I do not mean self-realization of the spiritual nature which Singleman pursues in his Zen search for his 'unborn face,' that self he was before he contrived to be born. Nor do I mean that other form of Zen self-realization where, by either gradual or sudden enlightenment, the mind perceives its own identity with heaven and earth . . ."

"Dear, dear, this is becoming rather heavy going. But if, Sneaze, you really do propose to make an exhaustive and scholarly analysis of the psychological maladies of our times, I feel that I, Waverhouse in person, must be granted an opportunity to lodge a full complaint against the civilization I seek to grace."

"You are always free to say what you like. But generally you don't say anything. You just talk."

"On the contrary, I have a very great deal to say. It was you, Sneaze, who, only a brief week back, fell down and worshiped a police detective. Yet here you are today, making ugly comparisons between detectives and pickpockets. You are an incarnation of the principle of contradiction. Whereas I am a man who, through every earlier life right to this present day of my present incarnation, has never wavered in the certitudes of my opinions."

"Police detectives are police detectives. The other day is the other day. And today's today. Never to change one's opinions is to demonstrate a petrifaction of mind that prevents its least development. To be, as Confucius put it in the *Analects,* willfully ignorant beyond all hope of education, is, my dear Waverhouse, to be you."

"That's really rather rude. Still, even a detective when he tries to speak his honest mind can be rather sweet."

"Are you calling me a detective?"

"I simply meant to say that, since you are not a detective, you're an honest man, and that that's good. There, there. No more quarrels. Let's listen to the rest of your formidable argument."

"The heightened self-awareness of our contemporaries means that they realize only too well the wide gap between their own interests and those of other people; and as the advance of civilization daily widens that gap, so this so-called self-awareness intensifies to a point where everyone becomes incapable of natural or unaffected behavior. William Henley, the English poet, once said that his friend Robert Louis Stevenson was so continuously unable to forget himself that, if he happened to be in a room with a mirror on the wall, he could not pass in front of the glass without stopping to study his reflection. Stevenson's condition is a telling example of the general modern trend. Because this overweening consciousness of self never lets up, not even when one sleeps, it is inevitable that our speech and behavior should have become forced and artificial. We impose constrictions on ourselves and, in that process, inhibitions on society. In short, we conduct our whole lives as if we were two young people at their first meeting in the context of a marriage-negotiation. Words such as serenity and self-composure have become no more than so many meaningless strokes of a writing-brush. It is in this sense that people nowadays have become like detectives and burglars. A detective's job is essentially to make profit by being sneaky and self-effacing; only by cultivating an intense awareness of himself can he even believe in his own existence. To no less a degree the rapacious burglar is obsessed with me, me, me because the thought of what will happen to him if he's caught is never out of his mind. Modern man, even in his deepest slumber, never stops thinking about what will bring him profit or, even more worrying, loss. Consequently, as with the burglar and the detective, his self-absorption grows daily more absolute. Modern man is jittery and sneaky. Morning, noon and night he sneaks and jitters and knows no peace. Not one single moment's peace until the cold grave takes him. That's the condition to which our so-called civilization has brought us. And what a mess it is."

"Most interesting. A penetrating analysis of our case," says Singleman who rarely resists any opportunity to thicken the clouds when high-flown cloudy matters are discussed. "I consider Sneaze's explanation is very much to the point. In the old days, a man was taught to forget himself. Today it is quite different: he is taught not to forget himself, and he accordingly spends his days and nights in endless self-regard. Who can possibly know peace in such an eternally burning hell? The apparent realities of this awful world, even the beastliness of Being, are all symptoms of that sickness for which the only cure lies in learning to forget the Self. This dire situation is well summarized in that ancient Chinese poem whose author was one of those

Who simply sit and, sitting all night
    through
Under a drifting moon, themselves
    withdrew
Themselves from Self and thereby
    came to be
Free of the world and from all Being
    free.

Modern man lacks naturalness even when performing acts of genuine kindness. The English, as is well known, are vastly proud of being nice, both in the sense of their refined behavior and in the sense of common kindness; but one may fairly suspect the hearts behind the niceness of the English as packed with self-regard. Perhaps I might remind you of the story of that member of the English royal family who, during some visit to India, was invited to a banquet. Among those present was an Indian prince who, momentarily forgetful of the nature of the occasion but perfectly naturally in terms of Indian custom, reached out for a potato, picked it up in his fingers and put it on his plate. Realizing his gaffe, he was terribly ashamed. But the English gentleman, immediately and with apparently equal naturalness, proceeded to help himself to potatoes with his fingers. An act of the most refined and kindly politeness? Or an act so-seeming but ultimately taken in order that it should be remembered, as it clearly has been, to the enhancement of English royalty?"

"Is it the English custom," asks Coldmoon, missing the point of the story, "to eat potatoes with their fingers?"

Disregarding Coldmoon's question, my master spoke. "I've heard another such story about the English. On some occasion at their barracks in England a group of regimental officers gave a dinner in honor of one of their non-commissioned officers. Toward the end of the meal, when finger-bowls filled with water were placed in front of each diner, the non-commissioned officer, a man not used to banquets, lifted the bowl to his mouth and swallowed the water down in a single gulp. Immediately, the colonel of the regiment raised his own finger-bowl in a toast to the non-commissioned officer's health and gulped its water down. His lead was promptly followed by every officer present."

"I wonder if you've heard this one," says Waverhouse who does not like to remain silent. "When Carlyle was presented to the queen, he, being an eccentric and anyway a man totally unschooled in court procedures, suddenly sat down on a chair. All the chamberlains and ladies-in-waiting standing ranged behind the queen began to giggle. Well, not quite. They were about to start giggling when the queen turned round toward them and signaled them also to be seated. Carlyle was thus saved from any embarrassment. I confess I find this courtly courtesy somewhat elaborate."

"I don't suppose," said Coldmoon rather shortly, "that, being the man he was, Carlyle would have been the least embarrassed if only he and the queen were seated while all the rest stayed standing."

"To be self-aware when one is actually being kind to other people may be all right," Singleman started up again, "but being self-aware does make it that much harder to be genuinely kind. It is widely held that the advance of civilization brings with it a moderation of combative spirit and a general easing of relationships between individuals. But that's all nonsense. When individual awareness grows so strong, how can mutual gentleness be expected? It's true of course that modern relationships seem superficially calm and easy-going, but they are in fact extremely tough; rather like the relationship between two *sumo* wrestlers who, immobilized by cross-grips in the middle of the ring, are nevertheless butting each other with their vast pot-bellies as hard as they can heave."

"In former times disputes were settled by the relatively healthy means of brute force, whereas nowadays the means and mentality have become so specialized that the intensity of the combatant's self-awareness has inevitably increased," says Waverhouse, taking it to be now his turn to talk. "Sir Francis Bacon observed in his *Novum Organum* that one can only triumph over Nature by obeying the laws of Nature. Is it not peculiar that modern quarrels so closely follow the pattern identified by Bacon in that, as in a *jūjutsu* contest, one defeats one's opponent by an exploitation of that opponent's own strength."

"Or again, it is, I suppose, something like the generation of hydro-electricity. One makes no effort to oppose the flow of water, but merely diverts its force into the production of power."

Coldmoon had obviously only just begun to express an interesting idea, but Singleman butted in to add, "And therefore, when one is poor, one is tied by poverty; when rich, entrapped in wealth; when worried, tangled by anxiety; and when happy, dizzied by happiness. A talented man falls at the hand of talent, a man of wisdom is defeated by wisdom, and a quick-tempered man like Sneaze is quickly provoked into rashness and goes rushing headlong out into the deadfalls dug by his artful enemies."

"Here, here," cried Waverhouse clapping his hands; and when my master, actually grinning, said, "Well, you won't in practice catch me quite as simply as that," everyone burst out laughing.

"By the way, I wonder what sort of thing

would finish off a fearful fellow like Gold-field?"

"His wife will obviously be toppled over by the weight of her nose, while the hardness of his heart will crush that usurer to death. His henchmen will be trampled to death by stampeding detectives."

"And the daughter?"

"Well, I'm not sure about her, and I have never in fact clapped eyes on her. But it seems likely that she'll be suffocated by clothes or food or even drinking. I can't imagine that she'll die of love, though I suppose she might end up as a roadside beggar like that fabled beauty Ono-no-Komachi."

"That's a bit unkind," objected Beauchamp who, after all, had written some new-style poems for the girl.

"And therein lies the importance of the moral injunction that one must have a merci-ful heart and never lose one's subjectivity. Unless one reaches and sustains that condi-tion of mind, one will suffer torment through-out eternity." That benighted Singleman waffles on as usual as though he were the sole proprietor of enlightenment.

"Don't be such a moralizing twerp. The chances are," said Waverhouse, "that you will meet your just deserts upside-down in one of your own oft-quoted flashes of Zen lightning. In the spring, of course."

"One thing at least is certain," said my master. "If civilization continues its rapid development along its present lines, I would not wish to live and witness it."

"The choice is yours. As Seneca advises, no man should carp at life when the road to freedom runs down every vein. Why don't you do yourself in?" Waverhouse helpfully enquired.

"I care rather less for dying than I do for living."

. "No one seems to pay much attention when he's being born, but everybody makes no end of a fuss about his departure." Coldmoon offers his own cool comment.

"It's the same with money," says Waverhouse. "When one borrows money, one does so lightly, but everyone worries like crazy when it comes to paying it back."

"Happy are they who don't worry about repayment; as happy as those who do not worry about death," intoned Singleman in his most lofty and unworldly style.

"I suppose you'd argue that the bravest in the face of death are those who are most enlightened?"

"Most certainly. Perhaps you know the Zen phrase 'The iron-ox-heart of an iron-ox-face: the ox-iron-heart of an ox-iron-face?' "

"And are you claiming to be so ox-and-iron-hearted?" Waverhouse, who happened to know that the phrase meant to have a heart so strong as to be undisturbed by anything, doubted that Singleman would dare make such a claim.

"Well, no, I wouldn't go that far. But,"

said Singleman for no very obvious reason, "the fact remains that neurasthenia was an unknown ailment until after people became worried about death."

"It's plain that you must have been born and bred before the invention of nervous prostration."

This weird dialogue held so little interest for Coldmoon and Beauchamp that my master had no difficulty in retaining them as an audience for a further airing of his grievances against civilization. "The key question," he announced, "is how to avoid repaying borrowed money."

"But surely no such question can arise. Anything borrowed must always be repaid."

"All right, all right. Don't get so up in the air. This is just a discussion between intelligent men, so listen and don't interrupt. I ask how can one borrow without repaying in order to lead in to the parallel question as to how can one contrive to avoid dying. Though it is no longer much pursued, that used to be the key question: hence the ancient concern with alchemy. However, the alchemists achieved no real success and it soon became deadly clear that no human being could ever dodge death."

"It was deadly clear long before the alchemists confirmed it."

"All right, but since this is just an argument, you just listen. Right? Now, once it became clear that everyone was bound to die, then the second question arose."

I Am a Cat (III) •

"Indeed?"

"If one is certain to die, what's the best way to do so? That is the second question. Once this second question had been formulated, it was only a matter of time before the Suicide Club would be founded."

"I see."

"It is hard to die, but it is much harder if one cannot die. Victims of neurasthenia find living far more painful than any death. Yet they remain obsessed with death; not because they shun it, but because they fret to discover the best means to that much-desired end. The majority will lack the nous to solve the problem. They will give up and leave nature to solve it for them or society itself will bully them to death. But there will also be a handful of awkward customers who will be unwilling to endure the slow death of such bullying. They will study the options into death and their research will lead to marvelous new ideas. Beyond all doubt, the main characteristic of the future will be a steady rise in suicides and, almost certainly, every self-destructor will be expected to work out his own original method of escape."

"People will be put to a great deal of trouble."

"Yes, they most certainly will. Henry Arthur Jones has already written a play in which the leading figure is a philosopher who strongly advocates suicide."

"Does he kill himself?"

"Regrettably, no. But within a thousand

years everyone will be doing it; and I am prepared to bet that in ten thousand years' time nobody will even think of death except in terms of suicide."

"But that will be terrible."

"Indeed it will. By that time the study of suicide, on a foundation of years of detailed research, will have been raised to the level of a highly respected and fully institutionalized science. At middle schools such as the Hall of the Descending Clouds the study of suicide will have replaced ethics as a compulsory subject."

"An intriguing prospect. A lecture-course on the theory and practice of suicide might well be worth attending. Hey, Waverhouse, have you been listening to Sneaze on the destiny of man?"

"Yes I have. By the time of which he has just been speaking the ethics teacher at the Hall of the Descending Clouds will be holding our current concepts of public morality up to reproof and ridicule. The young men of that far world will be instructed to abandon the barbarous customs of the ancients and to recognize that suicide is the first duty of every decent person. Moreover, since it is eternally right to do unto others as one would wish done to oneself, the moral obligation to commit suicide implies an equally moral obligation to commit murder. Consider, the teacher will say, the case of Mr. Peke Sneaze, that wretched struggling student-scholar dragging out his miserable existence just across from our school. Is he not obviously agonized by his persistent breathing yet lacks the ordinary physical courage to fulfill his moral duty to do away with himself? Is it not therefore, in common humanity, your compassionate duty to do him in? Not, of course, in any of the ancient cowardly ways involving such crudities as spears, halberds or any kind of firearm. In this day and age we are surely civilized beyond such coarse atrocities. No, he should be harassed unto death. Only the most refined techniques of verbal assassination should be employed. Which will be not only an act of charity toward that luckless sufferer but a credit to yourselves and to the school."

"This extension-lecture, Waverhouse upon Sneaze, is deeply interesting. I am truly moved by the high-mindedness of our descendants."

"Yes, but there's even more upon which to laud our unborn heirs. In our ill-governed times the police are intended to safeguard the lives and property of citizens. But in the happier times of our enlightened future, the police will carry cudgels, like dog-catchers, and go around clubbing the citizens to death."

"Why that?"

"Because today we value our lives and the police accordingly protect them. When in the future, living is recognized for the agony it is, then the police will be required to club the agonized to a merciful death. Of course, anyone in his right mind will already have com-

mitted suicide; so the necessary objects of
police attention will be only the gutless milk-
sops, those mentally impaired or deranged
and any persons so pitifully disabled as to be
unable to destroy themselves. Additionally,
anyone in need of help or assistance will, as
today, just stick up a notice to that effect on
the gate to his house. The police will call
round at some convenient time and promptly
supply to the man or woman concerned the
assistance requested. The dead bodies? Collected in hand-drawn carts by the police on
their regular rounds. The police themselves?
Recruited from criminals guilty of acts so
hideous they've been condemned to life. And
that's not all. Consider this further interesting aspect of . . ."

"But is there no end to this joke?" exclaims
Beauchamp from the daze of his admiration.
Before an answer could be given, Singleman
began to speak, very slowly and with great
deliberation, even though he still continued
worrying away at his ridiculous tuft of beard.

"You may call it a joke, but it might well,
and better, be called a prediction. Those
whose minds are not unwaveringly concentrated upon the pursuit of ultimate truth are
normally misled by the mere appearances,
however unreal, of the phenomenal world.
They tend to accept what they directly see
and feel, not as some empty froth of illusion
but as manifestations of an eternal reality.
Consequently, if someone says anything even
slightly out of the ordinary, such prisoners of

their senses have no choice but to treat the communication as a joke."

"Do you mean," says Coldmoon, deeply impressed, "something like that Chinese verse about small birds being unable to understand the minds of greater birds?"

The swallow and the sparrow see no use
In things that, to the eagle and the goose,
Are plainly useful. It could even be
That from their littleness the little see
Nothing whatever of Immensity.

And he smirks with delight when Singleman, with an approving inclination of his head, says, "Something like that."

Singleman, the even plodding of his speech unspurred even by adulation, slowly continues. "Once, years ago, there was a place in Spain called Cordoba . . ."

"Once? It's still there, isn't it?"

"That may be. The question of time past or present is immaterial. At all events, in Cordoba it used to be the custom that at the time of the angelus, the evening striking of the bells of churches, all the women came out of their houses and bathed in the river . . ."

"Even in winter?"

"I'm not sure about that, but in any case, every female in the place—young or old—jumped into the river, and no man was allowed to join them. The men simply looked on from a distance, and all they could see in

the evening twilight were the women's whit-
ish forms dimly moving above the rippling
waters."

"That's poetic. It could be made into a
new-style poem. What did you say the place
was called?" Beauchamp always shows interest whenever female nudity is mentioned.

"Cordoba. Now, the young men thought
it a pity that they could neither swim with
the women nor study their form in a better
light. So, one fine day, they played a little
trick . . ."

"Oh really? Tell me more," says Waverhouse immediately. The mention of any kind
of trick has, upon him, the same invigorating
effect as nudity works upon Beauchamp.

"They bribed the bell-ringer to sound the
angelus one hour early. The women, being
such sillies, all trooped down to the river-
bank as soon as they heard the bells, and
there, one after another in their various states
of undress, they jumped off into the water.
And then, too late, they at last realized that
it was still broad day."

"Are you sure that there wasn't a fierce
autumn sun ablaze?"

"A great number of men were standing
watching from the bridge. The women didn't
know what to do and felt terribly ashamed."

"And then?"

"The moral is simply this: that one should
always be wary of the common human failing of allowing oneself to be blinded by habit
to basic realities."

"Not a bad little sermon. A tale worth remembering. But let me give you another example, from a magazine story which I recently read, of someone rendered blind by an accustomed habit. Imagine that I've opened an antique-shop and that, up at the front, I've put on display some particularly excellent scrolls and works of art. No fakes, nothing shabby, only genuine first-class stuff. Naturally the prices are very high. In due course along comes some art-fancier who stops and enquires about the price of a certain scroll. I point out that the scroll is by Motonobu, that son of Masanobu who founded the Kano school in the early sixteenth century, and I then quote some quite astronomical sum, say, six thousand. The customer replies that he likes the scroll very much but, at such a price, and not carrying such large sums of money on his person, he'll have to let it go."

"How can you possibly know," asks my master, ever the wet blanket, "that the customer will answer like that?"

"Don't worry; he will. And anyway it's only a story, so I can make my customer answer as I like. So I then say to him, 'Please, for those of us who appreciate Motonobu, payment is hardly the point. If you like it, take it with you.' The customer can hardly do that. So he hesitates. I proceed in my friendliest manner to say that, confident that I shall be enjoying his future patronage, I would be happy to settle any difficulties about payment by accepting small sums paid monthly over a long period. 'Please don't feel under any obligation. But how about a hundred a month? Or shall we say fifty?' Finally, after a few more questions and answers, I end up selling him the Motonobu scroll for six thousand paid in monthly installments of only a hundred."

"Sounds like that scheme in 1898 for buying the ninth edition of the *Encyclopedia Britannica* through *The Times*."

"*The Times* is reliable, an honest sort of broker; but my scheme is of a very different character. As, if you listen carefully, you'll see. Now, Coldmoon, suppose you pay a hundred a month for my Motonobu, how long will you be paying installments?"

"For five years? Of course, isn't it?"

"Five years, of course. Now, Singleman, do you think five years is a long time or a short time?"

Singleman raised his head into its best position for the drone of Zen wisdom and intoned,

A single minute may be felt to be
As sempeternal as eternity,
While ten millenia can at times go by
In the mere flicker of an adder's eye.

"By which I mean your five years could be either long or short or simultaneously both."

"You're at it again, Singleman. Is there some deep moral message in that quotation? A sense of morals totally detached from common sense, eh? Anyway, a hundred a month for five years involves sixty separate payments, and therein lies the danger of habit. If one repeats the same action sixty times over, month after month, one is likely to become so habituated to payment that one also coughs up on the sixty-first occasion. And on the sixty-second. And on the sixty-third and so on because the breaking of an established habit irks the habitué. Men are supposed to be clever, but they all have the same weakness: they follow established patterns without questioning the reason for their establishment. My scheme simply exploits that weakness to earn me a hundred a month until my customer finally drops dead."

"Though I like your joke," tittered Coldmoon, "I doubt if you'll find a great many customers so profitably forgetful."

My master, however, did not seem to find the story funny. In a serious voice he said, "That sort of thing does actually happen. I used to pay back my university-loan, month after month on a regular basis, and I kept no count of the number of payments. In the end I only stopped because the university told me to stop." My master seems almost to brag of his half-wittedness as though it were the benchmark of humanity.

"There you are," cries Waverhouse. "You see, the reality of my imagined customer is sitting right here in front of us. Yet that very same person, a self-confessed slave to human habit, has the effrontery to laugh at my projection of his own vision of our future civilization into its likely and unlaughable reality. Inexperienced young fellows like Beauchamp and Coldmoon, if they are not to be defrauded of their human rights, should listen very carefully for the wisdom in our words."

"I hear and shall obey. Never, never shall I commit myself to any installment plan that involves more than sixty repayments."

"I know you still think it's all just a joke but I do assure you, Coldmoon, that it was a truly instructive story," said Singleman turning directly to face him. "For instance, suppose that someone as wise and experienced as either Sneaze or Waverhouse told you that you had acted improperly in going off and getting married without advising any of the interested parties of your intentions? Should they advise that you ought to go and apologize to that Goldfield person, what would you do? Would you go and make your apologies?"

"I should beg to be excused. I would not demur if they wished to go and offer an explanation of my behavior. But to go myself, no."

"What if the police ordered you to apologize?"

"I should refuse all the more strongly."

"If a minister of the government or a peer of the realm asked you to apologize?"

"Then, yet more firmly still, I would refuse."

"There, you see how times have changed.

Not so long ago the power of those in authority was unlimited. Then came a time
when there were certain things which even
they could not demand. But nowadays there
are strict limits upon the power of peers and
even ministers to compel the individual. To
put the matter bluntly, we are witnessing a
period when, the greater the power of the
authorities, the greater the resistance they'll
encounter. Our fathers would be astonished
to see how things which the authorities clearly want done, and have ordered should be
done, nevertheless remain undone. This era
takes for granted any number of things which
elderly people would once have thought unthinkable. It is quiet extraordinary how
quickly and how totally both men and their
concept of society can change. So, though
you may of course laugh as much as you like
at Waverhouse's version of the future, you
would be wise not to laugh so hard that you
fail to consider how much of it might prove
true."

"Flattered as I am to have found so appreciative a friend, I feel that much more
obliged to continue with my forecast of the
future. First I would emphasize, as Singleman has already indicated, that anyone nowadays who proudly thinks himself powerful
by reason of delegated authority or who seeks
to maintain an outdated power by marching
around with a troop of a hundred henchmen
brandishing bamboo-spears can only be compared to that antiquated bigot who imagined

that his spanking palanquin could travel fast-
er than a railway train. I fancy that the best
local example of such a fathead might actually be that usurer Goldfield, whom I consider the master-fathead of them all. So perhaps
we should simply relax and leave time to
slide over him. Anyway my forecast of the
future is not so much concerned with such
minor transitional matters as with a particular social phenomenon that will determine
the long-term destiny of the entire human
race. My friends, if you will take a long-term
view of the trends already obvious in the development of our civilization, you will have
no choice but to share my view that marriage
has had it. Are you surprised? That the sacred
institution of marriage should be so summa-
rily written off? Well, the grounds for my
forecast have already been stated and, I think,
accepted: that modern society is centered, to
the exclusion of all else, upon the idea of individuality. When the family was represented
by its head, the district by its magistrate and
the province by its feudal lord, then those
who were not representatives possessed no
personalities whatsoever. Even if, exceptionally, they actually did have personalities,
those characteristics, being inappropriate to
their place in society, were never recognized
as such. Suddenly everything changed. We
were all discovered to possess personalities,
and every individual began to assert his new-
found individuality. Whenever two persons
chanced to meet, their attitudes betrayed a

disposition to quarrel, an underlying determination to insist that 'I am I and you are
you,' and that no human being was any more
human than any other. Obviously, each individual grew a little stronger by reason of
this new individuality; but, of course, precisely because everyone had grown stronger,
everyone had also grown proportionately
weaker than their fellow-individuals. Because
it's now harder for people to oppress you,
certainly you're stronger; but because it's
now a lot more difficult for you to meddle
in other folk's affairs, you're clearly that
much weaker. Everyone, naturally, likes to
be strong; and no one, naturally, likes to be
weak. Consequently, we all vigorously defend the strong points in our position in society, scrapping like fiends over the merest
trifles; and at the same time, in an unremit-
ting effort to undermine the position of our
fellows, we lever away at their weakest points
at every opportunity. It follows that men
have no genuine living-space left between
them which is not occupied by siege-engines
and counterworks. Too cramped to live at
ease, the constant pressure to expand one's
individual sphere has brought mankind to a
painful bursting-point and, having arrived by
their own machinations at such an unpleasant state of affairs, men thereupon devised
a means to relieve the unbearable pressure:
they developed that system under which parents and their married offspring live sepa-
rately. In the more backward parts of Japan,

among the wilder mountains, you can still
find entire families, including their lesser
cousinage, all living together, perfectly con-
tentedly, in one single house. That life-style
was only viable because, apart from the head
of the family, no member of the group possessed any individuality to assert; while any
member who, exceptionally, happened to possess it, took good care never to let it show.
However, in more up-to-date and civilized
communities the individual members of families are struggling amongst themselves, no less
fiercely than do other and totally unrelated
members of modern society, both to guard
their own positions and to undermine those
of their so-called nearest and dearest. There
is therefore little real choice but to live sepa-
rately.

"In Europe, where the modernization of
society has proceeded much further than has
yet happened in Japan, this necessary disin-
tegration of the multi-generation family-unit
has long been common. If by chance European parents and sons do live in the same
house, the sons pay, as they would elsewhere,
for board and lodging. Similarly, if sons borrow money from their father, they pay it back
with interest as they would if they had borrowed from a bank. This sort of laudable
arrangement is only possible when fathers
recognize and pay proper respect to sons' individualities. Sooner or later such customs
must be adopted in Japan. It is many years
now since uncles, aunts and cousins moved

out of the family-unit to establish their separate lives: the time is now coming for fathers and sons to separate, but the development of individuality and of a feeling of respect toward individuality will go on growing endlessly. We shall never be at peace unless we move farther apart and give each other room for that growth. But when parents, sons, brothers and sisters have all so eased apart, what further easement can be sought? Only the separation of husband and wife. Some people today still persist in the mistaken view that a husband and wife are a husband and wife because they live together. The point is that they can only live together if their separate individualities are sufficiently harmonious. No question of disharmony arose in the old days because, being in the Confucian phrase 'two bodies but one spirit,' husband-and-wife was a single person. Even after death they remained inseparable, haunting the world as two badgers from a single sett. That barbarous state of affairs is now all changed. A husband now is simply a man who happens to be married, a wife a woman in the same lamentable condition. This wife-person went to a girls' school from which, after an excellent education designed to strengthen her individuality, she comes marching out in a Western hair-style to be a bride. No wonder the man she marries cannot make her do what he likes. If such a woman did in fact accomodate herself to her husband's beck and call, people would say she's not a wife but a doll. The

harder she works to become an intelligent
helpmeet, the greater the space demanded by
her individuality and the less her husband can
abide her. Quarreling begins. The brighter the
wife, the more bitter and incessant are the
quarrels, and there's no sense in boasting of
intelligence in a wife if all it produces is misery
for both of you. Now within this marriage a
boundary is established, a boundary as dis-
tinct as that between oil and water. Even that
would not be too awful if only it were steady,
but in practice the line of marital friction
bounces up and down so that the whole domestic scene is in a constant condition of
earthquake. By such experiences the human
race has come to accept that it is unprofit-
able to both parties that married couples
should live together."

"So what do they do?" asks Coldmoon.
"Divorce on the scale you imply is a worrying prospect."

"Yes, they part. What else can they do?
It's clear to me that, eventually, all married
couples will get divorced. As things still stand,
those who live together are husband and wife,
but in the future those who live together will
be generally considered to have disqualified
themselves from being a normal married
couple."

"I suppose that a man like myself will be
one of the disqualified. . . ." Coldmoon misses
no chance to remind us of his recent marriage.

"You are lucky to have been born in the
days of the Emperor Meiji when traditional

ways are still observed. Being a gifted proph-
et of things to come, I am inevitably two
or three stops ahead of my contemporaries
in all matters of any importance; and that,
of course, is why I am already a bachelor. I
know there are people who go around saying that I remain unmarried because of some
early disappointment in love, but one can only
pity such persons for their shallow minds and
their inability to see further than the ends of
their snooping noses." Waverhouse paused
for breath. "But to return to my far-seeing
vision of the future. . . . A philosopher will
descend from heaven. He will preach the un-
precedented truth that all members of mankind, both men and women, are essentially
individuals. Impairment of their individuality
can only lead to the destruction of the human
race. The purpose of human life is to maintain and develop individuality; and, to attain
that end, no sacrifice is too great. It is thus
contrary to the nature and needs of mankind
that the ancient, evil, barbarous practice of
marriage should continue. Such primitive
rites were, perhaps, understandable before
the sacrosanctity of individuality was recognized; but to allow the continuation of these
dreadful customs into our own civilized era
is quite unthinkable. The deplorable habit of
marriage must be broken. In our developed
culture there is no reason whatever why two
individuals should be bound to each other in
the highly abnormal intimacy of the traditional marriage-relationship. Once the reve-

lations of the heaven-sent philosopher have
been clearly understood, it will be regarded
as extremely immoral of young uneducated
men and women to allow themselves to be
so carried away by base and fleeting passions
that they even stoop to low indulgence in
wedding ceremonies. Even today we must do
our best to get such tribal customs discontinued."

"Sir," said Beauchamp so very firmly that
he even slapped his knee-cap, "I totally re-
ject your vile prognostication. In my opinion,
nothing in this world is more precious than
love and beauty. It is entirely thanks to these
two things that we can be consoled, be made
perfect and be happy. Again it is entirely due
to them that our feelings can be gracefully
expressed, our characters made noble and
our sympathies refined. Therefore, no matter
where or when one is born, here or in Tim-
buktu, now or in the future, love and beauty
remain the eternal guidestars of mankind.
When they manifest themselves in the actual
world, love is seen in the relationship between
husband and wife, while beauty shines forth
either as poetry or music. These are the
expressions, at its highest level, of the very
humanity of the human race; and I do not
believe, so long as our kind exists upon the
surface of this planet, that either the arts or
our current ideal of the married couple will
perish therefrom."

"It would be well, perhaps, if it were so.
But, for the reasons which the heaven-sent

philosopher has just given for his forecast, both love and beauty are bound to perish. You will just have to accept the inevitable. You spoke of the imperishable glories of art, but they will go the same way as the married couple: into oblivion. The irreversible development of individuality will bring ever greater demands by individuals for recognition of their singular identity. In a world where I and you both insist that 'I am I and you are you,' how can any art perdure? Surely the arts now flourish by reason of a harmony between the individualities of the artist and of each appreciative member of his public. That harmony is already being crushed to death. You may protest until the cows come home that you are a new-style poet; but if no one shares your conviction of the worth of your poems, I'm afraid you'll never be read. However many epithalamia you compose, your work will be dying as you write it. It is thus especially gratifying that, writing as you do in Meiji times, the whole world may still rejoice in its excellence."

"I'm not all that well known."

"If already today your splendid efforts are not all that well known, what do you imagine will be their fate in the future when civilization has advanced yet further and that heaven-sent philosopher has knocked the stuffing out of marriage? No one at all will read your poems. Not because the poems are yours and you are a bad poet, but because individuality has intensified to such an extent that anything written by other people holds no interest for anyone. This stage of the literary future is already evidenced in England where two of their leading novelists, Henry James and George Meredith, have personalities so strong and so strongly reflected in their novels that very few people care to read them. And no wonder. Only readers with personalities of matching force could find such works of any interest. That trend will accelerate and, by the time that marriage is finally recognized as immoral, all art will have disappeared. Surely you can see that, when anything that either of us might write has become quite meaningless to the other, then there will be nothing, let alone art, which we can share. We shall all be excommunicated from each other."

"I suppose you're right; but somehow, intuitively, I cannot believe the fearful picture you have painted."

"If you can't grasp it intuitively, then try it discursively."

"Discursive or intuitive," Singleman blurts out, "what's it matter? The point is that it's true. It's quite obvious that the greater the freedom of the individuality permitted to human beings, the less free their interrelations must become. I consider that all Nietzsche's glorification of a Superman is nothing but a philosophical attempt to talk a way out of the dead-end facing mankind. You might at first sight think that Nietzsche was enunciating some cherished ideal, but on reflection you'll recognize that he's simply voicing his bitter discontent. Twisting about in his bed, niggled by his neighbors, worried by their developing individualities, Nietzsche funked even the nineteenth century. Pouring out such jeremiads, he must have lived in an agony of despair. Reading his works, one does not feel inspired, merely sorry for their wretched author. That voice of his is not the voice of intrepidity and determination; it is nothing more than the whine of grievance and the screams of indignation. It was, perhaps, an understandable reaction in a rejected philosopher. When in ancient times a truly great man appeared, all the whole world flocked to gather under his banner. Which was no doubt very gratifying, certainly sufficiently gratifying for the great man in question to feel no need to resort to pen and paper with all that virulence one finds in Nietzsche. The superhuman characters portrayed in Homer's epics and in the Ballad of Chevy Chase are not demon-driven. Unlike Nietzsche's Superman, they are alive with life, with gaiety and just plain fun. Their times were truly merry and the merriment is recreated in the writing. Naturally, in days like that there was no trace of Nietzsche's atrabilious venom. But in Nietzsche's period things were sadly different. No hero shone on his horizons and, even if a hero had appeared, no one would have honored, respected or even noticed him. When, in a much earlier period, Confucius made his appearance, it was relatively easy for him to assert his importance because he had no equals as competitors. Today they're ten a penny and possibly the whole wide world is packed with them. Certainly no one nowadays would be impressed if you claimed to be a new Confucius; and you, because you had failed to impress, would become waspish in your discontent, in precisely the sort of discontent which leads to books which brandish Superman about our ears. We sought freedom and now we suffer from the inconveniences that freedom can but bring. Does it not follow that, though Western civilization seems splendid at first glance, at the end of the day it proves itself a bane? In sharp contrast, we in the East have always, since long long long ago, devoted ourselves not to material progress but to development of the mind. That Way was the right way. Now that the pressures of individuality are bringing on all sorts of nervous disorders, we are at last able to grasp the meaning of the ancient tag that 'people are carefree under firm rule.' And it won't be long before Lao Tzu's doctrine of the activating effect of inactivity grows to seem less of a paradox. By then, of course, it will be too late to do anything more than recognize our likeness to addicted alcoholics who wish they'd never touched the stuff."

"All you fellows," said Coldmoon, "seem hideously pessimistic about the future, but none of your moans and groans depress me in the least. I wonder why."

"That's because you've just got married,"

said Waverhouse hastening to explain away the mildest manifestation of hope.

Then, suddenly, my master began to talk. "If, my dear Coldmoon, you're thinking yourself fortunate to have found a wife, you're making a big mistake. For your particular information, I shall now read out something of pertinent interest." Opening that antique of a book which he'd brought from his study a short time back, my master then continued. "As you can see, this is an old book but it was perfectly clear, even in those early days, that women were terrible."

"Sir, you surprise me. But may I ask when the book was written?" said Coldmoon.

"In the sixteenth century, by a man called Thomas Nashe."

"I'm even more surprised. You mean to say that even in those early days someone spoke ill of my wife?"

"The book contains a wide variety of complaints about women, some of which will certainly apply to your wife. So you'd better listen carefully."

"All right. I am listening. Very honored too."

"The book begins by saying that all men must heed the views of womanhood propounded down the ages by recognized sages. You follow me? Are you listening?"

"We are all listening. Even I, a bachelor, am listening."

"Aristotle says that, since all women are good-for-nothings anyway, it is best, if you

must get married, to choose a small bride;
because a small good-for-nothing is less disastrous than a large one."

"Coldmoon, is this wife of yours hefty or
petite?"

"She's one of the heftier good-for-nothings."

They all laughed, more at the suddenness
with which Coldmoon had re-joined the eternal conspiracy of males than at anything inherently funny in his answer.

"Well," said Waverhouse, "that's an interesting book, I must say. Read us some more."

"A man once asked what might be a mira-
cle, and the sage replied, 'A chaste woman.' "

"Who, sir, is this sage?"

"The book doesn't give his name."

"I'll bet he was a sage who had been jilted."

"Next comes Diogenes who, when asked at
what age it was best to take a wife, replied,
'For a young man, not yet; for the old man,
never.' "

"No doubt that miserable fellow thought
that up in his barrel," observed Waverhouse.

"Pythagoras says that there are three evils
not to be suffered: fire, water and a woman."

"I didn't know," said Singleman, "that any
Greek philosopher was responsible for such
an ill-considered apothegm. If you ask me,
none of them are evil: one can enter fire and
not be burnt, enter water and not be drowned,
enter . . ." Here he got stuck till Waverhouse
helped him out by adding, "And entertain
a woman without being bewitched, eh?"

Paying no regard to his friends' interjec-
tions, my master went on with his reading.
"Socrates says that a man's most difficult task
is to try to control women and children.
Demosthenes says that the greatest torment
a man can invent for his enemy's vexation is
to give him his own daughter in marriage 'as
a domestical Furie to disquiet him night and
day' until he dies of it. The eminent Seneca
says that there be two especial troubles in this
world: a wife and ignorance. The Emperor
Marcus Aurelius compares women to ships
because 'to keep them well in order, there is
always somewhat wanting.' Plautus claims
that women 'deck themselves so gorgeously
and lace themselves so nicely' because, and I
paraphrase, such a mean trick disguises their
natural ugliness. Valerius Maximus in a letter
to one of his friends advises him that almost
nothing is impossible for a woman and goes
on to entreat God Almighty that 'his sweet
friend be not entrapped by woman's treach-
erie.' It was this same Valerius Maximus
who answered his own question about the
nature of woman by saying, 'She is an enemy
to friendship, an inevitable pain, a necessary
evil, a natural temptation, a desired calamity,
a honey-seeming poison.' He also remarked
that, if it is a sin to put a woman away, it is
surely a much greater torment to keep her
still."

"Please, sir," pleaded Coldmoon, "that's
enough. I cannot bear to hear any more awful things about my wife."

"There are still several more pages. How about listening to the end?"

"Oh, have a heart," said Waverhouse, "and anyway isn't it about time for your own good lady to come home?" He had hardly started his usual style of teasing when from the direction of the other room there came the sound of Mrs. Sneaze calling sharply for the maid.

"I say, that's torn it," Waverhouse whispered. "Had you realized she was back?"

My master permitted himself a spasm of muffled laughter. "What's it matter if she is?"

But Waverhouse was not to be dissuaded. "Oh, Mrs. Sneaze," he called, "how long have you been home?"

Answer, as the poets put it, came there none.

"Did you happen to hear what your noble spouse was just telling us, Mrs. Sneaze?"

Still no answer.

"I hope you understand he wasn't speaking his own thoughts. Just reading out the opinions of a Mr. Nashe from the sixteenth century. Nothing personal. Please don't take it to heart."

"It hardly matters to me," came the curt response in a voice so faint and distant that Mrs. Sneaze might well have been away in the sixteenth century pursuing the issue with Mr. Nashe himself. Coldmoon giggled nervously.

"Well, of course it hardly matters to me, either. I'm sorry to have mentioned it." Waverhouse was now laughing out loud when we heard the sound of the outside gate being opened and heavy footsteps entering the house. Next moment, and with no further announcement, the sliding-door of the room was yanked aside and the face of Tatara Sampei peered in through the gap.

Sampei hardly looked himself. His snow-white shirt and his spanking new frock-coat were surprises in themselves but he was also carrying, their necks string-tied together, a clutch of bottles of beer. He set the bottles down beside the dried bonitos, and himself, without even a nod of greeting, hunkered down heavily on his hams with all the self-confident resolution of a warrior. "Mr. Sneaze, sir," he immediately began, "has your stomach-trouble got any better lately? It's all this staying at home, you know; it does you no good."

"I haven't said whether my stomach was better or worse," my master tartly objected.

"No, I know you haven't. But your complexion speaks for itself. It's not good, yellow like that. This is the right time of year to go fishing. Why not hire a boat at Shinagawa? Bracing. I went out last Sunday."

"Did you catch anything?"

"No, nothing."

"Is it any fun when you don't catch a sausage?"

"The idea is to buck yourself up, to get the old juices flowing again. How about all of you? Have you ever been out fishing? It's terrific fun. You see," he began speaking to them as a group, somewhat loftily as though to a ring of children, "you set off in this tiny boat across the vast blue ocean . . ."

"My preference," said the irrepressible Waverhouse, "would be to set off in a vast blue boat across the smallest possible ocean."

"I can see no point," said Coldmoon in his most detached voice, "no fun at all in setting off on a fishing expedition unless one expects to catch at least a whale. Or a mermaid."

"You can't catch whales from cockleshells and mermaids don't exist. You scribbling men of letters have no common sense whatever."

"I'm not a man of letters."

"No? Then what the devil are you? I'm a businessman, and for us businessmen the one thing you must have is common sense." He turned toward my master and addressed him directly. "You know, sir, over the last few months I have amassed a very great stock of common sense. Of course, working as I do in a great business-center, it's only natural that I should become like this."

"Like what?"

"Take, for instance, cigarettes. One can't expect to get very far in business if one goes around smoking trashy brands like Shiki-shima or Asahi." At this point, he produced a pack of Egyptian cigarettes, selected a gold-tipped tube, lit it ostentatiously and began to puff its scented smoke.

"Can you really afford to chuck your money around like that? You must be rolling in the stuff."

"No. No money yet, but something will turn up. Smoking these cigarettes builds one's image, confers considerable prestige."

"It's certainly an easier way to gain prestige than by polishing glass balls. A real short cut to fame. Far less troublesome than all your labors, wouldn't you say, Coldmoon?"

Waverhouse had scarcely closed his mouth and before Coldmoon could utter a syllable, Sampei turned and said, "So, you are Mr. Coldmoon. The chap who's given up on his doctorate. For which reason it's become me."

"You're studying for a degree?"

"No, I'm marrying Miss Goldfield. To tell the truth, I felt rather sorry for you, missing a chance like that; but they pressed me so hard that I've agreed to marry her. Nevertheless I can't help feeling that somehow I've wronged Mr. Coldmoon. Can you follow my feelings, Mr. Sneaze?"

"But please, my dear sir," said Coldmoon, "you are most welcome to the match."

"If she's what you want," my master mumbled vaguely, "then I suppose you might as well marry her."

"How absolutely splendid," burbles Waverhouse. "All's well that ends well, and all that. It just goes to show that nobody need ever worry about getting his daughters married. Wasn't I saying only just now that someone suitable would quickly come along and, sure enough, she's already found this very cool customer to be her unblushing bridegroom. Think of it, Beauchamp, and rejoice.

It's a gift of a theme for one of your new-style poems. Waste no time. Get going." Waverhouse was off again.

355
•
吾輩は猫である

"And are you," asked Sampei somewhat obsequiously, "the poet Mr. Beauchamp? I should be deeply grateful if you would deign to compose something for our wedding. I could have it printed right away and have it sent out to all concerned. I will also arrange for it to be printed in the daily press."

"I'd be happy to oblige. When would you like to have it?"

"Any time. And any piece which you already have on hand would do. And for that I'll invite you to our wedding reception. We'll be having champagne. Have you ever tried it? It tastes delicious. I'm planning, Mr. Sneaze, to hire an orchestra, a small one, for the occasion. Perhaps we could get Mr. Beauchamp's poem set to music and then it could be played while the guests are eating. How about that, Mr. Sneaze? What do you think?"

"You do as you like."

"But Mr. Sneaze, could you write the musical setting for me?"

"Don't be silly."

"Isn't there anyone among you who could handle the music?"

"Mr. Coldmoon, the unsuccessful marriage-candidate and failed ball-polisher, happens also to be a fine violinist. Ask him if he'll oblige. But I doubt if he'll squander his wealth of soul in return for a mere sipping of champagne."

"But there are champagnes and champagnes. I shan't be offering anything cheap or nasty. No filthy pops. Nothing but the best. Won't you help me out?"

"Of course, and with pleasure. I'll write the music even if your champagne is mere cider. Indeed, if you like, I'll do the job for nothing."

"I wouldn't dream of asking you to aid me unrewarded. If you don't enjoy champagne, how about this for payment?" Reaching into his jacket-pocket, Sampei pulled out some seven or eight photographs and scattered them on the floor-matting. One was half-length, one was full-length, one standing, another sitting, one dressed somewhat casually, another very correctly in a long-sleeved kimono and yet another wearing a formal Japanese hair-do. All of them were photographs of young girls.

"Mr. Sneaze, sir, these were all prospective brides in whom I am, of course, no longer interested. But if any of these marriage-candidates happened to interest Mr. Coldmoon or Mr. Beauchamp, I would gladly, in recognition of their assistance to myself, act as their agent in effecting introductions to any of these fanciable ladies. How about this one here?" he asks, thrusting a photograph under Coldmoon's nose.

"Oh nice," says Coldmoon, "very nice. I rather fancy that one."

"And how about this?" He shoves another picture into Coldmoon's hand.

"Very nice too. Quite charming. Yes, I certainly fancy her."

"But which one do you want?"

"I don't mind which."

"You seem a bit feckless," Sampei commented dryly. Then, turning to my master, he went on with his sales-pitch. "This one, actually, is the niece of a doctor."

"I see."

"This next one is extremely good-natured. Young too. Only seventeen. . . . And this one carries a whacking great dowry. . . . While this one here is a daughter of a provincial governor." All alone with his imaginings, Sampei rattles on.

"Do you think I could marry them all?"

"All? That's plain gluttonous. Are you some kind of polygamist or something?"

"No, not a polygamist. But a carnivore, of course."

"Never mind what you are. Sampei, put those snaps away at once. Can't you see," said my master in a tone of sharp scolding, "that he's only leading you on?"

"So you don't want an introduction to any of them," said Sampei, half in question and half in statement, as, one by one, slowly, giving Beauchamp and Coldmoon a last chance to relent, he put the pictures back into his pocket.

There was no response.

"Well now, what are those bottles for?"

"A present. I bought them just now at the dramshop on the corner so that we might drink to my forthcoming marriage. Come, let's start."

My master clapped his hands for the maid and asked her to open the bottles. Then the five of them, my master, Waverhouse, Single-man, Coldmoon and Beauchamp, solemnly lifting their glasses, congratulated Sampei on his good fortune in love. Sampei fairly glowed with self-esteem and assured them, "I shall invite you all to the ceremony. Can all of you come? I do hope so."

"No," my master answered promptly. "I shan't."

"Why ever not? It'll be the grandest once-in-a-lifetime day of my life. And you won't attend it? Seems a bit heartless."

"I'm not heartless. But I won't attend."

"Ah, you haven't got the things to wear? Is that the snag? I can gladly arrange for the right kit to be made available. You really ought to go out more and meet people. I'll introduce you to some well-known persons."

"That's the very last thing I would wish."

"It might even cure your stomach-troubles."

"I don't care if they never get better."

"Well, if you can't be budged, you can't. But how about you others? Will you be able to come?"

"Me? I'd love to," said Waverhouse. "I would even be delighted to play the role of the honored go-between. A verse leaps to my lips:

Evening in spring:
The marriage rite
And nuptial bonds made champagne-
        tight.

What's that you said? Suzuki's going to be
the go-between? I might have known it. Well,
in that case, I'm sorry, but there it is. I suppose that it really would be a bit too much
to have two lots of go-betweens. So I'll attend
your party as an ordinary human being."

    "And how about you? Will you come with
your friends?"

    "Me?" said Singleman apparently sur-
prised.

Having this fishing-rod to be my friend,
I live at ease in nature and am free
Of every care the red-dust world might
        send
Like some hooked promise to entangle
        me.

    "And what the hell is that?" asked Waver-
house. "Something from the hallowed guide
on how to write a poem in Chinese?"

    "I really can't remember where I picked it
up."

    "You really can't remember? How tire-
some for you. Well, come if your fishing-rod
can spare you. And you, Mr. Coldmoon, I
hope I may count on you. After all, you have
a special status in this matter."

"Most certainly I'll be there. It would be a pity to miss the chance of hearing my own music played by an orchestra."

"Of course. And what about you, Mr. Beauchamp?"

"Well, yes. I'd like to be there to read my new-style poem in front of the couple themselves."

"That's wonderful. Mr. Sneaze, sir, I've never before in all my life felt so pleased with the world. And, to mark the moment, I'll have another glass of that beer." He filled a tumbler to the brim and sank it at one go. Slowly his face turned shining red.

The short autumn day has grown dark. The charcoal fire in the brazier has long ago burnt out and its crust of ash is studded and strewn with an ugly mess of cigarette-ends. Even these happy-go-lucky men seem to have had enough of their merriment and in the end it was Singleman who, climbing stiffly to his feet, remarked, "It's getting late. Time to be on our way." The others followed suit and, politely apopemptic, vanished into the night. The drawing-room grew desolate, like a variety hall when the show is over.

My master ate his dinner and went off into his study. His wife, feeling the autumn chill, tightens her collar, settles over her sewing-box and gets on with her re-modeling of a worn-out kimono. The children, lying in one row, are fast asleep. The maid has gone out to a bathhouse.

If one tapped the deep bottom of the hearts

of these seemingly light-hearted people, it would give a somewhat sad sound. Though Singleman behaves as though enlightenment had made him a familiar of the skies, his feet still shuffle, earthbound, through this world. The world of Waverhouse, though it may be easy-going, is not the sweven-world of those painted landscapes which he loves. That winsome donzel Coldmoon, having at last stopped polishing his little globes of glass, has fetched from his far home-province a bride to cheer his days. Which is pleasant and quite normal; but the sad fact is that long-continued, pleasant normality becomes a bore. Beauchamp too, however golden-hearted he is now, will have come in ten years' time to realize the folly of giving away for nothing those new-style poems that are the essence of his heart. As for Sampei, I find it difficult to judge whether he'll finish up on top of the pile or down the drain, but I'd like to think he'll manage to live his life out proud and happy in the ability to souse his acquaintance in champagne. Suzuki will remain the same eternal groveling creeper. Grovelers get covered in mud; but, even so be-sharned, he'll manage better than those who cannot creep at all.

As for me, I am a cat, still nameless though born two years ago, who has lived his life among men. I have always thought myself unique in my knowledge of mankind, but I was recently much surprised to meet another cat, some German mog called Kater Murr.

I Am a Cat (III)

who suddenly turned up and started sounding off in a very high-falutin' manner on my own special subject. I subsequently made enquiries and discovered that my visitor was in fact the ghost of a cat who, though he'd been in Hell since dying a century ago, had become so piqued with curiosity about my reputation that he re-materialized for the express purpose of upsetting me. This cat, I learnt, was a most unfilial creature. On one occasion when he was going to meet his mother, he was carrying a fish in his mouth to give her as a present. However he failed to control his animal appetites and broke his journey to guzzle the fish. His combination of talents and greed was such as to make him virtually human, and he even once astonished his master by writing a poem. If such a feline culture-hero was already demonstrating superior cat-skills so long as a century ago, perhaps a good-for-nothing specimen like me has already outlived its purpose and should no more delay its retirement into Nothingness.

My master, sooner or later, will die of his dyspepsia. Old man Goldfield is already doomed by his greed. The autumn leaves have mostly fallen. All that has life must lose it. Since there seems so little point in living, perhaps those who die young are the only creatures wise. If one heeds the sages who assembled here today, mankind has already sentenced itself to extinction by suicide. If we don't watch out, even cats may find their individualities developing along the lethal crushing pattern forecast for these two-legged loons. It's an appalling prospect. Depression weighs upon me. Perhaps a sip of Sampei's beer would cheer me up.

I go round to the kitchen. The back-door is half-open and rattles in the autumn wind. Which seems to have blown the lamp out, for the room's unlit. Still, there are shadows tilting inward through the window. Moonrise, I suppose. On a tray there are three glasses, two of them half-filled with a brownish liquid. Even warm water, if kept in a glass, looks cold. Naturally this liquid, standing quietly beside the jar of charcoal-existinguisher, looks, in the icy moonlight, chill and uninviting. However, anything for experience. If Sampei, as I recall, could after drinking it become a bright warm red and start breathing as heavily as a man who's run a mile, perhaps it's not impossible for a cat that drinks it to feel livelier. Anyway, some day I too must die so I might as well try everything before I do. Once I'm dead, I tell myself, it will be too late in the grave to regret that I never tasted beer. So, take courage and drink up!

I flicked my tongue into the stuff but, as I began to lap, I got a sharp surprise. The tip of my tongue, as though it had been pricked with needles, stung and tingled painfully. What possible pleasure can human beings find in drinking such unpleasant stuff? I've heard my master describe revolting food as not fit for a dog, but this dark drink is truly not fit for a cat. There must be some fundamental antipathy between cats and beer. Conscious of danger, I quickly withdrew my tongue. But then, on reflection, I remembered that men have a pet saying about good medicines always tasting filthy and that the drafts they down to cure their colds invariably make them grimace with disgust. I've never worked out whether they get cured by drinking muck or whether they'd get well anyway without the face-making business. Now's my chance to find out. If drinking beer poisons my entire intestines, well, that will be just too bad: but if like Sampei, I grow so cheerful as to forget everything around me, then I'll accept the experience as an unexpected joy and even, perhaps, I'll teach all the cats of the neighborhood how sweet it is to drown one's woes in drink. Anyway, let's take a chance and see. The decision made, I drooped my tongue out cautiously. But if I can actually see the bitter liquid I find it hard to drink it; so closing my eyes tight shut, I began to lap.

When, by sheer strength of will and tiger-like perseverance, I'd lapped away the beer-lees in the first glass, a strange phenomenon occurred. The initial agony of my needled tongue began to ease off and the ghastly feeling in my mouth, a feeling as if some hand were squeezing my cheeks together from the outside, was pleasurably relieved. By the time I'd dealt with the first glass, beer-swilling was no longer much of a problem. I finished off the second glass so painlessly that, while I was about it, I even lapped up all the spill on the tray and slurped the whole lot down into my stomach.

That done, in order to study my body's reactions, I crouched down quietly for a while. My body is gradually growing warm. I feel hot around my eyes and my ears are burning. I feel like singing a song. I feel like dancing the Cat's High Jinks. I feel like telling my master, Waverhouse and Singleman that they can all go to hell. I feel like scratching old man Goldfield. I feel like biting his wife's vast nose off. I feel like doing lots of things. And in the end I felt I'd like to wobble to my feet. As I stood up, I felt I'd like to walk. Highly pleased with myself, I felt like going out. And as I staggered out, I felt like shouting, "Moon, old man, how goes it?" So I did. Oh, but I felt wonderful!

So this, I thought, is how it feels to be gloriously drunk. Radiant with glory, I persevered in setting my unsteady feet one in front of each other in the correct order. Which is very difficult when you have four feet. I made no effort to travel in any particular direction but just kept going in long slow wayward totter. I'm beginning to feel extremely sleepy, and indeed I hardly know if I'm still walking or already sunk in sleep. I try to open my eyes, but their lids have grown unliftably heavy. Ah, well, it can't be helped. Confidently telling myself that nothing in this world, neither seas nor mountains nor anything else, could now impede my cat-imperial progress, I put a front paw forward when suddenly I hear a loud sloppy splash. . . . As I come to my senses, I know that I'm done for. I had no time to work out how I'd been done for because, in the very moment that I realized the fact of it, everything went haywire.

When I again came to myself, I found I was floating in water. Because I was also in pain I clawed at what seemed its cause, but scratching water had no effect except to result in my immediate submersion. I struck out desperately for the surface by kicking with my hind-legs and scrabbling with my fore-paws. This action eventually produced a sort of scraping sound and, as I managed to thrust my head just clear of the water, I saw that I'd fallen into a big clay jar against whose side my claws had scraped. All through the summer this jar had contained a thick growth of water-hollyhocks, but in the early autumn the crows had descended first to eat the plants and then to bathe in the water. In the end their splashing about and the heat of the sun had so lowered the water-level that the crows found it difficult either to bathe or to drink, and they had stopped coming. I remember that only the other day I was thinking that the water must have gone down because I'd seen no birds about. Little did I then dream that I myself would be the next to splash about in that jar.

From the water's surface to the lip of the

jar, it measures some five inches. However much I stretch my paws I cannot reach the lip. And the water gives no purchase for a jump. If I do nothing, I just sink. If I flounder around, my claws scrabble on the clay sides but the only result is that scraping sound. It's true that when I claw at the jar I do seem to rise a little in the water but, as soon as my claws scrape down the clay, I slide back deep below the surface. This is so painful that I immediately start scrabbling again until I break surface and can breathe. But it's a very tiring business, and my strength is going. I become impatient with my ill success, but my legs are growing sluggish. In the end I can hardly tell whether I am scratching the jar in order to sink or am sinking to induce more scratching.

While this was going on and despite the constant pain, I found myself reasoning that I'm only in agony because I want to escape from the jar. Now, much as I'd like to get out, it's obvious that I can't: my extended front leg is scarcely three inches long and even if I could hoist my body with its outstretched fore-paws up above the surface, I still could never hook my claws over the rim. Accordingly, since it's blindingly clear that I can't get out, it's equally clear that it's senseless to persist in my efforts to do so. Only my own senseless persistence is causing my ghastly suffering. How very stupid. How very, very stupid deliberately to prolong the agonies of this torture.

"I'd better stop. I just don't care what happens next. I've had quite enough, thank you, of this clutching, clawing, scratching, scraping, scrabbling, senseless struggle against nature." The decision made, I give up and relax: first my fore-paws, then my hind-legs, then my head and tail.

Gradually I begin to feel at ease. I can no longer tell whether I'm suffering or feeling grateful. It isn't even clear whether I'm drowning in water or lolling in some comfy room. And it really doesn't matter. It does not matter where I am or what I'm doing. I simply feel increasingly at ease. No, I can't actually say that I feel at ease, either. I feel that I've cut away the sun and moon, they pull at me no longer; I've pulverized both Heaven and Earth, and I'm drifting off and away into some unknown endlessness of peace. I am dying, Egypt, dying. Through death I'm drifting slowly into peace. Only by dying can this divine quiescence be attained. May one rest in peace! I am thankful, I am thankful. Thankful, thankful, thankful.